SUPERNATURAL

HEART OF THE DRAGON

COMING SOON FROM TITAN BOOKS:

Supernatural: The Unholy Cause
by Joe Schreiber

Supernatural: War of the Sons
by Rebecca Dessertine & David Reed

SUPERNATURAL™
HEART OF THE DRAGON

KEITH R.A. DeCANDIDO

Based on the hit CW series SUPERNATURAL created by Eric Kripke

TITAN BOOKS

Supernatural: Heart of the Dragon
ISBN: 9781848566002

Published by
Titan Books
A division of Titan Publishing Group Ltd
144 Southwark St
London
SE1 0UP

First edition February 2010
10 9 8 7 6

Visit our website: www.titanbooks.com

Did you enjoy this book? We love to hear from our readers. Please email
us at readerfeedback@titanemail.com or write to us at Reader Feedback
at the above address.

To receive advance information, news, competitions, and exclusive Titan
offers online, please register as a member by clicking the "sign up" button
on our website: www.titanbooks.com

A CIP catalogue record for this title is available from the British Library.

Printed and bound in the United States.

Dedicated to *Shihan* Paul and
everyone else at the dojo.

The writing of this novel coincided with
the preparation for taking my first black-belt promotion,
which I consider one of the great accomplishments of
my life. The study of karate has proven to be such an
enlightening and glorious experience, and I will always be
grateful to my fellow *karateka* for their
encouragement, wisdom, and spirit.

Osu, Shihan; osu, senpais; osu, my dear friends.
This one's for you guys.

HISTORIAN'S NOTE

The 2009 portions of this novel take place shortly after
the fifth-season episode "Changing Channels."

1859

ONE

The rain had not let up for the better part of an hour.

Yoshio Nakadai knelt in the shelter on the side of the road in *sei-za* position—knees and shins on the floor, feet crossed under his buttocks—waiting for the rain to cease. He was in no hurry. This shelter had been built for the very purpose of shielding travelers from rainstorms. The repetitive rhythm of the rain pelting the roof gave him a focus for his meditations.

Yet such focus had been difficult to achieve of late. Even now, emptying his mind proved nigh on impossible.

Once, a *samurai* such as Nakadai would have committed *seppuku*—ritual suicide—when his master's holdings were seized, his lands taken, his title stricken. But such days were in the past. No one knew the ways of honor anymore, and the code of *bushi* had become a story told to children around the fire, rather than the way of life it was meant to be.

Now Nakadai was just another of the many lordless *ronin* who wandered the countryside in the hope of using his skills to survive. During the year that had turned since his master had fallen out of favor with Edo, he had worked as a sword for hire protecting people and caravans, and had taken work as an investigator, an arbitrator settling a dispute between two merchants, a builder, and a teacher showing a rich man's son how to defend himself.

His reputation had served him well, particularly in the towns nearer to Edo. Unlike so many *ronin*, Nakadai always acted honorably.

He knew no other way. Besides, if a person hired him and he did his job properly and well, they were more likely to hire him again.

However, while Nakadai was able to acquire enough coin with which to live, he was unable to obtain the contentment he longed for. Had he actually committed *seppuku*, as tradition demanded, he might well have found peace. But to die out of loyalty to a dishonorable man?

Nakadai felt no great love for the *shogunate*, but in this instance, they had been right to censure his master, who had proven himself a coward and a thief. The dishonor was his master's, not Nakadai's.

There was no reason to die for the likes of *him*.

Yet honor demanded that he do so. He'd pledged fealty, and the fact that his master did not deserve such loyalty didn't change the fact that Nakadai had so sworn.

That conundrum continued to plague him. His mind

refused to empty.

The rhythm of the rain was suddenly broken by the rapid sound of feet squelching in the mud.

Nakadai opened his eyes and peered into the obscuring rain. He saw a short man running toward the shelter. As soon as the man arrived he futilely tried to wipe the water off his face and brush it from his clothes. Finally surrendering to his sodden state, the newcomer laughed and spoke.

"Greetings, I hope you don't mind if I share the shelter with you."

"Of course not," Nakadai replied quietly. Then he closed his eyes once again, hoping the man would understand that he wished not to be disturbed.

However, such understanding was not forthcoming.

"I honestly thought this rain would have passed by now," the man continued, peering out from under the roof's edge. "I figured to myself, 'Cho, you just have another hour to go before you reach town, you can make it before the rain gets too bad.' Instead, the downpour just got worse!" Turning back to his companion, the man named Cho studied him more closely.

"Hey, you look familiar."

Nakadai sighed and opened his eyes. Clearly, he would not achieve a proper meditative state with this Cho person present. Not that he had been in any danger of doing so without him, either.

Rising to his feet, he started to walk the perimeter of the shelter in order to restore full feeling to his legs. The space

was so small that he had to step around the newcomer more
than once.

"You heading into town, too?" the man asked, following
Nakadai with his gaze. "I'm guessing you're a *ronin*, aren't
you?" Then he shook his head. "Okay, it wasn't a great guess,
'cause you've got a nice-looking katana and you seem like
you could kill me just by looking at me. But those clothes
have seen better decades, if you don't mind me saying. You
hoping to find work?"

"Yes."

Nakadai continued his perambulations around the
shelter, never making eye contact, and looking to the skies
from time to time to see if there was a sign that the storm
would break.

Despite his most fervent wishes, his companion
continued.

"You know, you really do look familiar. I'm a messenger,
see, and I get around a lot. Would've loved to have been a
samurai or even a *ronin*, but you should see me with a sword.
Or I guess you shouldn't, because I'm *very* bad at it. Still have
the scar, actually."

Finally, Nakadai turned his head to look at Cho, and he
had to admit to himself that he was less than impressed. The
messenger possessed muscular legs, as might be expected
from one of his profession, but he also had huge eyebrows,
unfortunate teeth, flabby arms, and his clothes hung sloppily
about his torso. The latter, at least, could be attributed to the
storm. But the rest....

One of those flabby arms, the left one, had a lengthy scar running from the elbow to the wrist.

"Pretty sad, huh? But I could always move fast, so I became a runner. Soon enough, folks were hiring me to carry messages. It's good—I get to travel to other towns and meet lots of people.

"You know, I'm just *sure* that I know you from somewhere," he insisted again.

Nakadai turned away. The scar was old and healed, and also rather straight. It probably came from an accident— tripping while holding the sword, perhaps, with the edge slicing into his arm on the way to the ground.

"That's it!" Cho exclaimed, pointing in his direction. "You're *Doragon Kokoro*, aren't you?"

Nakadai winced.

"I am called Yoshio Nakadai." He had never liked that nickname. The *samurai* had singlehandedly killed seven bandits who attacked his master's caravan while they were on the way to Edo for an audience with the *shogun*. The bandits had been unskilled, and also drunk, so they could easily have been dispatched by a poorly trained monkey, but his master observed the quantity rather than the quality, and lionized Nakadai's defense against so many foes. When they arrived in Edo, he referred to Nakadai as having the heart of a dragon, and the nickname of *Doragon Kokoro* had stayed with him ever since.

Cho shook his head and grinned unevenly, then bowed formally.

"It is an honor to meet you."

"Thank you," Nakadai said out of politeness. If Cho was honored, then so be it. He stared out at the sky to find that the downpour was lighter and the horizon was turning blue. "The rain will end soon," he observed.

"Excellent," Cho responded, but then his face fell. "Or, perhaps not. You see, while I normally take pride in my work as a messenger, today I am the bearer of bad tidings."

"That is unfortunate," Nakadai said, but he didn't press. He had no interest in the private communications of others.

"Very unfortunate. I have come from the local *daimyo* with news that will greatly displease the people I represent. You see," Cho continued, despite Nakadai's desire to respect the privacy of both the sender and recipient, "there are two maidens whose fates remain undetermined."

Nakadai turned to face the messenger.

"What do you mean?"

"A man named Kimota promised his son to two different women. The fathers of both maidens paid the bride-price. Before the deception was discovered, however, Kimota took ill and died."

"Why did the son not simply repay one of the fathers?" Nakadai asked. "Or both, and choose another woman as his wife?"

"Unfortunately, Kimota engaged in his duplicity in order to pay off gambling debts," Cho explained. "The money is long gone, and the poor young man is under obligation to two women."

"It is a difficult problem," Nakadai agreed, shaking his head. "I assume you were sent to the *daimyo* to receive judgment."

"Exactly," Cho said with a sigh, "but the *daimyo* has refused to judge on the matter, deeming it beneath his notice to settle the disputes of gamblers."

Nakadai rubbed his chin. The patter of the rain lessened, and within a minute or two it would be light enough to allow them to continue on their separate journeys.

Then he spoke.

"I have at times," he said slowly, "acted as an arbitrator in just such disputes, ones that were too sensitive—or too meager—to cause the *daimyo* to intervene. Perhaps I may be of assistance."

Cho brightened at the idea.

"Perhaps," he said. "Both maidens' fathers had rather expected that the *daimyo* would solve all their problems."

Nakadai allowed himself a small smile.

"In my experience, it is rare for a *daimyo* to solve any problem that is not his own."

Cho laughed loudly at that.

"Very true," he agreed, then he straightened and looked directly at the fallen *samurai*. "We would be honored to have the Heart of the Dragon serve as mediator."

Wincing again at the nickname, Nakadai walked out from under the shelter.

"Shall we, then?" He turned and strode down the road at a brisk pace.

"Absolutely," Cho replied enthusiastically, and he ran to catch up and then pass the *ronin*, until he was leading the way.

As the messenger passed, Nakadai thought he caught a glimpse of a strange expression on his new companion's face. A trick of the changing light made the man's eyes appear pitch black.

But he quickly dismissed it as a momentary illusion.

The dispute proved a difficult one for Nakadai to mediate.

Both women were insistent that they were promised to Kimota's son—a befuddled youngster named Shiro.

First he spoke to one of Shiro's prospective brides, a woman named Keiko.

"The *daimyo* is a filthy worm!" she said stridently. "How *dare* he treat my future as something so horribly unimportant! What kind of a *daimyo* just leaves us twisting in the wind like that? I tell you, he ought to be hanged! Or at least stripped of his position! He's almost as bad as Kimota, taking advantage of us like that!

"You're a *samurai*, you should *do* something about it!"

Nakadai listened patiently to Keiko's shrieking, which only got louder as she continued. Then he thanked her and spoke to the other woman, whose name was Akemi.

Unfortunately, all Akemi did was cry. Nakadai tried asking her questions—something that had been unnecessary with Keiko, who spoke without prompting—but each question received only another sob in reply.

Next, Nakadai spoke to the fathers. He had been

concerned that there would be bitterness between the two men, but their shared misfortune had apparently brought them close together as comrades.

"Kimota convinced me," Keiko's father started, "to keep the engagement a secret until harvest day."

Akemi's father continued.

"He made the same request of me. It's been a poor year for crops, you see."

"Kimota's explanation was that the news of an impending marriage would cheer the rest of the townsfolk, after what we knew would be a poor harvest," Keiko's father finished.

Nakadai nodded. He'd wondered how Kimota had managed to keep the twin engagements quiet in so small a town as this, where everyone generally knew the details of everyone else's affairs.

Finally, Nakadai spoke to Shiro.

"I don't know what to do," the young man moaned. He was sitting with his head down, staring at his sandals rather than looking up at Nakadai. "Both women are worthy wives, of course, and I would be happy with either of them. I honestly never expected to marry a woman as fine as either Akemi or Keiko. But Father never even *told* me any of this. The first I heard of either engagement was when Keiko and Akemi's fathers both came to me after the funeral."

Normally when he performed such arbitration, Nakadai's queries would eventually reveal some critical fact that had remained hidden, and that would point to his best course of action. But in this case, all he could find was what he had learned from Cho at the shelter: Kimota had tricked two men into paying a bride-price for Shiro. Since Shiro could only marry one, he'd be obligated to return the other's money, which would leave both him and his new bride utterly destitute.

For the first time since his master had been disgraced, Nakadai found himself uncertain of how to proceed.

The town boasted a modest inn, and on his third night there, Nakadai sat up late, cleaning his katana by candlelight. The rhythm of wiping the cloth on the curved blade helped him organize his thoughts.

He heard footsteps moving through the town's main street. At this hour, most of the populace was asleep, so the steps echoed loudly through the night.

They also grew closer to the inn.

Within moments, the swathed shadow of a female figure, cast by a wavering candle, fell across the paper door that led to Nakadai's room. The shadow's arm thrust forward, and the door slid open.

It was Akemi. She fell to her knees.

"Forgive my intrusion at this late hour, *Doragon Kokoro*, but I must speak with you."

Nakadai gritted his teeth. Cho had introduced him to the townspeople as the Heart of the Dragon, and he was not pleased that the name had taken hold. Nor did he like the idea of people simply entering his room unannounced.

However, he had yet to actually hear from Akemi, as these were the first words that had come from her mouth while in his presence. So he nodded to her, sheathing his sword.

She rose, shut the door, then walked toward him, kneeling again in front of him and bowing low.

"I wish to plead with you to rule for my father."

"You were both equally wronged," he replied. "Why should Keiko suffer and you benefit?"

Suddenly, Akemi's eyes changed from pale blue to pitch black.

"Because, oh mighty Heart of the Dragon, I won't give you a choice." As she spoke, her tone became strangely guttural.

Instantly Nakadai was on his feet with his sword unsheathed. With the transformation of her eyes came an alteration in her face. It morphed into something not quite human.

"What are you?" he demanded.

"Originally? Just a demon trying to set the people of this town against one another. For amusement, really. Turning humans against people they trust—now *that's* a party." Akemi's head shook back and forth. "But these peasants refuse to cooperate! Instead of fighting over who gets to marry that tiresome little rodent Shiro, as I was hoping they would, they whined to the *daimyo*, begging for assistance.

"But then I found you."

Now Akemi's face formed an expression that could barely be called a smile.

"Now I get to do something that'll provide a *lot* more than simple entertainment. And you'll be the one to assist me."

Nakadai remained in a defensive posture, but he resisted the urge to launch himself at the intruder.

"I will never assist a creature such as yourself, demon, if that is what you truly are."

"Really? So what happens next?" the demon purred with a voice like gravel. "You attack me? If you do so, then you harm poor, helpless Akemi—and the peasants will condemn you as the murderer of an innocent woman."

Nakadai knew that the monster spoke true—yet he could hardly stand defenseless, either.

So he retained his stance and let the demon speak.

"You see," it said with a hint of Akemi's voice, "one day I will have need of you. Not today, nor even soon, but when the day of this task arrives, it will require the sacrifice of a hero." The black eyes stared hard at Nakadai. "Do you know how hard it is to find a true hero, especially in these wretched days?

"By the time I possessed Cho—seeking to pass the time—and pretended to go to the *daimyo*, I had given up hope of ever again meeting a virtuous man. But then I saw you in the shelter, and I realized I had my hero. Then it was just a matter of luring you here, and that was the easiest thing in the world."

"I will not participate in any plan of yours."

"Your cooperation is neither required nor necessary," the thing that controlled Akemi said with a chuckle.

Before the stunned *ronin* could react, the demon

proceeded to rend Akemi's garments and slam her head into the inn's support pillar.

Then she screamed.

As she continued to do so, Nakadai's heart sank, and he realized that there was no defense against this. He knew he had only a few seconds before someone responded to her screams. His only option was to stay and try to explain what had happened. The alternative was to choose the coward's path and flee.

Honor would not permit him to run.

Footsteps clattered in the street, mixing with the woman's cries to shatter the stillness. The door to the inn was thrown open, and a half-dozen men stared in horror at the sight of Nakadai with his sword drawn, and Akemi, lying naked, bleeding, and writhing on the floor.

One of the men was Akemi's father. He called out his daughter's name and knelt beside her, cradling her wounded head, wiping the blood from her eyes.

"What did he do to you, my precious daughter?"

Whimpering, the demon—whose eyes had returned to normal—replied in Akemi's voice, "I tried to plead with him to rule for our side, and he attacked me!" She lifted her head and glared malevolently at Nakadai. "Said I wasn't fit to be a bride, and that when he was done, I'd never be!"

Akemi's father whirled on him.

"You *dare* violate my daughter?"

Another of the townspeople spoke up.

"We thought *Doragon Kokoro* was a man of honor!

But you're just more filthy *ronin* scum!"

"I did not touch your daughter," Nakadai said, knowing it was futile. "She has been possessed by a demon."

The voice of Akemi pierced the night air.

"He's lying!"

"Of course he is," her father said. Then he turned to the men who stood in the doorway. "Seize him!"

Nakadai could have resisted with the greatest of ease. These were peasants, after all. He could have killed all six of them—and Akemi as well—without difficulty, and made his escape.

But his katana had never claimed the blood of an innocent. It would not do so now, even if that meant Nakadai's own death.

No, he knew then that his fate had been sealed the moment the demon entered his room, wearing Akemi's skin. Or perhaps it had been sealed the moment he took shelter from the rain.

So he let the men grab him, take his sword, bind him, and take him to the town square. More townspeople gathered along the way, roused by the hubbub. He was bound to a post and guards were assigned to watch him. But they need not have bothered—he would await the sunrise with dignity.

At sunrise, the entire town was called to the square to mete out justice. Akemi's father told everyone what *Doragon Kokoro* had done to his daughter, and he spat in the dust as he spoke.

"Will anyone speak in defense of the *ronin*?" he challenged.

Nobody spoke.

Ropes biting into his wrists at his back, Nakadai regarded the crowd that had gathered before him. In their eyes, he saw revulsion at what they thought had been done to Akemi, and disappointment that the Heart of the Dragon was apparently less than his reputation. He longed to speak the truth, but knew it would do no good.

Akemi's father turned to look at him. His eyes swam over with black.

So the demon has found a new vessel, Nakadai mused.

"It seems that you have been condemned, *ronin*," it said, no hint of the guttural in its voice. "You should have sought your pleasures in a whorehouse instead of with my daughter, *filth*." He spat again, this time at Nakadai's feet.

Of Cho and Akemi, the prisoner saw no sign. He wondered what became of those who had been possessed, after the demon departed. He suspected that it didn't bear thinking about.

His eyes returning to normal, Akemi's father spun to face the crowd.

"Yoshio Nakadai, the so-called Heart of the Dragon, will be burned to death for his crimes!"

The crowd cheered their assent, hurling epithets.

Nakadai was appalled.

"I demand the right of *seppuku*!" he cried.

Turning back, the demon snarled with the voice of Akemi's father.

"You have violated my daughter! You are in no position

to 'demand' anything, *ronin* scum!"

Nakadai moved to protest, and then silenced himself. To refuse a proper death for a *samurai*, even a *ronin*, was unheard of. But he also knew that any further objection would be fruitless.

Several of the townspeople pounded a bamboo pole into the ground, well away from their dwellings, while others grabbed him, dragged him over, and tied him there. Some made certain his bindings were firm, while others placed sticks at his feet, piling them up to his knees.

Akemi's father left, then reappeared holding a torch.

The townspeople all backed away.

"You die today for your crimes, *Doragon Kokoro*," the demon shouted, loud enough for all to hear. An amused grin briefly twisted its mouth.

He bent over to thrust the torch into the sticks. As he did so, he whispered words in a language that Nakadai did not know, and that only the *ronin* could hear.

There was a foul purpose here, but as the flames licked his legs and his battered robes caught fire, he could not divine what it was.

Though the flames burned the living flesh from his bones, the Heart of the Dragon died without screaming, while the population of an entire town cheered his death.

The demon watched through Akemi's father's eyes as Yoshio Nakadai burned. Even as the flames consumed the *ronin*'s body, a fire of a different kind was consuming his soul.

The creature was pleased with itself. So many of its kind were concerned with quick fixes—a soul here, some political influence there. Such things were so—so *trivial*.

No, it preferred to play for the bigger stakes.

Not that the small stakes didn't have their rewards. He looked around at the people of this town, who had been so easily manipulated by Kimota. The demon hadn't had anything to do with that—in fact, it was Kimota's manipulations that had drawn its attention to this otherwise insignificant little spot in the first place.

Such delightful machinations attracted him like a fly to shit.

But once the demon had realized what was happening, it had decided to have some fun. It had gifted Kimota with a fatal illness, turned the people even more against one another, and then wore the town messenger to guarantee that no help would be forthcoming from the *daimyo*, thus enraging them further.

That anger, the outrage—*that* was fun. But being able to lure a noble soul to the town, that was *art*. And it was art that would survive long past this delicious moment.

While it had no idea how long it might take, the demon was fully aware that one day the demons and the angels were going to go to war, that Lucifer's minions and God's minions would launch their epic final battle.

Most demons would be little more than foot soldiers, and they'd be happy with their lot. But *this* demon had plans. It had managed to escape Hell, thanks to a bored man who possessed an ancient scroll and didn't value his own soul particularly highly. Since that day it had roamed the Earth, getting ready for the big one.

It wasn't sure how long it would take, but being an immortal demon, it could afford to be patient.

The eldritch flames, summoned through a whispered spell, entwined themselves around the Heart of the Dragon, blackening his purity and his nobility even as the physical flames melted his flesh and muscle and bone.

When the time came, the spirit of Yoshio Nakadai would become a weapon of unimaginable power in the hands of demonkind: a noble soul put to ignoble use.

2009

TWO

Dean Winchester stared calmly across the table at the man with the white goatee.

They were the only two players remaining in an all-night poker game, and Dean had a substantial pile of chips in front of him. White Goatee only had one hundred-dollars' worth left, and he was contemplating his cards nervously while puffing on his twelfth cigar of the night. That he did so while sitting under the red NO SMOKING sign had been a source of amusement when the game started, but now it was just tiresome.

Dean doubted he'd ever get the smell of cheap cigar out of his leather jacket, but that was the price he had to pay. Well that and the game's 600-dollar buy-in, which Dean had been forced to borrow from Bobby Singer. He and his brother Sam had been reduced to an almost penniless state, which meant that they needed a big score in order to keep doing things like eating and putting gas in Dean's 1967 Chevrolet Impala. After all, starving to death or being stuck on the road without gas were extra inconveniences when you were trying to prevent the Apocalypse.

White Goatee stared at Dean's four up cards: a two of hearts, three of clubs, four of hearts, and a six of spades. As for him, he had three aces showing, as well as a four of diamonds. Dean had consistently matched his opponent's bets, never raising him. He could afford to be magnanimous, given his monster pile of chips and the fact that White Goatee was on his last legs.

I really ought to learn this guy's name, Dean mused.

Then he thought about it.

Nah. Why bother?

The problem for White Goatee was that he couldn't be sure if Dean was betting for the fun of it or not. After all, Dean was able to match all bets, even with a crap hand. His up cards indicated a likely straight, or maybe two pair or three of a kind.

On the other hand, White Goatee could easily have a full house, or even four aces. *Not likely, though, judging from his expression.*

What worried White Goatee, Dean figured, was that his pile of chips had been slowly but surely increasing all night and into the morning. That wasn't an accident. The other five players had all dropped out, with most of their money now represented by clay disks that were either stacked in front of Dean or in the middle of the table.

In many ways, he felt ridiculous playing poker when the world was about to end, but they had to get cash somehow. Besides, he felt even more ridiculous thinking so matter-of-factly about the end of the world.

Yet it was true, and there was no escaping it. Sam had been manipulated by a demon named Ruby into freeing Lucifer from his prison. The angels and the demons were squaring off, and humanity was going to pay the price.

The angels insisted that Dean was the vessel for the Archangel Michael, while the demons were just as insistent that Sam was destined to become the vessel for Lucifer. They had been told that this was inevitable, and that they should accept their fates.

Both brothers declined to accept a damned thing. *So to speak.*

They had no idea how they were going to triumph, but they also knew that they'd find a way, or go down fighting.

First things first, though.

"C'mon, Colonel Sanders," Dean said, breaking the silence and making everyone in the room jump. "Bet or fold."

White Goatee sighed.

"Ain't got me no choice, do I?" He pushed all his chips in. "Hunnert."

Dean tossed in two fifty-dollar chips.

"Call."

Grinning, White Goatee flipped over the ace of hearts he had in the hole alongside the three he had up.

"Quads."

Letting out a long breath, Dean first flipped over the six of hearts. Then he flipped over the four of hearts.

Thinking Dean only had two pair—sixes and fours— White Goatee started to make a grab for the chips.

Then Dean flipped over his third hole card: the five of hearts.

Which gave him the two, three, four, five, and six of hearts: a straight flush, which was the only hand that could beat four of a kind.

He grinned like the cat who ate the canary.

"Oh, *hell*, no!" White Goatee yelled.

Behind Dean, three men laughed. One was the bartender, who also ran the game. The other two were the only players who'd stuck around after they had lost all their money, curious to see how the rest of the game would go.

The bartender could afford to laugh, since one hundred dollars of everyone's buy-in went straight to him, in return for the use of the hall. Once Dean paid Bobby back, that left him with three grand in his pocket. And as likely as not, Bobby would let him keep the 600.

Or perhaps not. Bobby hadn't exactly been in as charitable a mood lately. *Being stuck in a wheelchair will do that to you.*

"A pleasure, gentlemen," Dean said as he pushed his chair back. He stepped over to the bar to collect his winnings, and to reclaim his cell phone.

Scowling, White Goatee just slumped in his seat.

"The pleasure's all yours, boy," he growled.

Chuckling, the bartender counted out a stack of bills.

"Don't mind Hal, son," he said when he was done. "He just ain't used to losin'."

"Not surprised," Dean commented, loud enough for everyone to hear. "He's good." Then he broke into a grin again. "But I'm better."

The two remaining players both rolled their eyes. One of them spoke up.

"Come on back next time you're in town. I think I can speak for all of us when I say that we'd appreciate a rematch."

"I'll bet," Dean replied cheerfully. Then he headed for the exit, ignoring the daggers that Hal was staring at him from under the cloud of cigar smoke.

Opening the door, Dean winced as the rising sun caught him right in the eyes. For some reason, he had thought the sun wouldn't be up for at least another hour yet.

Walking out into the parking lot, he reached into the pocket of his leather jacket and pulled out his cell phone, turning it back on. There were two messages waiting for him, and he put the phone to his ear to listen.

One was a *how're-you-doing* from Ellen Harvelle, who'd been fanatical about checking in with the Winchesters ever since the mess in River Pass.

The other was Sam, letting him know that the omen they had thought was manifesting in East Brady, Pennsylvania, had turned out to be just a crazy old person with an arson fetish.

By the time Dean finished listening to the messages, he had arrived at the Impala, parked between an SUV and a pickup. Putting the phone away, he hopped in and started the car, checked the rearview mirror—

—and nearly jumped out of his skin at the sight of Castiel's stubble-covered face and blank expression, suddenly there in the passenger seat.

"Hello, Dean."

"What the *hell*, Cass?!"

"Sam and Bobby told me that you were here. Bobby did not wish me to remain in his house."

Backing the Impala out of the space, Dean peered over his shoulder.

"How many times do I have to remind you about personal space, Cass, huh?"

But despite the moment of panic he'd experienced, Dean found it difficult to be angry with Castiel—an angel who had rebelled against his fellows, convinced that they weren't truly following the wishes of God.

The angels had killed Castiel for his actions, but then for no discernable reason, he was resurrected. Cass believed that God had done it; the other angels figured it to be Lucifer's doing, in an attempt to sow the seeds of discord within the heavenly host.

Dean didn't give a crap about any of that—he just wanted the angels and demons gone.

Cass had become the Winchesters' friend and ally, and while he had lost some of his abilities—such as healing others—he still had enough angel mojo left to be a big help to Sam and Dean when they needed him.

"I need you and Sam to go to San Francisco," Castiel continued without acknowledging Dean's question, as Dean pulled onto the back road on which the bar sat. "The Heart of the Dragon has risen again."

"Uh, okay," Dean replied as he turned onto the empty road. "And that means what, exactly? There's gonna be a dragon in San Francisco?"

"No. But a spirit is returning to this plane—one the demon hordes will be able to use in their war with the angels. There have already been deaths."

"Okay, then." That wasn't much more than he'd started with.

"I know it's a long way, but this is important, Dean."

Dean sighed.

"I have to talk to Sam and Bobby first, Cass."

"Sam already knows, he's been researching all night."

"Glad you're giving us an option," Dean responded angrily. He squeezed the steering wheel and let out another deep sigh. "All right, all right, let me gas up the Impala and we'll leave—"

"I can simply send you there," Castiel suggested.

"*No*," Dean said emphatically.

"It's 1,500 miles from here to San Francisco, Dean. It will take you a day just to drive…."

"I've told you before, Cass, when you do that, it turns my sphincter inside out." He felt queasy just at the thought.

"No, I'll pass."

Castiel shook his head.

"Very well, then. Sam has been researching the two previous manifestations of the Heart of the Dragon."

Dean made a right turn, putting the Singer Salvage Yard in sight. *Bobby's not gonna like seeing Cass here*, he thought grimly. And as if the angel had read his mind, he saw Castiel flinch slightly.

"You okay, Cass?"

Castiel swallowed and cleared his throat.

"Bobby is not comfortable with my being in his home. He's still very… angry about his condition, and my inability to heal him. I don't think he wants me back there."

"Cass, I'm sure he'll get used to—"

"I will leave you to it, then," Castiel interrupted, and then disappeared.

Suddenly wishing he had something to drink, Dean shook his head and kept driving. One moment Castiel was there, the next he wasn't. No matter how many times he saw it, he still found it disturbing. No *way* was he going to actually go through it himself, not unless it was a dire emergency. Getting Dean away from Zachariah—that had qualified.

This didn't.

He pulled into the driveway, parking the Impala next to a junker Bobby had been working on prior to his recent injury, which had gone untouched ever since. It was still an open question as to whether or not he would ever walk again. While it was still possible to run a salvage yard from a wheelchair, Dean knew Bobby wasn't happy about it.

Can't exactly blame him.

Of course, if the four of them couldn't stop the world from going down in flames, it wasn't going to matter a whole helluva lot, either.

Inside, Sam was sitting at the kitchen table, a steaming mug of coffee next to him. Glancing at the coffeemaker on the counter, Dean saw that a fresh batch had just been made, the pot almost full.

"Hey," Sam said, without even looking up from the reams of paper he was going through, all probably fresh from Bobby's laser printer. "How'd it go?"

"Well, gas, food, and lodging won't be a problem for a while," he replied, stepping over to the counter. "Cass filled me in on the 'Frisco thing."

Nodding, Sam looked up now.

"Yeah, based on what he told me, I've been checking it out. This spirit appeared in December 1969 and again in December 1989."

"Every twenty years, huh? So no surprise that it's back now," Dean said, grabbing a mug from Bobby's dry-rack and pouring himself some coffee. "Cass said it wasn't really a dragon."

"Well, I'm not so sure about that," Sam said, handing over some of the papers. "We've got bodies sliced open and burned to a crisp."

"Yeah, but *dragons*?" Dean asked, taking the papers.

"I mean, c'mon. That's straight out of a fairy tale."

"Dean, you've been to Hell, I started the Apocalypse, and we're supposed to be possessed by an archangel and the devil. *Now* you're being skeptical?"

"Yeah, well...." Dean glanced down at the printout at the top of the stack.

Then he did a double take.

"*Sonofabitch*...."

Sam frowned.

"What?"

Dean shoved the printout under his brother's nose. It was a copy of a December 1969 article from the *San Francisco Chronicle*, complete with the original photographs. He jabbed a finger at someone in one of the crowd shots.

"Look at that guy."

Sam squinted.

"I don't—" Then he peered closer. "Sorry, I'm not recognizing him."

"Oh. No, I guess you wouldn't." Dean took the printout back and started to read. The story was about the death of a young couple near the Winterland Ballroom—the site, Dean knew, of some great concerts in the 1960s and '70s. And the person he'd pointed at was a bald man with a heavy scowl.

Dean had seen that face at two junctures in his life. Once was when he was a young child, and pictures of him had adorned the wall of their house in Lawrence, Kansas. Those pictures were lost when the house caught fire during the demon Azazel's attack in 1983. Dean and Sam's mother Mary was killed in the process. Sam, who was only six months old at the time, wouldn't have remembered those photos.

The second time had come a year ago, when Castiel had sent Dean back in time to 1973 and he'd met Samuel and Deanna Campbell and their daughter Mary; his grandparents and his mother—who, to Dean's abject shock, were also hunters. The elder Campbells were killed by Azazel in '73.

The bald man was Samuel Campbell—his grandfather. And apparently, on one of the Campbell family hunts, they had gone after the Heart of the Dragon....

1969

THREE

Moondoggy thought this whole thing was just completely uncool.

It started out the way it always did: Moondoggy needed money for grass. This wasn't unusual, since Moondoggy frequently had trouble securing gainful employment, and dealers had trouble giving him grass when he couldn't pay for it.

It wasn't that he didn't *want* to work. Michael James Verlander—who had started calling himself "Moondoggy" after he turned on, tuned in, dropped out, and moved to San Francisco six years earlier—just wasn't always hip to the whole "taking instructions" scene. It had derailed his career as a roadie. He'd been a good one, too, for the Dead and Ten Years After, and a few others.

Lately, though, the gigs had been drying up.

Finding things, though, Moondoggy had always been good at that.

So when Albert Chao came to him in the bar one night, and told him he was looking for a piece of paper that was part of a spell, Moondoggy was with it. His ex was a waitress at the bar, and Albert was one of the regulars.

Moondoggy knew some guys who knew some guys who dealt with that kind of spooky stuff. Albert promised some serious bread, and that meant Moondoggy could buy more grass.

So first he went to the head shop in Haight-Ashbury where Ziggy sold his comic books. Ziggy used to hunt freaky stuff all the time, till he lost his legs. Now he went around on crutches and wrote and drew comic books about a guy who hunted monsters.

Moondoggy bought one of his comics, and in exchange Ziggy gave him the name of a guy in the Tenderloin. The guy in the Tenderloin passed on another name to Moondoggy in exchange for the comic book, which was handy, since Moondoggy hated Ziggy's comics and was just going to throw it out anyway.

That was when he hit the snag.

The guy in the Tenderloin sent Moondoggy back to the Haight to a chick named Sunflower, who'd been looking to score some really *good* LSD. Her usual supplier had got himself pinched by the fuzz, and her other pushers had stuff that had been stepped on way too many times.

That wasn't the snag. That was the easy part. Moondoggy never bothered with acid—that stuff supposedly broadened your horizons, but he generally preferred to deaden his. But he knew how to get the best LSD in the Bay Area. In exchange for introducing Sunflower to the acid king, Moondoggy could finally score the spell fragment for Albert Chao.

No, the snag was that he had to go to Dolores Park.

Moondoggy walked down 25th Street, rubbing his arms against the November cold, approaching an imposing Victorian façade halfway down the block. He was only wearing his bell-bottoms, Birkenstocks, and the tie-dyed shirt his ex had given him as a birthday present before they broke up. He used to have a denim jacket, but it had disappeared at some point. He might even have sold it for some grass. He couldn't remember.

The place he was apartment-sitting was in the Inner Mission on Guerrero near 22nd. It was only a ten-minute walk to Dolores Park, but it may as well have been another planet. There were very few people on the street, and the ones he did see were going straight from their fancy sports cars to their front doors. Other people peered at him from behind their lace curtains.

None of them bothered with the cold. Weather was for peasants.

Any minute, he just *knew* someone was gonna call the fuzz.

His knobby knees wobbling, he walked up the stairs to the Victorian's front door, which had been painted a sickly green color.

Knocking on the door, he felt a chill that had nothing to do with the wind coming in off the bay. The door made a hollow sound, like he was banging on someone's coffin.

For several seconds, nobody answered. This was all starting to get too heavy for Moondoggy.

Just as he was about to give up, go back to his pad, and figure out what to tell Albert, someone opened the door a crack. It made a piercingly loud creak, and he winced.

Someone was standing on the other side, but it was dark in there, and Moondoggy couldn't make out a face.

"Uh, how's it hangin', man?" he said haltingly. "Sunflower sent me?"

"Are you Moondoggy?" replied a voice that sounded like crumpled paper.

"Uh, yeah, that's me, man. I'm just here to pick up the spell fragment."

"Do you understand that what I am about to hand you is not complete?"

Now he had recovered his nerves, Moondoggy was starting to get cranky.

"Look, man, I didn't go to college or nothin', but I know what the word 'fragment' means, okay? I'm just here to pick the thing up, know what I'm sayin'?"

There was a pause.

"Wait here," the crumpled-paper voice said, and then the door shut with a loud slam that ruffled the hairs in Moondoggy's beard.

"Coulda at least let me in," he muttered, rubbing his arms again. "Shoulda made Albert pay me in advance."

He wasn't sure how much time passed—Moondoggy had never owned a watch, which was another reason his roadie career hadn't lasted all that long—but eventually the green door squealed open again.

It opened wider this time, so that Moondoggy could see the cat who was standing on the other side. He had skin that was more wrinkled than the elephants at the circus, and wispy white hair in spots on his mostly-bald head. Liver spots covered his crown.

There were some concert posters on the wall, which surprised Moondoggy. He wouldn't have thought that cats who dealt in spells would like good music, but there was the poster from when the Dead played at the Fillmore back in February and March.

Was that this year, or last? He was never good with dates.

A gnarled hand held out a scrap of paper that was as crumpled as the old man's voice.

"Be very wary of this," the man said. "It is part of a spell that can summon a vile spirit from the very depths of Hell."

"Uh, yeah. Heavy." Moondoggy took the proffered scrap and looked it over. It looked like a bunch of nonsense. He didn't know any languages except for English and Spanish, and this didn't look anything like either one. With a shrug, he shoved the piece of paper into the back pocket of his bell-bottoms.

"Thanks, man. Hey, were you at that Dead show at the Fillmore? 'Cause it was—"

The door slammed again.

"Guess not." Turning around, he started down the stairs. With each step, he felt an ever-increasing desire to put as much distance as he could between himself and the gloomy Victorian house.

So he walked as fast as his legs could carry him back to the Inner Mission. Moondoggy felt more at home here. There were *people*, and nobody looked twice at him. Best of all, there weren't creepy old cats with weird voices and spell fragments.

Finally he arrived home.

Of course it wasn't exactly *Moondoggy*'s home. The pad actually belonged to his friend Freddy, who had gone east for Woodstock back in August. Then he'd decided to stay in New York and become a famous folk musician. Last Moondoggy heard, Freddy had got a gig at Gerde's Folk City in Greenwich Village. Lots of people got their start at Folk City, Bob Dylan, Arlo Guthrie, Judy Collins, and Doc Watson, so Freddy had figured if they could do it, he could do it.

Of course, Freddy didn't even know how to tune his guitar right, so Moondoggy wasn't holding out much hope. But as long as Freddy was chasing his dream, he had a place to sleep, and that was all that mattered.

He just hoped that Freddy wouldn't mind what had happened to that fancy mug of his. Freddy claimed he'd been cutting down on the caffeine anyhow, so he probably wouldn't even notice.

He climbed the three flights of rickety stairs up to the apartment, fumbling through the pockets of his bell-bottoms for the keys. His arrangement was handy—Freddy didn't charge him rent, just asked him to feed Viola Lee, his cat, and that hadn't been an issue for weeks.

Reaching his destination, Moondoggy instinctively stretched his hand out towards the doorknob.

But then the door opened.

"Far out," Moondoggy muttered, and a chill ran up his spine, but he quickly calmed his nerves. "Musta forgot to lock it." It certainly wouldn't have been the first time. In fact, that was why Viola Lee was no longer his concern.

Stepping inside, he heard the sounds of Led Zeppelin playing from his—okay, Freddy's—turntable. That was when Moondoggy *knew* something was wrong. For one thing, he *hated* Zeppelin. For another, he'd been gone for a couple of hours now. If he'd left a record on, the needle would be at the end of the side. No way would it still be playing.

Walking cautiously down the short hallway and into the pad's tiny living room, he found someone sitting on the couch.

"Albert?" Moondoggy asked, relief palpable in his voice. "Are you early, man? Not that I'm complainin' or nothin'." He vaguely recalled asking his neighbor to look out for Albert. Timing wasn't one of Moondoggy's strong points.

Albert just smiled. He was a young Asian, and if Moondoggy remembered right, he was half Chinese and half Japanese. He had his dark hair in a bowl cut that made him look like an Eastern Paul McCartney—or at least what McCartney looked like back in the day, before he grew the beard—and he had a flat face. The tip of his nose stuck out a bit, which was freaky. Albert wore a white Nehru jacket and black slacks, and looked way too elegant to be hanging out in a dump like this.

He stood up.

"I'm working on a timetable, 'Doggy. You see, this spell functions best on the night of the new moon." The look on his face said that he expected that to mean something.

"Far out, man," Moondoggy answered with a nod. He'd never really paid much attention to the lunar cycle, so he had no idea when the new moon might occur. Digging a hand into his back pocket, he pulled out the scrap of paper the old man had handed him. "Here you go, man. You got my bread?"

Snatching the crumpled paper from Moondoggy's hand, Albert peered at it intently.

"All in good time, 'Doggy. I have to make sure that these are solid goods."

Moondoggy nodded.

"I can dig that." There'd been plenty of occasions when he'd bought some grass without checking to make sure it was good, often to his regret. *Always best to inspect the merchandise.*

Albert pulled a much more pristine slip of paper out of the pocket of his Nehru jacket. Unfolding the paper, he held it next to the wrinkled one Moondoggy had given him.

Then he broke into a wide grin.

There was something *wrong* in that grin.

"Excellent."

"So can I have my bread now?" Moondoggy asked. He really wanted to get this over with.

But Albert seemed to have forgotten that he was there. He was chanting something now, and while Moondoggy didn't recognize the words, he had a creepy feeling they were the strange ones he'd seen on the scrap of paper.

While he usually prided himself on being pretty laid back, he was beginning to get pissed off. He didn't like being ignored, and he had important things to do.

"Hey, man, go cast your spell on your own time. I gotta go score me some grass before I meet up with my old lady, and...."

Then the coffee table caught fire.

"Aw, man!" Moondoggy cried, jumping back. Freddy might not miss the mug, and cats ran away all the time, so he wasn't sweating that, but the coffee table? That Freddy would *notice*! He grabbed a blanket and moved to smother the flames.

But then he froze.

The coffee table was already burned to a pile of ash, but now Moondoggy could see a figure standing inside the fire. The flickering light of the flames cast odd shadows.

Albert had a huge grin on his face.

"Yes! It worked! Finally! It's even better than I thought!" Then he regarded Moondoggy with a pitying expression. "I must apologize, 'Doggy. You see, I misled you in the bar last week when I informed you that I would be able to pay you handsomely for the service of providing the rest of the spell."

Moondoggy couldn't take his eyes off the figure inside the fire. The man exuded waves of malevolence, and he was holding something, but he couldn't figure out what it was. The flames licked higher toward the ceiling.

As Albert's words sunk in, with a shudder Moondoggy turned his attention back to his visitor.

"Whaddaya mean, man?" he said plaintively. "You're not gonna stiff me, are you?"

"I mean," Albert said slowly, "that if I had the money to pay you, I would not require the spell needed to bind the Heart of the Dragon."

"The who of the *what?*" Moondoggy was still enraptured by the fire that kept burning but didn't move or spread to the rest of the apartment. And by the man inside it. This was as heavy a scene as he'd ever encountered.

Then the man raised his arms, and Moondoggy saw a curved sword that was also on fire. The man waved the sword back and forth several times, sending the weapon whistling menacingly through the air, the fire sparking and dancing.

Albert spoke again.

"And I'm afraid I can't leave any witnesses to what I've done, either."

FOUR

Samuel Campbell hated Christmas.

He had nothing against the holiday itself. He didn't dare, honestly, since every time he brought it up, Deanna would give him one of her looks and then lecture him about the winter solstice. *Many cultures celebrate the death and rebirth of the sun, since the sun gave life*, and so on, and so forth.

Samuel understood, truly he did. He understood that it was why Christians celebrated the birth of Jesus Christ at this time of the year. Early Christianity was very good at co-opting pagan and Jewish rituals, all to make conversion more palatable. He had always found it ironic that the early church had been so much better at it than the modern one.

It didn't even bother Samuel how commercial the holiday had become, with images of Santa Claus on Coca-Cola cans, and department stores doing their best to separate the people from their money.

Nor was he terribly annoyed at the fact that every year, it seemed like the ramp-up started earlier and earlier. The calendar had only just turned to December, and already it was beginning—with commercials on the TV announcing special Christmas bargains and sales.

Even the whole "peace on Earth, good will to Man" notion had been co-opted by the hippies, which left a bad taste in Samuel's mouth. But still, the sentiment was a good one, if naïve.

No, what he hated about Christmas was the timing. The monsters just loved the solstices, especially the winter one. Nothing they liked better than to come out at night, after all, and the longest night of the year was fast approaching.

And nothing liked the darkness more than vampires. Right now, Samuel was crouched in the bushes outside a remote house that stood alone at the end of an unlit cul-de-sac in Big Springs, just off the turnpike. It was colder than a well-digger's ass out here, but the information they'd got from Father Callapso said that this was where the vampire lived.

He'd spent the past few days tracking this particular bloodsucker. Most of his victims were girls, primarily teenagers too stupid to say "no" to a man who wanted to bring them home. Of course, in Samuel's experience, most teenage girls were that dumb, and he thanked the God he didn't entirely believe in that his fifteen year-old daughter Mary didn't fit that mold.

Willful, annoying, disrespectful, yes—Mary was all those things. Samuel had hoped for a dutiful little girl, but she'd already seen too much of the ugliness of the world. When you trained a child practically from birth how to defend herself, how to fire a weapon, how to use a knife, and that not only was the monster in the closet real, but it could and *should* be shot, hoping for "dutiful" was a waste of time.

The roar of a car's engine sounded in the distance and quickly grew closer. Samuel soon saw the vehicle that made the noise: a gussied-up show-off car with fins of the kind that boys used to impress girls. He didn't know the specifics—all he knew about cars was that they started moving when he stepped on the gas, and stopped when he hit the brakes.

Most likely Mary would've been able to quote chapter and verse, since she'd been spending what spare time she had at an auto mechanic's shop. Some boy who worked there after school was sniffing around her, and Samuel had been meaning to check him out. He just hadn't had the time.

His only consolation was that Mary's own after-school activities would probably keep her too busy to do anything other than talk. The life of a hunter wasn't exactly built for romance.

He'd tried explaining that to her once.

"But what about you and Mom?" she'd asked defiantly.

"That's different," Samuel had protested weakly.

"How?" Mary had pressed, and Samuel had given up, knowing he didn't have an answer.

The car pulled into the driveway that ran alongside the house. Samuel checked the ground next to him where he'd set the bow and arrows, and the machete. He'd use the arrows to slow the vampire down, and then the machete to cut off his head.

Cutting the engine of his ostentatious muscle machine, the creature leapt out of the driver's side and ran around to open the passenger door for his victim. The bloodsucker fit the image nicely: tall, dark, and handsome. He had long sideburns, like most kids these days who weren't hippies, and wore a blue jacket and tie. Despite himself, Samuel admired his clean-cut approach.

Most vampires looked a few years out of date—immortals tended to have a wonky time-sense. Like that one who appeared to be about forty, but talked about fighting "Jerry" during "the Great War." Plenty of World War I vets still called it "the Great War," but for anyone who'd fought in World War II—as Samuel himself had—it was all about "the Nazis" or "the Krauts."

When the vampire opened the door to let the girl out, Samuel heard a familiar-sounding giggle.

"What a groovy house!" Mary said in a much higher, squeakier voice than was normal for her. Even in the gloom, he could see that her eyes were wide, and her mouth fell open.

He had to admit to a certain pride at his daughter's ability to put on a character—pride which was tempered by the fact that he was using his fifteen year-old daughter as bait for a bloodsucker. But that was the job. This vampire liked teenagers, and Samuel had a teenager for a daughter. So she had to be the one who would lure the creature back to his house without endangering any more innocent girls.

Then he heard the low hum of another engine and turned to see the Campbell family pickup truck moving slowly down the road. There was hardly any moon, and its lights were out, so the truck was nearly invisible. If he hadn't been expecting it, he might not have seen it himself.

Even knowing it was there, he couldn't see the driver, but he knew his wife Deanna was behind the wheel.

Reaching down into the brush, Samuel picked up the bow and grabbed an arrow. He'd need to break cover in order to aim the bow—if he didn't stand up straight, he'd never get a good shot off, and with Mary that close, he couldn't risk it—so he got to his feet, notched the arrow, and pulled the string back.

The arrow flew free and lodged itself right in the vampire's back, cutting through his blue jacket and embedding itself in his spine.

The vampire jerked slightly with the impact.

"Ouch," he said calmly, and turned, frowning, to see where the arrow had come from.

Then he laughed.

"Ah, I see." He clapped. "Bravo for your excellent skills, sir, but you've made one rather critical error."

Samuel scowled. "I don't think so."

"Did you really think this arrow would *hurt* me?" the vampire continued, grinning.

"By itself? No."

Suddenly, the creature stumbled.

"What…?"

"But before I came here," Samuel said, "I dipped the

arrowhead in the blood of a dead man.”

Hissing, the vampire fell to the ground, and started to roll on the lawn in front of his house. Dead man's blood was poison to his kind. As he did so, Mary calmly stepped aside, finding a safe vantage point.

Samuel reached down to pick up the machete.

He heard the door slam on the pickup truck, and spotted Deanna walking toward the house, gas can in hand. In the dim light of a crescent moon, it looked as if she had grown a tail, but that was just the scabbard for Samuel's Claymore, dangling from her waist. After Samuel cut off the bloodsucker's head—which would kill it—they'd burn the body.

Suddenly, the front door to the house slammed open, the noise of cheap metal crashing against wood paneling and echoing into the night. Samuel glanced over, only to see five people moving onto the front porch, all of them looking very unhappy.

All five had noticeably pointed incisors.

“Aw, hell, it's a *nest*!” he cried, reaching for the bow and arrow once again.

Before he could even notch the arrow, one of the vampires was on him, snatching the bow away.

“I don't think so, meat,” it snarled.

The arrow, however, was still clutched in Samuel's right hand, so he shoved it into the vampire's belly.

Snatching the bow back from the now-stunned creature, he grabbed the quiver and slung it onto his shoulder, yanking out another arrow and quickly surveying the situation.

Two of the vampires were attacking Mary, with the remaining two on Deanna. Both women were fighting back, and the quarters were too close for Samuel to risk a shot.

Grabbing his machete, he sliced down at the neck of the one he'd stabbed in the belly. It didn't cut the head clean off, but combined with the paralysis from the dead man's blood, the wound would keep the creature down. They could always finish him off later.

He moved in to help Mary, and as he did so one of the vampires grabbed his arm and pulled him close. He could smell gore on its breath, and he recoiled. That gave it the opening it was looking for.

The vampire moved in to bite him on the neck.

The report of a gunshot echoed in Samuel's ears, as Mary fired the .22 calibre pistol that she always carried, just in case. The bullet ripped into the vampire's knee. It wouldn't kill it, of course—in fact, a knee wound would heal in short order—but the impact was enough to make the monster stumble.

Samuel gave her a quick nod, then turned to face the downed monster while Mary spun to deal with the one that was still plaguing her.

Gripping its knee tightly with its left hand, blood seeping through the wound and staining its fingers, the vampire on the ground looked up and snarled at Samuel.

"You'll die slowly for that one, baldy."

With astonishing speed, the creature leapt to his feet and took a swing at Samuel with its right hand. Instinctively, Samuel raised the machete to deflect the blow. The blade cut through the vampire's flesh and struck bone with a sickening squelch.

While the vampire yanked its arm back in an attempt to free it from the blade, Samuel kicked him in the stomach. The bloodsucker fell backward, and Samuel was forced to let go of the machete's hilt.

Snarling, the creature—machete still lodged in his forearm—prepared to leap again, but moving swiftly Samuel once again used a poisoned arrow like a spear and stabbed his attacker in the stomach.

Then he elbowed the monster in the face—which hurt Samuel's arm as much as it did the vampire's glass jaw—and grabbed for the machete hilt, tearing it loose from the vampire's flesh with a bloody yank. He felt the hot splash of ichor on his face.

For a few seconds, the vampire flailed, but quickly the dead man's blood on the arrowhead left him helpless. Samuel beheaded him quickly.

Wiping his face with his sleeve, Samuel looked around to see how the women were doing....

As soon as the five other vampires appeared on the front porch of the house, he saw Deanna drop the gas can. While it hit the pavement with a sharp clank of metal on asphalt, she had reached for the scabbard and pulled out Samuel's grandfather's Claymore. Since she was a better swordsman, while he was more skilled with a bow and arrow, he had entrusted the precious weapon to her for that evening's hunt.

The provenance of the *claidheamh mór* had been a subject of great discussion in the Campbell family, due in part to the fact that Grandpa Campbell himself told a different story every time you asked him where the basket-hilt sword had come from. Sometimes it came from a member of the Clan who had fought alongside Bonnie Prince Charlie. Other times it was William Wallace's sword—a neat trick, since the basket-hilt Claymore hadn't existed in the fourteenth century. Once, Grandpa Campbell claimed that he himself had used it to help steal the Stone of Scone.

In fact, pretty much every significant event in Scottish history, Grandpa tried to tie to his sword.

The only story Samuel actually believed was the one that his grandfather told him on his deathbed, when he bequeathed it to him. By then, Samuel had already learned the truth about the things that go bump in the night. A wraith had literally sucked out the brain of his best friend, and Samuel had narrowly managed to kill it.

But somehow, Grandpa Campbell knew all about the monsters. As he lay in his four-poster bed, staring at young Samuel as intently as he could with rheumy eyes, the cancer ravaging his stomach and sending him into frequent fits of coughing, he told him about the family *claidheamh mór*, and how since the 1700s, the sword had been used to slay any number of malevolent creatures.

"And now," Grandpa had said to Samuel between coughs, "I want you to slay your own monsters with it."

* * *

Deanna pulled the sword out just in time as two vampires attacked her—one from the front, the other from the rear. She thrust the sword upward, impaling the first creature through his rib cage. Hot blood spurted everywhere, and the vampire snarled at her.

She elbowed the other one in the face—a temporary stopgap. Tightening her grip on the silver basket-hilt of the Claymore, she yanked it out of the first vampire's chest and used the momentum of that to swing it around at the one that staggered behind her.

The sword bit into the vampire's arm, causing more blood to spurt.

But the first one—unperturbed by the stab wound she had inflicted—grabbed her by her hair. As the roots tugged at her scalp, Deanna struggled to fight the creature off, whilst trying to keep tabs on the second as it stumbled, grasping its bleeding arm.

Predictably, the first vampire went straight for her neck. However, he only got a mouthful of linen, fooled by her thick, flesh-colored scarf. But she knew that would only delay him for a second—as soon as the surprise wore off, he'd tear into her carotid artery.

But a second was all Deanna needed.

She swung again with practiced ease, bringing the sword around in a smooth arc. At such close quarters the Claymore cleaved through the vampire's neck, even though the angle was awkward.

The head didn't quite come off, but it was lolling

awkwardly as the vampire collapsed to the ground.

"You filthy strumpet!" the other one breathed as he wrapped a meaty hand around Deanna's neck. Breathing became impossible as the vampire's grip tightened, and Deanna felt her feet lift off the ground.

"You will pay for what you've done!"

Deanna grabbed frantically at the vampire's wrist with her free hand, while trying to bring the Claymore around with the other.

Neither tactic was successful.

A whistle through the air signaled an arrow; there was a *thunk* and a jolt as the shaft struck the vampire in his wounded arm. Despite the pain that had to be shooting through its body, it stubbornly maintained its grip on her neck for a few more seconds.

Deanna was beginning to see spots dancing in front of her eyes, when the creature collapsed to the ground. Finally the grip lessened, and she fell in a heap alongside it, just as she found herself able to suck in precious air again.

Clambering to her feet, she finished the job of decapitating the first vampire, then beheaded the paralyzed one who had almost killed her.

Only then did she turn to flash a smile at her husband.

"Nice shooting."

"My pleasure," Samuel replied. Then he finished using his machete on the vampires who had attacked him and Mary.

"I think," Deanna said, "that we need to have a talk with Father Callapso."

Mary stared at her.

"Why? He was the one who led us to this."

"His information was wrong," Samuel explained. "There's a huge difference between a single bloodsucker and a *nest.*"

Deanna hefted the Claymore, unwilling to sheathe it until it had been cleaned. Picking up the gas can with her free hand, she approached her husband and daughter.

"It's not like *any* of our sources are one hundred percent unimpeachable," she said. "We just need to make sure what he gives us is as reliable as it can be. Still, we're lucky that the Father passes information to us at all—and that he doesn't think it's all insane."

Samuel scowled at that.

"Yeah, well, that exorcism we did for him three years back probably helped. He owes us."

Deanna started to reply, then stopped herself and nodded in the direction of the bloody corpses.

"I really don't want to start an argument...."

Mary let out a dramatic sigh.

"Oh, come *on*, Mom—it's not like I've never heard you two fight."

"She wasn't talking about you, Little Miss," Samuel said. "She meant when we have six vampire corpses we need to dispose of, and a house to burn down so it can't be used again. Once a nest, always a nest."

"Right on," Mary said emphatically. "Let's get this over with, so I can wash the blood off me."

Deanna reached up to touch her face with the wrist of her sword hand. Sure enough, the sticky sensation of blood was there. For that matter, they were all drenched in it.

"And Dad?" Mary continued. "I'm fifteen now, so can we *please* stop with the 'Little Miss' thing?"

"I'll think about it," Samuel answered with a wry smile. Mary just shot him a dirty look.

Deanna shook her head and hefted the gas can.

"Come on, my darlings, let's get to work."

Mary always thought it was kind of corny that the mailbox in front of the house said THE CAMPBELLS on it. It was like something out of the good old days, like when she was a little kid.

But the old days weren't really all that good—indeed, not as good as most people thought. What people saw on their televisions was what they *believed* was real, but Mary had learned the hard way just how much of a fiction life really was.

The world was changing. Everyone knew that, of course. Thanks to television they all saw what was happening—Woodstock, Kent State, Watts, Vietnam, the Civil Rights Act, the March on Washington, the assassinations of Dr. King and Senator Kennedy, Neil Armstrong on the moon—and no one expected things to stay the same.

Mary, though, had known just *how* different things were from when she was eleven years old and watched her parents exorcise a vengeful spirit.

The moon landing had only been a few months ago. To Mary, it was a wondrous thing. Neither Deanna nor Samuel seemed all that interested, especially since it looked as if there was a shapeshifter on the loose in St. Louis, and they were preparing to take the truck onto the turnpike to check it out.

"But Dad," Mary had said back then, "what if we go into space and get away from the monsters?"

Samuel hadn't had a good answer to that, so he'd just shrugged and continued his preparations.

There were times when Mary wondered what it would be like to have a normal life. Most of the time she was happy not to have one, because the only way to live a normal life was to remain ignorant. Sure, she'd be able to go to birthday parties and hang around with her friends and do all the other things teenagers did, but she wouldn't have known that at any moment a vampire or a shapeshifter or some icky creature might come and kill her.

No, knowledge was power. She preferred to know what was coming. If that meant fewer dates, then that was fine.

They drove back from Big Springs after burning the vampires and their house. As soon as they arrived, Mary's first destination was the bathroom. Her long blonde hair was all sticky with vampire blood, and it was just *awful*. Besides, if she let her mother or father go first, they'd take *forever*.

She peeled off her blouse and dungarees, tossing them into the bathroom hamper. Once they'd all showered, Deanna would put the clothes in the laundry with that special soap that Xin—a fellow hunter—had turned her on to.

As she stood under the hot water and rubbed baby shampoo into her hair—she'd learned early on that baby shampoo was best at getting out organic stains—she thought about the fact that she'd be following a night of vampire hunting with a day at school and her ignorant classmates.

There were times when she wished she could have it both ways. Have the normal life *and* still be a hunter. But she knew that was impossible. Sadly, it left her a bit of an outcast at school, both with her fellow students—who thought she was weird—and the school's teachers and administrators—who were frustrated by her all-too-frequent absences. Much to their chagrin, parent-teacher conferences didn't seem to do any good.

That was probably why she was spending so much time at the mechanic's place after school, whenever she could. John Winchester worked there. He was a nice boy, and refreshingly normal. But he wasn't like so many of the other high-school students, who just seemed so *stupid*. John was always so thoughtful about everything, whether it was homework, the war, politics....

Plus he didn't judge Mary the way the other kids did. He respected her privacy and in a time when women were burning their bras and demanding equal opportunity, he treated her like a person, instead of a girl.

Of course, there were times when she *wanted* to be treated like a girl. Despite the hot shower, she shuddered at the thought of what her dad would say if he knew what she was thinking.

Such thoughts were *nothing* compared to what some of the girls at school were doing. In fact, some of them really *were* tossing out their bras, and not shaving their armpits, and doing other far-out things.

Laughing to herself, she turned the shower off. She'd have gladly stayed under for several more minutes, but that wasn't fair to her parents, who probably stunk pretty bad by now. Toweling herself off, she found herself giggling that she—who'd just spent her evening being bait for a vampire who'd intended to suck her blood—thought that bra-burning and armpit hair were "far-out."

Normally she'd blow-dry her hair, but she decided to let it air-dry so Deanna could get in next. Wrapping herself in a towel, she opened the bathroom door to a burst of cool air.

Deanna was standing outside, arms folded, foot tapping.

"About time."

"Sorry," Mary said, even though she'd moved as fast as she could.

"You've got a letter," Deanna said as she retreated into the bathroom. "I left it on your dresser."

"Thanks, Mom," Mary said as she padded down the hall to her bedroom.

Closing the door behind her, she slipped the towel off and tossed it onto the floor. It fell into a crumple near the hamper with all the other dirty clothes that always wound up on the floor instead of in the hamper that her mother had wasted her money buying—as she always put it. Mary opened the top drawer of the dresser to pull out some underwear.

As she did so, she saw the envelope Deanna had left for her.

It had one of the "Plant for More Beautiful Cities" commemorative six-cent stamps for postage, and a San Francisco postmark. There was no return address, but she didn't need one, because she recognized the handwriting immediately.

She tore open the envelope and read both the letter and the *San Francisco Chronicle* clipping that it came with. Then she threw on a tie-dyed T-shirt and a fresh pair of bell-bottom dungarees over her underwear.

As soon as she opened the door, she hesitated. Pulling the T-shirt off, she went with a white button-down blouse instead. If she was going to convince her father to go to San Francisco, she needed to do it without wearing what he called "hippie clothes."

Deanna, as usual, had showered in record time, and was already toweling off by the time Mary left her room. Dressed in her terrycloth bathrobe, she walked downstairs with Mary. They found Samuel seated at the dining room table looking over the *Lawrence Journal-World*'s sports section. Unwilling to wait for the women to finish in the bathroom, he had chosen to sponge himself off in the kitchen sink, which meant he was clean, but his shirt and pants were water-stained.

Mary plunged straight in.

"There may be a job in San Francisco," she announced.

Her father looked up from his paper.

"Excuse me?"

"The letter I got in the mail?" Mary offered the letter and

clipping. "It was from—"

Samuel winced.

"Do *not* tell me it was from Yaphet. That crazy hippie is—"

"—in Florida," Deanna said. "Remember, he went down there last year?"

"No, I *don't* remember," Samuel said with a sigh. "I don't keep track of bad poets." Then he turned his attention back to Mary. "So who is it from?"

"Jack Bartow," she replied. "Remember him?"

Grimacing, Samuel snatched the letter and clipping out of her hand.

"Yeah, I remember him." He looked as if he'd just stepped in something foul.

"C'mon, Dad, he was cool."

Ever the diplomat, Deanna joined in.

"He was a very skilled observer of the supernatural, Samuel."

"And an even more 'skilled observer' of our daughter." Samuel said without looking up.

The Campbells had been in San Francisco a year earlier, tracking a witch who was working her way west on a mystical killing spree. Bartow—who was only a few years older than Mary, and whose family had also hunted until they were killed by a pack of hellhounds—had helped track the witch down.

Mary had thought Bartow was incredibly groovy, which of course made Samuel a little crazy. They had a great deal in common, really, but all Samuel cared about was that Jack was a boy who was interested in her.

Samuel didn't like anybody anyhow, and he especially didn't like boys who "sniffed around her," as he put it. She'd always hated that phrase.

Deanna went over to stand behind him, and she read the letter and clipping over his shoulder.

Then she looked up.

"He thinks it's a dragon?"

"There's no such thing," Samuel said emphatically.

"Maybe," Mary said, "but *something* killed those people in a way that sure *looks* like a dragon did it. The corpses were sliced to ribbons *and* burned to a crisp."

Deanna gently took the *Chronicle* clipping from Samuel's hand.

"It says here that the first body—the one in the Inner Mission—was found on the morning of the fourth of November."

Mary was confused.

"So?"

Samuel scowled again.

"November third was the last new moon."

Abashed, Mary lowered her head.

"Right. Sorry." Her parents had trained her to know the phases of the moon. New moons and full moons were always rife with supernatural activity. It was stupid of her to have forgotten.

"It may just be a spirit that happens to act like a dragon," Deanna said. "But it doesn't help that the second and third killings were both in Chinatown."

"So will we go?" Mary asked hopefully. She'd enjoyed San Francisco the last time, and she *really* wanted to see the city again.

Besides, she had a history test tomorrow that she hadn't had time to study for, and this was the perfect way to get out of it.

Samuel looked up at Deanna, who nodded.

"Fine," he said, "let's pack."

"I'll call Marty," Deanna said, referring to Martin Jankowitz, their travel agent. He was always able to get them quick flights relatively cheaply.

Mary ran up to her room. Since it was San Francisco, she was definitely packing her tie-dyed shirts, no matter *what* her father might say....

FIVE

Deanna Campbell had to resist the urge to kick her husband under the table, again.

She was sitting with Samuel, Mary, and Jack Bartow at an Italian restaurant on Columbus Avenue. Upon their arrival at the airport in San Francisco, Mary had found a pay phone, called Bartow, and set up a time and place to meet and get more information on this supposed dragon. Meanwhile, Samuel and Deanna had waited for the luggage.

They'd packed two suitcases, one with enough clothes to last them all for a week, and the other with all the supplies and weapons they might need. It took forever for the second suitcase—the one with the clothes—to arrive, and Samuel was close to just abandoning it when it finally was disgorged onto the carousel.

"Could've been worse," Deanna had whispered to her husband, "it could've been the other one that got lost."

Samuel just scowled. Both suitcases were too large to fit into the overhead compartments, so they'd had to check them before boarding, which made Samuel nervous. The weapons they'd amassed—pistols, crossbows, shotguns, longbows, machetes, swords—would be prohibitively expensive to replace. Samuel's dry-cleaning business and Deanna's occasional substitute teaching work provided them with enough money to pay for Mary's education and allow them to keep their armory stocked.

And occasionally buy last-minute plane tickets.

Yet here were times when the bills threatened to overwhelm them. That was the problem with hunting—it was a calling, not a profession, and callings didn't feed the bulldog.

Mary was *still* on the phone when Deanna and Samuel found her.

"Look," she was saying as they approached, "that was my last dime, and I really need to—Oh! Here's Mom and Dad. I'll see you soon, okay? Right on, Jack. *Bye!*"

"You used *all* your change?" Deanna asked before Samuel could say anything.

"Just catching up," Mary said, then she shot a look at her father. "It's not like we warned him we were coming."

Samuel hadn't wanted to pay the long-distance charge for a call to California.

Turning back to Deanna, Mary continued.

"Anyhow, he's going to make reservations for six o'clock tonight at a place in North Beach."

With that they rented a car and proceeded to their

hotel—the Emperor Norton Lodge on Ellis Street in the Tenderloin—to unpack and make sure the weapons were all clean and ready.

It was Deanna's idea to take the bus to North Beach—more popularly known as "Little Italy"—so they wouldn't need to deal with trying to park in that busy neighborhood.

"But I don't want to go weaponless," Samuel had protested.

"The killings are in Chinatown, Samuel."

"It's not the dragon I'm worried about."

Deanna just sighed, and Mary rolled her eyes.

They weren't wholly unarmed, of course, but they did leave their firearms at the motel. It wasn't wise for civilians to wander around a big city armed in these days of civil unrest. The local law tended to take a dim view of people carrying guns, and the last thing the Campbells wanted to do was gain the attention of the San Francisco Police Department.

On three separate occasions as they walked towards the restaurant, someone with long hair and bare feet tried to give Samuel a flower. It made his scowl so deep that Deanna feared his face would collapse in on itself.

Bartow was late for dinner, leaving the three of them waiting outside the restaurant. The reservation was in his name, and Samuel refused to wait at the bar with an underaged girl, even though nobody in the restaurant seemed to mind.

Finally, Bartow limped up the hill of Columbus Avenue,

after having come out of the front entrance to the City Lights bookstore. Since the last time they'd seen him, he'd exchanged his plain wooden cane for an ornate walking stick sporting a dragon's head handle.

Samuel's eyes naturally went straight to Bartow's left foot—or what was left of it. He'd had the injury before they met him last year—when he'd just turned seventeen—and claimed it was an accident due to a poorly maintained handgun. But Samuel was sure the young man had shot himself in the foot deliberately to avoid the draft.

"Sorry I'm late," Bartow said. "Ferlinghetti was doing a reading, and it ran over."

"Wow, that sounds swell," Mary said with a smile, but Samuel just looked confused.

Deanna rode to his rescue.

"Lawrence Ferlinghetti. He's a poet, and the owner of that bookstore down the street."

That just prompted a grunt, and with nothing more left to be said, they all went into the restaurant.

Once they were all seated and had ordered drinks, Bartow started asking Mary about school. His brown hair was Brylcreemed into a duck's ass style, and he had a pencil-thin mustache that was almost black. He was exactly the type of boy Deanna would have swooned over when she was fifteen.

Before long, the conversation turned to the young girl's social life, and that was what prompted the kick. As soon as the personal questions began, Samuel's mood darkened—

if such was possible—and he started glaring openly. He was about to interrupt when she let him have it.

Samuel jumped slightly, and looked at his wife.

She frowned at him, and her expression said, *Let the young people talk*. She knew how these things went, and didn't want to be thrown out of such a nice restaurant.

He sighed, and held his tongue as long as he could. After a while, as Mary was telling Bartow what a nerd her math teacher was, he glanced at Deanna again, and she nodded.

"So, Jack," Samuel said sharply, "what can you tell us about this so-called dragon?"

Bartow smiled.

"I'm not the only one calling it that, Sam," he said.

Samuel's face twitched, and Deanna sighed. He hated any diminutive of his name, and it would only serve to make an unpleasant conversation even more so.

Where are those drinks, she thought, glancing around for the waiter.

"It's 'Samuel,'" Her husband said evenly. But to his credit, he didn't snap. "Or better still, 'Mr. Campbell.'"

"Dad…" Mary started, but Bartow put a hand on her arm.

"No, it's all right, Mare," Bartow said in a suddenly subdued tone. Then he turned back. "I apologize for my disrespect, sir."

Samuel looked surprised, not knowing how to react. Deanna smiled into her napkin.

"Apology accepted," he muttered.

Nodding confidently, Bartow reached into his shirt

pocket and took out a pack of cigarettes.

"Anyhow, like I said, folks are referring to whatever it is that's killed these four folks as 'the heart of the dragon.'"

"Four?" Deanna interrupted. "I thought it was three."

Placing a cigarette in his mouth, Bartow lit it with a zippo.

"It was, ma'am, but there was another last night. SFPD's keeping this one out of the newspapers to avoid a panic, but I got a buddy on the job." At Samuel's dubious expression, he added, "I helped my parents exorcise a demon that had taken the guy's son—sometimes a little Latin goes a long way. And that sort of thing buys a lotta gratitude."

Samuel relented a bit.

"My buddy couldn't get me the files, but he did provide some details about the victims. The first was named Michael Verlander, but everyone called him 'Moondoggy.'"

"A hippie," Samuel said.

"Yes, sir. But the place where he was found belongs to a guy named Frederick Gorczyk, whereabouts unknown. The next two were ordinary citizens of Chinatown. One was the manager of a laundry, and the other owned a restaurant. But the victim last night was different—a woman named Marybeth Wenzel, a student at Berkeley."

"Do the victims have anything in common?" Samuel asked.

Bartow shook his head while dragging on his cigarette.

"At least not that anybody could find. Hard to say for sure, since the Chinese don't usually talk to cops, so nobody knows much about those two. And this latest victim, the girl? She just makes it even worse. That's why mum's the word with the PD on the latest one. A hippie and two Chinese is one thing—they'll barely get noticed. But this is a nice college girl, and that usually means lots of attention from the fourth estate."

Their drinks arrived at that moment. Deanna sipped her 7-Up in annoyance at how right Bartow was. Immigrants and a dropout wouldn't garner much press attention, but the newspapers would become a lot more interested once word of the girl's death was made public.

"Do you *really* think it's a dragon?" Mary asked eagerly.

Bartow shrugged and sipped from his glass of red wine.

"Dunno, Mare, but word all over Chinatown is whispered talk of 'the heart of the dragon.'"

Samuel slugged down some of his beer.

"All right. You girls hit the books. See if you can find out what this 'heart of the dragon' is, and how it might relate. I'll see if I can track down who summoned it."

Bartow sat up straighter in his chair.

"What do you want me to do, sir?"

"We can take it from here, son," Samuel said a little dismissively.

"Dad," Mary said with a glare, "that's not fair. We wouldn't be here if it wasn't for Jack."

Samuel was about to argue, but Deanna cut him off.

"We can probably use his help on the research end," she said.

Her husband tossed her a look of irritation, but she just stared right back. Samuel didn't like working with other hunters, she knew, but given that Jack had actually called them in on this, it didn't seem right to cut him off now.

"The three of us have our own way of doing things," Samuel said in a tight voice. "I'm sure Jack understands that."

Taking a final drag on his cigarette, Bartow stamped it out in the ashtray just as the waitress brought their food. He waited until after she'd placed all four plates in front of them before speaking.

"Look, I realize I can't do much with my bum hoof, but I know my way around the public library, and I know this town. I can help." Then he began cutting his veal parmigiana into neat rectangles with his knife and fork.

Samuel ignored his own meal and stared at Jack.

"It's the bum hoof I'm concerned about, Jack. I'll be honest with you—I'm not comfortable trusting my back to somebody who shot himself in the foot."

Jack's mouth was full, and Mary—who was twirling her spaghetti pomodoro around her fork—spoke before he could swallow and defend himself.

"Dad, what's got into you," she demanded. "Why are you being such a butthead?"

"I'm not being a—"

"He didn't shoot himself in the foot!"

"So *he* says."

"And so *I* say, because last time we were out here he showed me the wound. The angle's wrong—it couldn't *possibly* be self-inflicted."

Deanna couldn't help but smile with pride. She also

hoped her husband didn't pick up on the fact that Mary and Jack had been in such an intimate situation without his knowledge.

"Why didn't you mention that before?" Samuel asked.

"Why didn't you just trust me?" Mary shot back.

"Or me?" Jack asked, finally able to get a word in edgewise. "Look, I dig that you don't like me, Mr. Campbell, but you knew both my parents. And I get the scene, believe me. I can help."

Samuel glanced at Deanna, which told her that he felt outnumbered.

Deanna just dug into her pasta primavera, signaling to him that he was on his own.

Samuel finally speared his osso bucco with a fork, which prompted her to smile again. He'd never admit to losing the argument, but not trying to claim the last word was usually enough.

Six

Josh Friedrich loved working the overnight shift in the morgue.

Sure, a lot of people thought that made him a loony, but Josh had long ago stopped caring what other people thought. It made it easier to sleep through the night.

Or, rather, sleep through the day, since he spent his nights here, in "the frigidaire"—his nickname for the freezer where the bodies were kept—and in the lab doing his thing.

The best part was that the cops usually didn't bother him all that much. Josh loved his job as a coroner, but he hated dealing with the police. While they were impossible to avoid completely, they didn't come to the morgue at night unless it was absolutely necessary.

As a result, most of Josh's reports were either delivered by messenger, or left for someone to pick up during the day.

Which suited Josh fine. He got to investigate the human body at his leisure, he got to help solve crimes, and he rarely had to talk to the fuzz. Or to reporters.

Reporters were worse, and every day of his life Josh was thankful he wasn't part of the Zodiac killer nonsense. Anybody came to him to talk about it, he just said he wasn't on the case, and ran away.

One downside to working late was that he had to work on the Sabbath. That didn't bother Josh all that much, but his mother suffered from serious diarrhea of the mouth whenever the subject came up. To silence her, he either told her that his job was important, or tried to get Friday nights off.

But he'd never request the day shift. He liked it quiet.

So it was kind of a drag when the FBI agent showed up. The guy just stormed in like it was his living room or something. Josh knew he was a Fed the minute he walked in the door, just by the way he carried himself. He was bald, so he didn't have the trademark slicked-back hairdo, but the rest of him just *screamed* Bureau.

As soon as he got into the morgue, he put his hands on his hips and stared straight at Josh.

"You Dr. Friedrich?"

"Uhm, yessir. What can I—"

"You're the coroner on the Wenzel case, right? And the other burnings?"

Josh blinked. *Rude sonuvabitch, isn't he?*

"Uh, yes—yessir, I am. I didn't realize this was a federal case."

"Why are you surprised at that, exactly, Doctor?" the Fed asked tersely.

Swallowing nervously, Josh thought for a moment before he replied.

"Well, uh—to be honest, the fuzz here don't really like Feds, sir."

"Well, we're not all that fond of them, either."

"I don't blame you," Josh said quickly. "Anyhow, I'm surprised they called you guys in."

"They didn't—we called ourselves in." Then he looked around the room. "I need to see the body."

"Sure," Josh said. "Follow me."

Josh led the Fed—*did he say his name?*—back to the frigidaire.

"Sorry about the cold," he said, knowing that the fuzz always yammered about the temperature.

"I've been in worse," the man said with a shrug. He was definitely a cool cat.

Walking over to the south wall—that was where the most recent cases were kept—Josh went immediately to the metal door behind which lay Marybeth Wenzel's body.

He didn't even need to look at the file to find the right drawer, since he'd been fascinated by this case—or, rather, these cases, since this was the fourth body that had come in like this.

"I'm glad you guys are here," Josh admitted. "The fuzz ain't gonna be with-it on this one, if you know what I mean."

Pulling back the sheet, he revealed a body that was badly charred and cut up. Josh wondered briefly if the Fed would be a puker, but the guy didn't even blink.

"That's pretty bad," he said flatly.

"You said it, brother. We were only able to identify her from dental records. She had *great* teeth," he added with a smile that showed his really bad ones. His mother was always bugging him to see a dentist. "Anyhow, she's got third-degree burns *all* over her. And that's the really weird part."

The Fed had bent over to peer at the cuts, but looked up at Josh's last words.

"What do you mean by 'weird,' Doctor?"

"Well, the burns are even, all the way from head to toe. The only way for that to happen is for the body to be completely immersed in fire, all at once. But there's too much left for it to have been an explosion, so it doesn't make sense."

The Fed raised an eyebrow that made him look *just* like Mr. Spock on TV.

"So?"

"Well, she had to have been killed where she was found— the burns made the body too fragile, so if she'd been moved postmortem, there'd be signs, and there aren't. But the place where she was found? No signs of fire *at all*. Now, with burns like this, that just isn't possible."

"What's your theory, then?"

That threw Josh for a loop. He wasn't used to law enforcement asking for his opinion—or, rather, hypotheses, since that was all he usually had, even though the fuzz always misused the word "theory" that way. He would often volunteer one, and sometimes they'd even pay attention, but no one had ever *asked* before.

He kind of liked it, though he'd have liked it more if he actually *had* a hypothesis.

"I don't know," he admitted ruefully. "I'm sorry, but—well, I'm at the end of my rope with this one. It's the same with two of the others—Hsu and Ding have the same burns, with the same lack of *any* kind of fire at the crime scene. Even with Verlander, the only other damage was to a small table. Isn't that freaky?"

"That's one word for it." The Fed took another look at the wounds. "Are these animal cuts?"

Josh barked a laugh, which prompted a withering look. Again, Josh swallowed—this cat knew how to glare and mean it—and he hastily answered.

"Uh, no, sir, no they aren't. The cuts are clean and almost—uh, surgical. Looks like they were made with a long blade, like a big knife."

"Or a sword?"

That resulted in another barked laugh—he couldn't help himself.

"What, Basil Rathbone killed him? Sorry," he added quickly, "but who uses a sword anymore?"

"You'd be surprised," the Fed replied, his face an expressionless mask. "And you say that the other three are the same?"

"Yup."

"Can I see Hsu and Ding's files? And Verlander's?"

"Sure." Josh went back out into the main office and stepped over to the file cabinet. The manila folders were all still in the wire-frame basket on top of the cabinet, since these were "hot" cases. Too soon to stuff them into a drawer.

The Fed flipped through each folder like he'd been doing it all his life—which, Josh supposed, he had—then just handed them back.

"Thanks."

He'd been trying to be good, but Josh found himself unable to resist asking.

"Is this another serial killer, like the Zodiac?"

The Fed just shook his head.

"I'm not at liberty to say right now, son. And the FBI would appreciate if you kept this meeting to yourself, savvy?"

Nodding quickly, Josh replied eagerly.

"Oh, absolutely." Besides, who was he gonna tell?

The man took his leave, and Josh smiled. For once he had actually been treated like a person, instead of a loony who played with dead people all night.

He wondered what kind of job options there were for coroners working with the Feds. And if they had a night-shift available.

SEVEN

One of the lessons Deanna Campbell tried very hard to instill in her daughter was that a hunter's best weapon wasn't a shotgun. Nor was it holy water. It wasn't even a Claymore that killed a vampire, a demon, or a family of ghouls.

It was a library card.

But convincing her fifteen year-old skilled fighter of a daughter of this fact was an uphill battle in itself.

Early in the morning on their second day in San Francisco, Deanna took Mary with her to the giant white edifice of the San Francisco Public Library. The main branch sat on the corner of Larkin and Grove Streets, part of the city's Civic Center.

It was a chilly day, and as they entered the building, there wasn't much change in the temperature. Walking across the lobby, Mary spoke in a low voice.

"Mom, you know, we could handle this ourselves—me and

Jack, I mean," she added hastily. "You could go with Dad."

"No thanks," Deanna said. "You know how much I hate acting. Let your father play dress-up—he's good at it."

"I guess," Mary responded, a hint of disappointment in her voice.

Samuel had been up late the previous night, posing as an FBI agent, so they had opted to let him sleep in. The visit with the coroner hadn't yielded a lot of useful information, but once he caught up on his rest, he was going to do what he could with it and try to find a common denominator among the four victims.

Deanna smiled. She could see right through her daughter—who just wanted to spend time alone with young Mr. Bartow. She couldn't really blame her, all things considered, but there was no *way* she was leaving her fifteen year-old unchaperoned with an eighteen year-old boy. Sure he came from a family of hunters, but that didn't stop them from being teenagers.

Mary looked down, probably embarrassed at having been so transparent.

Then she brightened when she saw Bartow waiting for them at the entrance to the research room, leaning on his cane.

"We ready to go?"

"Absolutely," Mary replied, a grin replacing her frown.

Deanna chuckled, and they made a beeline for the reference desk, where a young woman with long, straight dark hair, a large nose, and a bright smile sat on a tall chair. She was wearing a dark blue sundress and a light blue cardigan sweater.

"How may I help you?"

Putting on her brightest smile and over-emphasizing her midwestern accent, Deanna responded.

"Hi, miss—I sure hope so! We all just had the most *swell* time in Chinatown, and we wanted to learn more about the people there. Can you recommend some good books for us to read?"

The librarian nodded briskly.

"Well, I'll see what I can do. You see, most of our books on the Oriental culture are in Chinese, and they're at our Chinatown annex. We have a few books on Chinese culture here, though, and several of them are in English. Is there any particular aspect you have in mind?"

"It's funny you should ask that, because everywhere we went, my daughter kept hearing people talking about something called 'the heart of the dragon,' and we're just *dying* to find out what that might be."

"Okay, that gives us a start," the librarian continued, stepping down from her perch. "Well, the dragon is a very important part of Chinese culture. Let's see what we've got."

She took them to a huge cabinet with dozens of narrow drawers—the card catalogue where the titles were filed by subject. She deftly chose specific drawers, labeled in a system of numbers and categories, starting with "180 – Oriental Philosophy," and within moments she'd turned up several books with historical references to dragons.

Ancient Chinese secrets, eh? Deanna noted with admiration. *This woman really knows her business.*

Several hours of reading later, however—covering every category from "Paranormal Phenomena" to "Paleozoology"—turned up very little that seemed germane to this particular hunt. They found plenty on dragons, but nothing quite matched what the clues seemed to indicate.

Closing the last of the books the young librarian had brought them, Mary looked up at her mother and Jack.

"Lots of references to people fricasseed by a big lizard, but nothing that explains the way the bodies were cut up," she said. "Maybe it's not a dragon we're looking for, but somebody who's been possessed by one. Somebody with a sword?" she offered skeptically.

Deanna shook her head to clear the cobwebs. Every depiction of dragons they had been able to find showed creatures with claws that were similar to those of an eagle, or a bear—none of them matched the precise cuts Samuel had described.

"I don't know," she said. "There's nothing like that in any of the books I read, but it makes about as much sense as anything else."

What was worse was that nothing they found made a single reference to a dragon's heart, except in the vaguest possible sense. A person with the "heart of a dragon" was said to possess great strength of character—which didn't exactly fit with running around 'Frisco cutting people to shreds.

Deanna closed her own tome with a *thump*, then she, Mary, and Jack brought their books to the wooden hand truck that rested under a sign marked "returns" in precise block letters.

"Well, this was a waste of time," Mary said with a sigh.

"Hey, c'mon," Jack protested. "Sometimes knowing what you're *not* hunting helps you figure out what you *should be*." But even he didn't look entirely convinced. Nevertheless, Mary clutched at the idea.

"You think so?" she said.

Deanna shot the young man a grateful look. She'd been saying the same thing for the last couple of hours, but Mary didn't want to hear it, coming from her mother. So hearing it from someone closer to her own age helped a lot. It didn't hurt that the source was a cute young boy.

The woman in the blue cardigan sweater was gone, and an older lady with dark hair done up in a beehive now sat at the reference desk. She looked to be of Oriental descent and was, in fact, the third librarian to sit back there since they had arrived that morning. Unlike the first, younger librarian who'd helped them, this one was a bit more formally dressed: a white blouse, a gray sweater, and a long maroon skirt.

"Did you find what you were looking for, ma'am?" the librarian asked.

"Not everything, I'm afraid," Deanna said, exaggerating the disappointment in her tone. She almost forgot to put her "Midwestern Mom" voice back on, but caught herself just in time. As she had said to Mary, character acting was Samuel's scene. Deanna preferred to either read about something, or shoot it.

"Oh, I'm sorry," the librarian said, sounding like she meant it.

"It's all right, I suppose," Deanna replied with a game smile. "We learned bunches about Chinese culture and about dragons, which was really swell. I just wish I knew what all those people meant when they talked about 'the heart of the dragon.'"

The librarian frowned.

"What an interesting subject," she said curiously. "Are you sure it's Chinese culture you're looking for?"

The question brought Deanna up short.

"Why do you ask?"

"Well, although there are many references to dragons in Chinese lore, the only reference I've ever heard to 'the heart of the dragon' was in relation to a Japanese warrior from one hundred years ago," the woman explained. "In fact, he was *called* the Heart of the Dragon."

Her interest piqued, yet managing to stay in character, Deanna pressed for more information.

"I don't know," she said slowly. "This was something we heard them talking about in Chinatown, not Japantown." Then she chuckled. "For that matter, is there even any such place as *Japantown*?"

Mary elbowed her in the ribs.

"Mom! C'mon, this could be what we're looking for." She tugged nervously at her ever-present charm bracelet.

"Yes, dear," Deanna said. Rubbing her side, she tossed the librarian a conspiratorial smile. "Teenagers—what can you do?"

"They certainly can be impatient," the woman agreed.

"But to answer your question, there is a section of the city we call Japantown—in fact, that's where my parents live."

"Would you have any books that talk about the warrior you mentioned?" Deanna asked. "I'm afraid my daughter won't let me rest until we find *something*."

"There's at least one I can recall—but it may not help you much, I'm afraid. You see, it's a text in Japanese. I can have it sent over, but unless you read the language...." She trailed off with a shrug.

Jack stepped forward.

"That won't be a problem," he said crisply. "How soon can the book be delivered?"

The librarian shrugged again.

"It usually takes an hour or so," she said. "But I'm afraid we wouldn't be able to have it before the library closes for the day."

"Can you hold it for us, though, to look at tomorrow morning?" Jack asked eagerly.

"Absolutely!" the librarian said, caught up in his enthusiasm. "I'll just need your name."

"John Riet. That's R-I-E-T."

"Very well, Mr. Riet, I'll put in the request right away, and set the book aside for you to look at in the morning. Just come back to this desk and give your name."

"Groovy." He turned to Deanna. "I've got a friend who's in the Oriental Studies Department at Berkeley. He owes my parents a favor, so he should be able to help out."

That settled, they headed for the lobby and out the door into the brisk San Francisco afternoon. The sun was bright in the sky, so the air was warm now, and there was a pleasant breeze. One of the things Deanna had loved about this city the last time they visited was the constancy of the weather. It was as if the place was enmeshed in a permanent spring.

Mary peered curiously at Jack.

"John Riet?"

"John's my real name, but since it was also Dad's name, everyone called me Jack," he explained. "You know, like Jack Kennedy. And 'riet' is Dutch for 'cane.'"

"Oh," she said. "Groovy."

Deanna interrupted them.

"Mary, you and I need to go back to the hotel to see if Samuel has checked in or not." Then she turned. "Jack, we can give you a call when we know what the next step is."

"Right on," he said. "Actually, I could come back with you, and we could have some lunch. I know a great place...."

Mary's face brightened, but Deanna knew how Samuel would feel about that. Beyond the fact that he was certain Jack wanted to get Mary alone, his disdain for other hunters was nigh-on legendary. He was sure to balk at sharing yet another meal with the young man, especially so soon.

"I'm sorry, Jack," she said sincerely, "but not today. We'll call you, all right?"

"Sure thing." Jack sounded as disappointed as Mary looked, so Deanna grabbed her daughter's hand and practically dragged her toward the bus stop. It was just as she had said to the librarian.

Teenagers—what can you do?

* * *

Samuel hadn't held out much hope for assistance in Chinatown as long as he was posing as an FBI agent. In fact, just generally being Caucasian would work against him. Maybe he'd send Mary in later, have her play the open-minded hippie trying to grok the Oriental culture, and shadow her.

So, after taking a nap, he decided to head to the first crime scene, where Michael "Moondoggy" Verlander met his death, located in the Inner Mission.

He still wasn't happy that Deanna had convinced him to keep Bartow involved. Samuel had tolerated his presence, and yes, he'd been the one to bring them this job, but Samuel just didn't like being around other hunters. They always assumed you felt the same way they did, but as far as Samuel was concerned, a jackass was still a jackass—and a lot of them had turned out to be jackasses.

As he walked down Guerrero Street, he saw a bunch of kids gathered together, shouting slogans. One of them was standing on a milk crate at the center of the group, making a speech. Some of the kids held signs that read things like PEACE and MAKE LOVE, NOT WAR. More than half of them were wearing tie-dyed shirts that gave Samuel a headache just to look at, and most of them were in desperate need of a haircut—including the women. Some were barefoot, others wearing sandals.

There was a boy sitting next to the speaker strumming on a guitar, but the tune couldn't be heard over the shouting.

On the one hand, Samuel understood those who didn't wish to fight in the war in Southeast Asia. Having served in both World War II and Korea, he knew there was a big difference. The former *needed* to be fought—the latter was mostly just an excuse to get people killed for no good reason. Vietnam seemed to be more of the same after Korea. But Samuel couldn't in good conscience agree with the song by one of the Beatles who crooned: "Give peace a chance."

Because if you did that, then you'd already lost.

The enemy wasn't the Viet Cong, though, and it wasn't the Chinese or the Soviets or the North Koreans. Hell, it wasn't even the Nazis. The real enemy was largely unseen, and unknown, and a lot worse.

The only way to stop the *real* enemy was to fight. The only alternative was to lose and die. And Samuel had no intention of dying any time soon.

Still, he mused as he continued down Guerrero toward the apartment building, he couldn't really bring himself to blame most people for feeling the way they did. Unless you knew—really *knew*—what the world was like, you'd think that giving peace a chance might be preferable to dying in a faraway jungle nobody cared about.

They still needed haircuts, though.

When he reached the third floor of the apartment building, he saw that the crime-scene tape was still attached to one side of the doorframe, hanging loosely toward the floor and fluttering in an almost imperceptible breeze. Given that the hallway hadn't been swept and the windows not cleaned since before the Japanese bombed Pearl Harbor, this particular bit of failed maintenance wasn't much of a shock.

He was about to knock on the door, which was covered with peace-sign stickers and other odd decals, when it opened to reveal a very angry face. A huge hook nose was framed by tiny eyes and a thin-lipped mouth, which was ameliorated somewhat by the thick mustache its owner wore. Unfortunately, it was brick red, while his hair—including sideburns in dire need of a trim—was dark brown. The contrast was comical, and only Samuel's experience with disguises assured him that the facial hair was real.

"Whaddaya want, man?" the face demanded.

Recalling something from both Bartow's conversation and Verlander's casefile, Samuel put on his most stentorian voice.

"Are you Frederick Gorczyk?"

"Who wants to know?"

Holding up the false identification, Samuel answered authoritatively.

"I'm Special Agent Jones." One thing he'd learned early on was that FBI agents never referred to themselves as just "Agent So-and-so," and they never called themselves "FBI agents," either. It was a small thing, but it could make or break an impersonation.

Gorczyk blinked, some of the anger fading.

"Okay."

Samuel continued.

"If you *are* Frederick Gorczyk, I have some questions for

you regarding the death of Michael Verlander."

"And if I *ain't* him?"

Samuel gave a very small smirk.

"Then I'll have to arrest you for trespassing."

Gorczyk made a noise like an exploding pipe.

"I ain't trespassin', man, I'm Freddie Gorczyk." Samuel noted that he pronounced it "gore-chick," not "gore-zik."

"My apologies for the mispronunciation, Mr. *Gorczyk*," he said, and he motioned into the apartment. "May I come in?"

"Sure, fine." Gorczyk, who'd been blocking the doorway the entire time, opened the door wide, turned, and led him into the small living room.

On the left was a wall filled with metal braces screwed into it, used to hold up wooden bookshelves. Most of them were stuffed with books, but one shelf had a record player, with speakers sitting on the floor beneath it.

On the right was a couch, and several stained posters decorated the wall advertising various concerts, festivals and exhibits. Samuel recognized a few of the bands from records Mary had asked him to buy for her as birthday and Christmas presents.

The carpet was cheap, stained and faded, but he could clearly see that it had been vacuumed recently. There was also a rectangular section cut out of it, right in front of the battered leather couch. Samuel recalled a mention in Verlander's file about the coffee table being burned and the ashes and carpet going to the lab for analysis. That explained the cutout.

After looking over the living room in silence, Samuel turned to Gorczyk.

"I need to know what Mr. Verlander was doing in your apartment."

"Messin' it up, is what he was doin'! Look, I went east for Woodstock back in August, okay, man?" When Samuel didn't respond, he continued. "And once I got there I realized that New York City, man, that's where it's at! So I stayed. I'd already asked Moondoggy—that's 'Mr. Verlander,' okay?—to house-sit while I was at the festival, and I called him and told him to keep on keepin' on while I tried to break in, okay?"

"Break in?"

"You know, get gigs. For my music, man."

"So what happened?" Samuel asked.

Gorczyk started waving his hands wildly.

"He lost my cat, man! Broke my stuff, even scratched my LPs! Practically burned down my whole apartment. And then he got himself killed, so I can't even get no restitution or nothin'."

"I'm sorry for your problems, Mr. Gorczyk," Samuel said with as much sincerity as he could muster—which wasn't all that much, really—then added, "but I need details. Do you know who he might have entertained while he was here?"

"Anybody who got him grass, is who." Gorczyk swallowed, adding hastily, "Uh, not that I know nothin' about that, man. Not my thing."

A glance into the kitchenette revealed a lot of empty

potato-chip bags, and Samuel smiled to himself.

"I'm investigating a murder, son—I couldn't care less about what you or Mr. Verlander smoke."

"Yeah, okay." Gorczyk didn't sound like he believed that. Then he brightened. "Oh, hey, man, you know who you oughtta talk to? Mrs. Holzaur. She lives next door in 3C, and she's always seein' stuff. I asked her to keep an eye on Moondoggy, okay? She mighta seen somethin'. I don't know if the pi—uh, the cops talked to her or not."

Again, Samuel smiled to himself, but he decided not to respond to the veiled reference.

Instead, he crouched down near the cut-out bit of carpet, where he noticed some yellow crystals.

Sulfur.

Not that Samuel harbored any doubts at this point, but the sight of sulfur confirmed that this was something he and his family needed to take care of, and quickly.

It may or may not have been a dragon, but a demon was *definitely* involved.

Getting to his feet, he motioned to leave.

"Thank you very much for your assistance, Mr. Gorczyk," he said. "You've been a great help."

"Sure, man. Just hope you catch the guy. Moondoggy was a jerk, but he didn't deserve what he got."

Stepping out into the hall, the door clicking shut behind him, Samuel knocked on the door to apartment 3C. Unlike the door to Gorczyk's apartment, 3B, Mrs. Holzaur's door was empty save for the tarnished brass number and letter.

A short, wrinkled woman wearing a faded housedress, curlers in her hair, answered the door. A lit cigarette dangled from between her lips.

"Are you Mrs. Holzaur?"

"You a policeman, mister?" she asked in a raspy voice.

"Federal agent, actually—Special Agent Jones."

"Too bad. I was hopin' you'd be a policeman, on account'a I ain't heard from none of 'em." She took a drag on her cigarette.

"I'm sorry, ma'am?"

Blowing smoke in Samuel's face, Mrs. Holzaur coughed, then spoke.

"I told them policemen when that man was murdered, I told 'em to talk to me, that I knew stuff about the yippies and the aliens and the Chinee and whatnot."

"You're talking about the murder of your next-door neighbor, Michael Verlander, yes?"

"He ain't my neighbor. He was watchin' the place for my neighbor. One'a them yippies, or whatever they call 'em. My husband was still alive, he'd'a shot 'em both, and that's the truth."

"No doubt, Mrs. Holzaur," Samuel said quickly. "Now what's that about aliens and—and the Chinee?"

"The aliens, see, them's the ones who made the mary-jew-ana. Smokin' that stuff, see, that's what leads to people turnin' into aliens, and then they're gonna take over. Been *tellin'* the policemen this, every chance I get, but they don't do nothin'!" She took another drag on her cigarette.

One thing the Campbell family had learned early on was that the crazy ones were worth paying attention to—often there was good wheat among all that chaff. So he waited to see if Mrs. Holzaur would carry on about marijuana and the alien plot to destroy the youth of America. When she seemed to have abated, he began to ask questions.

"And how does the Chinese person fit into this?"

"It's *obvious* ain't it? That yippie fella asked me to let in his friend while he went out to meet with his alien buddies. Told me to let this guy—Albert—have something to eat."

Samuel brightened.

"Albert?"

"Yeah, told me to give Albert some chow. Like I need to feed some Chinee kook."

"Did you feed him?"

More smoke in Samuel's face for that one.

"'Course not! Albert can chow down on his own damn time, you ask me. Damn Chinee, them people're takin' over! You watch, 'fore too long, we'll all be slant-eyed devils like *them*, and then where'll we be, huh?" She dragged on her cigarette, then dropped it to the linoleum floor of the hall. "If my husband was alive, he'd take his shotgun to 'em all, and that's no lie."

Samuel nodded noncommittally, careful not to show any sign of the elation that swept over him.

"Thank you for your time, Mrs. Holzaur. The FBI appreciates your input, and rest assured we'll be giving your allegations the full attention that they warrant."

"Yeah, right—you're just like all men, all talk and no action, that's your problem. If my husband was alive, he'd take a shotgun right to your head, I'll tell you *that* for free."

Samuel turned his back on Mrs. Holzaur, who continued to natter on to herself about aliens and yippies and the Chinee and what her husband would do with his shotgun. He had a spring in his step, because now he had a name.

Albert.

He somehow doubted that Moondoggy would want the loony lady next door to provide Albert with chow. But he might well ask her to let in someone named Albert *Chao*.

Now Samuel just had to figure out who Albert Chao was and what he had wanted with Moondoggy....

EIGHT

David Severn would have been perfectly happy, except for the pain in his ankles.

But it had been worth it. He'd been trying to find the perfect date, and this seemed to be it. Debbie was his best girl, and after a hard week working as a supermarket manager, he was darn well going to show her a good time.

Their first three dates had been busts. She had sneezed a lot at Golden Gate Park, and didn't enjoy Ghirardelli Square, saying that shopping wasn't romantic—it was something she did with her mother. And then there was the Fillmore.

It had been against David's better judgment to go to one of those loud music shows: a bunch of weirdos dressed like circus clowns playing music that was far too loud and not remotely melodious. David preferred his musicians to be clean-cut and well dressed and actually proficient, like The Ventures or Buddy Holly, God rest his soul, or like The

Beatles before they started taking drugs.

For Debbie's sake, however, he had pretended to enjoy himself—she was his best girl, after all, and an absolute sweetheart—but he hoped she wouldn't want to do that again.

But as they'd left the Fillmore that night, they'd walked down Geary Boulevard and up Steiner Street to where David had parked his car. On the way, they passed Winterland. David knew it was an ice-skating rink, but Debbie mentioned that the owner of the Fillmore sometimes rented it for concerts that were too big to fit in the smaller venue.

Then she commented on her love of ice-skating.

Right then and there, David had the next Friday's date planned out.

Sure enough, she loved it. Debbie was an excellent skater, too—which was more than David could say for himself. He fell over several times, more than once on his rear end, but Debbie just laughed and helped him up and showed him how to do it properly.

After a while, he'd gotten it down pat. But *boy*, did his ankles hurt.

Still, on the whole the date had gone very well. Debbie had so much fun that they wound up making out near the locker room until the place closed down and the staff had to throw them out.

As they exited onto Steiner Street, David put his arm around Debbie's waist.

"You really skated beautifully, doll."

"Thanks." She smiled up at him. She loved it when he called her "doll." "When I was growing up," she said, "I used to watch Sonja Henie's movies all the time. She was my hero."

"Wow—it's kismet," he said profoundly.

"What do you mean?" she asked, a puzzled look crossing her face.

"Well, you know that Buddy Holly's my hero. That means that both of our heroes died in plane crashes!"

She stiffened under his arm.

"She died of *leukemia*," Debbie said sternly. "She just happened to die while she was flying home to Oslo."

Crestfallen, David didn't know how to respond.

"Oh," he said. Before he could try to salvage the conversation, a voice came from behind them.

"Hello, David."

Whirling around, he saw a young pointy-nosed Oriental in a Nehru jacket and green slacks. But despite the man's unique appearance, David didn't recognize him at all, and was a bit insulted at the familiarity from someone like him.

"Excuse me? Have we met?"

Debbie moved in closer, and he held her more tightly. He shifted slightly to place himself between her and the Oriental.

"David, who is this?" she asked nervously.

"That's what I'm gonna find out, doll."

The Oriental shook his head.

"You really don't remember, do you?"

"Remember what?" David asked angrily. "Who *are* you?"

"You have the unmitigated gall to ask me that?" the man responded, his voice rising with each word. "I'm Albert Chao! I'm the man you *fired* just because I talked to the wrong girl!"

Debbie looked up at him.

"Is that true, David?"

He swallowed now, trying to remember. The supermarket's owner, Mr. Wilhelm, had always insisted on hiring Orientals as stock boys, but he'd left the firing to David. He supposed this Chao character was one of them.

"Look, buddy," he said, putting on his best manager's voice, "if I did fire you, it was for a good reason, all right? So let me and my girl here move along, and you can go back to your opium den or wherever."

The Oriental broke into a big grin.

"Oh, I'm going to enjoy this."

Something about that grin got under David's skin, and he didn't want to look at it anymore. Remembering the boxing classes he'd taken at school, he extricated himself from Debbie, stood in a proper fighting stance, and punched Chao right in the face.

The Oriental tried to duck, but he wasn't fast enough. The impact of David's fist on the man's nose sent sharp knives of pain cascading up and down his arm, and as he heard the crack of bone breaking, he hissed out a sharp breath. He didn't remember it hurting this much to punch someone. Of course, he'd worn gloves back then....

Debbie, bless her, ran right up to him.

"Are you okay?"

"I think so."

But the Oriental hadn't budged. His pointy nose was bloodied but he seemed unfazed.

David couldn't believe it—that was his best punch!

Then the man started muttering something. David couldn't understand a word he was saying, but there was something in the way he whispered it that sent a chill through his bones.

Debbie held him tighter.

"David, what's he doing?"

"I—I don't—" David stammered. Then he found he couldn't catch his breath.

What the hell is *he doing?*

Then Chao stopped speaking, and the sudden silence was even more frightening. David found that he couldn't even hear the noises of the street. It was a Friday night in the middle of San Francisco, there was noise everywhere, but David couldn't hear anything except the ragged sounds of his own breathing and the beating of his heart against his rib cage.

Suddenly, hot air pushed hard against his face. Sweat formed almost instantly, even as he saw a huge fire erupt from the Steiner Street sidewalk.

A man stood in the center of the fire. David couldn't make out his features, but he somehow just knew that the figure was staring right at him.

It was like something in one of those bizarre psychedelic songs that that band had played at the Fillmore. This couldn't *possibly* be happening. Yet he could feel the fire on his face, see the flames flickering into the night air—and hear Debbie's strangled cry.

The man in the fire raised a giant sword.

The last thing David heard was his own scream.

The Campbells converged on the Emperor Norton Lodge.

Much to Samuel's chagrin, Mary also called Jack and told him about the sulfur that had been found at the first murder scene. He promised to see if he could find out whether or not there had been any signs of demonic activity recently.

Deanna revealed that they had found a lead on "the heart of the dragon," but that it was in Japanese. Samuel was dubious—Chao was a Chinese name—but every little bit helped. They'd know more when Bartow's professor friend at Berkeley translated the texts.

Then—armed with a name—they split up, each trying to find the man known as Albert Chao, and any connection he might have with the other victims.

They all returned to the Lodge late that night. Deanna ordered them a room-service meal, and the family compared notes.

Samuel went first.

"I found a lead on a possible target, but I got there too late. First I checked the bars near where Verlander was killed, and found a place where the name Albert Chao rung a bell. The bartender told me that Albert had been fired from a supermarket job two months ago, and he was angry about it.

"So I tracked down the supermarket and found out who did the firing. They said the guy was taking his girlfriend to Winterland tonight."

Mary perked up.

"Ooh, who was playing?"

"It's a skating rink, Mary," Samuel said with a frown.

"Really? I thought it was a concert hall. Hendrix and the Dead play there all the time."

Samuel didn't even pretend to know what she meant.

"Anyhow, when I got to Winterland, the cops were already there, just down the street, and so were reporters. Both the supermarket manager and his girlfriend had been burned to death and cut to ribbons."

Deanna winced.

"Oh no!"

Mary's mouth set in a line.

"We've got to stop this guy, Dad."

"Well, I'm open to suggestions," Samuel said bitterly, angry at having failed to get there in time. "What did you find out at Berkeley?"

Mary had headed to Berkeley to talk to some of Marybeth Wenzel's fellow students, under the guise of being a high-school student who was looking into Berkeley as a possible college. Her cover was that she was concerned at the news that one of the students had been killed.

"Marybeth got straight As, and all her friends thought she was pretty swell. The only thing was that people said she had weird taste in men."

Samuel frowned.

"What does 'weird' mean, exactly?"

Mary's expression mirrored his own, a look of distaste on her face.

"The girls wouldn't say, but there was one boy who claimed, 'She only liked slant-eyes.' I think he meant Orientals."

Samuel nodded.

"So this is one of Chao's old flames?"

"That's my guess."

Deanna went next.

"Not surprised it's an 'old' flame. I talked to the people at the laundry and the restaurant where the two Chinatown victims worked, pretending to be one of Albert's old teachers, and in both cases I was told that he had worked there. Both of them said he was fired, and our two corpses are the ones who did the firing.

"What's especially interesting is that one of the reasons he was fired from the laundry is that he lied on his application: Chao said he was Chinese—when he's really half-Chinese and half-Japanese."

Samuel sighed.

"So the only people Chao had a grudge against, that any of us could find out about, are dead." If that was true, they were at a dead end.

"You think maybe he's done?" Mary asked hopefully.

Deanna shook her head.

"There's a demon involved here, Mary, remember? That

means that it's not going to end. Chao may *think* he has control of this, but he doesn't. And the demon won't stop the killing just because Chao's run out of grudges."

"Besides, a guy like that probably has a long list of people who've pissed him off," Samuel said, then he sighed. "We need to find out where Chao lives. That was one thing I couldn't get out of anyone."

"We should call Jack, and see if he found out anything," Mary said brightly, ignoring the shadow that crossed her father's face.

"Okay," he said. "Call him, but—"

Mary bounded up from the bed.

"—use the pay phone outside, I know."

Samuel called after her as she headed to the door.

"I just don't want to pay what the hotel charges for calls!" But she was gone before he could finish.

When the door closed behind her, Samuel looked at Deanna and started to speak, but she cut him off.

"This is why you lost your hair, right?"

At first, Samuel scowled, then he broke down and laughed. She laughed with him.

Then he pulled her into an embrace.

"You still love me, even though I'm a broken-down old bald man?"

"You're darn tootin', Mr. Man," she said with a mischievous grin, then she kissed him.

NINE

Albert showed them. He showed them *all*.

I'm sorry, Albert, you're nice and all, but—you're just too heavy *for me. I just can't handle all that intensity, you dig? Call me when you lighten up....*

"*Lighten up?*" Pfagh.

He was destined for great things. He just *knew* it.

If only all these people wouldn't keep getting in his way.

I don't want liars on my payroll, nor half-breeds. Remove yourself from my establishment before I throw you out.

Before she died, his mother used to tell him stories of her ancestor, the legendary Heart of the Dragon: a *ronin* who had traveled the countryside of feudal Japan righting wrongs and punishing the guilty, until he was condemned by a mob of ignorant peasants.

I saw you talking to that girl. We don't like that kind of behavior around here, mister. Consider yourself fired.

People liked to think that ignorant peasants didn't exist in this day and age. After all, a man had walked on the moon, which meant mankind had evolved, right?

Wrong.

It took different forms these days, but it was the same old song.

After that bastard at the supermarket fired him, he fell into a deep state of depression. All he could imagine, all he could see, all he could dream about were the people who kept him down.

Stupid half-breed! You don't belong in Chinatown with the real *people!*

It had started when he was a child, with the other Chinatown kids taunting him because his mother was Japanese. His parents both told him they were just ignorant, that they were kids who didn't know any better, and things would improve when he grew up.

But things didn't improve. Everywhere he turned he was met with rejection, disgust, and revulsion.

But always he remembered his mother's stories about the Heart of the Dragon.

Once he was unemployed, he had plenty of time on his hands. So he took a trip to the library, tried to see if there was anything in their collection of Japanese texts.

And he found more than he had bargained for.

The stories told of a demon who had imprisoned *Doragon Kokoro*'s soul. Yet according to the texts, the power of blood could supersede the power of the demon's incantation.

A descendant of the Heart of the Dragon could summon his demon-tainted ancestor back to the land of the living, where it would wield great power.

The problem was that the texts were incomplete, so he wasn't sure of the entirety of the spell, nor its ultimate effect. Still, he was certain that it would tether the Heart of the Dragon to him, thus granting him the ability to right all wrongs, and remove the petty people from his life.

There was another spell—this one complete—that would banish the spirit again for eighty seasons, but what use had he for that? Why would he wield great power, only to surrender it?

At first he hadn't entirely believed everything he read. But what did he have to lose?

He had no girl.

No family, no job, no friends.

Nothing.

But he had a destiny. He was a descendant of the Heart of the Dragon. He deserved better—and he would have it.

Someone in a bar he frequented told him about Moondoggy Verlander, a burned-out hippie who was good at tracking down the arcane, and Albert hired him. Moondoggy became his first test subject, and he had felt a bit of remorse about that, but the results were exactly what he had hoped for. Guilt quickly gave way to euphoria.

Then Albert was finally able to avenge himself on those who had wronged him, who had kept him from his destiny.

Now they were gone, he found himself at a crossroads.

What was next for him and his very own ancestral *ronin*?

It had caught him off guard, when that idiot supermarket manager had punched him. But, though startled, Albert had only felt a brief sensation of pain. And even though he was pretty sure he'd heard the crack of his nose breaking, when he had wiped away the blood, he had found no injury.

It seemed as if he was indestructible as long as he had the Heart of the Dragon bound to him. That hadn't been in the texts, and he wondered what other unknown facets existed in this great union between him and his ancestor. What else had been contained in that lost text?

Looking around now, he knew there had to be more that he could do.

Enough dwelling on the past, he mused. He needed to think about his future.

The apartment in which he lived was, charitably speaking, a dump. The "pad," as the landlord had referred to it, was tiny, with warped wood floors in the living room, a frayed and stained carpet in the bedroom, and cracked linoleum in the kitchen. He could barely afford a hammock to sleep on, and macaroni in the cabinet. The only reason he had a chair was that he'd found it on the street.

He needed to move up in the world.

And the Heart of the Dragon would accomplish that for him.

With a small smile at the thought of what he might be able to achieve, he once again started to chant the spell. Perhaps spending more time with the *ronin* would allow him to take what was rightfully his from society.

The fires of the netherworld burned bright, and the form of the *ronin* appeared within the flames that licked toward the ceiling. Just as fire had consumed Yoshio Nakadai in his death, so did flames continue to follow him across the centuries. Albert felt the warmth of the fire dance on his face, driving out the chill of the inadequately heated apartment.

Yet it wasn't just heat he felt. No, it was *power*. He had in his possession a creature who could kill *anyone*. It was time he used his ancestor for something other than petty revenge.

The Heart of the Dragon had been a great hero, renowned throughout Japan. Albert Chao was determined to be at least as famous.

He hadn't had the money to pay Moondoggy, but now he could get all the money he wanted.

A loud noise from behind him prompted him to spin around, only to find a bald man standing in the doorway. He had apparently kicked the door in, splintering the lock, which irritated Albert. Not so much that he'd kicked in the door, but that his apartment was so awful that its door could so easily *be* kicked in.

The man had a handgun, but he didn't look like a robber.

"Who are you?" he demanded.

"My name doesn't matter," the bald man said. "But I know yours. You're Albert Chao, you've killed six people in cold blood—and I'm here to stop you."

Albert broke into a large smile.

"I doubt that."

And wordlessly he willed the Heart of the Dragon to kill the bald man. Surrounded by the eternal fires, the spirit married Albert's thoughts to immediate action. The *ronin* raised the katana over his head at an angle, ready for an immediate downward *sokutso* slice at the bald man's collarbone. As he did so, Albert spoke again.

"I control the Heart of the Dragon, *gaijin*. He is mine to command for as long as I live."

"Fine," the bald man said. He raised his gun and shot Albert.

Samuel had to admit to enjoying the look of utter shock on Albert Chao's face as the Smith & Wesson Model 60 revolver's .38 calibre bullet slammed into Chao's knee, blood blooming into a stain on his pants leg as the young man fell to the warped wood floor.

Chao's head collided with the wall on the way down, slicing open a nasty gash on his forehead.

Unfortunately, while it put Chao down for the count, the man with the sword was still moving toward him, wreathed in flames that flickered cruelly in the dimly lit apartment.

Samuel pointed his revolver at the spirit.

"That's not going to do any good, Samuel," Deanna said from behind him. She and Mary had waited in the hallway, preparing the counter spell that they'd found in the library, helpfully translated by Bartow's professor friend at Berkeley.

"Yeah, I know," Samuel snapped over his shoulder as he

hastily backed away from the spirit as it bore down on him. "I was just hoping it might flinch a bit. Handguns weren't all *that* common in feudal Japan."

The extensive notes Bartow had provided told of a masterless *samurai* named Yoshio Nakadai who had lived in nineteenth-century Japan and who had been given the nickname of *Doragon Kokoro*, which translated to "heart of the dragon."

Bingo.

They chronicled his death, allegedly at the hands of a demon, and revealed that his spirit could be resurrected by a descendant possessing the proper incantation, a portion of which was included amidst the papers at the library.

Since Chao was half-Japanese, they realized he may well have been kin to Nakadai.

The demon's role in Nakadai's death explained the sulfuric residue. Bartow hadn't found any other omens that indicated demonic activity—which was pretty rare, in any case—so he and the Campbells chalked it up to the spirit's origins, rather than any specific demonic intent.

Also amidst the texts was a spell that could send the spirit back—and this one was complete. It didn't banish the spirit permanently, but it beat the alternative....

The most valuable piece of information gleaned from their research, however, had been an SFPL call slip that was stuck between two pages. Bartow had pocketed it immediately, because the slip had revealed the name and address of the last person who had taken the book out.

Albert Chao.

Once they had transcribed the counterspell, and gathered the materials they'd need to cast it, they headed to Chao's apartment, hoping to stop him before he instructed the Heart of the Dragon to kill anyone else. Just now that next victim looked likely to be Samuel himself, as he barely dodged a powerful slice from the spirit's katana.

Samuel put a hand to his cheek, which was hot from the proximity of the flames. Strangely enough, though he could feel the heat, the fire hadn't set the apartment alight.

"How's that spell coming, Little Miss?" Samuel called to Mary.

"Don't call me that!" she shouted from the hallway.

Then she came into view in the doorway. In her right hand she held a piece of notepaper with the phonetic spelling of the words to the spell. In her left she had a pinch of pulverized kihada root, which they had purchased from a small drugstore in San Francisco's tiny Japantown.

The Heart of the Dragon swung his sword once again.

Samuel tripped over a battered chair, which was all that saved him as the fiery blade of the katana singed his bald scalp. The apartment was very sparsely furnished, but it was also very small, and very soon Samuel was going to run out of places to dodge.

"Where's the damn Claymore?" he asked Deanna, who was keeping herself between the spirit and Mary.

"Are you out of your mind? That's a katana! It'd slice the Claymore in two!"

The spirit reared above him wielding its flaming weapon, without realizing it, Samuel suddenly found himself literally backed into a corner.

He heard a voice. Mary was speaking the incantation slowly, making sure to get the pronunciation right. He knew she had to do it right in order for it to work, but if she didn't hurry up, he was going to be skewered and burned to a crisp.

Samuel thought quickly: there was a window nearby, but a quick glance revealed that it wasn't the one with the fire escape. Albert lived on a fifth-story walk-up, so jumping out wasn't an option.

In the moments before the creature struck, he really wished that shooting Albert had broken the man's hold on the spirit.

Dammit.

The warrior raised his katana. Heat from the demonic flames licked across Samuel's face. He'd been half tempted to fire his revolver, just to see what would happen, but knew that he'd only be wasting a bullet.

Now, though, he'd take whatever he could, because there was nowhere to dodge, nowhere to run....

He raised the pistol.

Mary finished the incantation and threw the pulverized root into the flames that surrounded the *ronin*.

Though the katana remained raised, the spirit threw its head back and screamed. The flames grew hotter, and Samuel had to put his hands in front of his face to try to ward off the pounding heat.

A flash of light.

Then nothing.

Mary was grinning.

"Guess it worked," she said triumphantly.

"For the time being," Deanna said. "Remember what the professor's notes said: all this spell does is banish it for twenty years."

Mary shrugged.

"So we come back in twenty years and stop it again. We can come down in a shuttle from our house on the moon."

Samuel rolled his eyes.

"Moon shuttle. Right. If we're on the moon, we'll be too busy fighting the monsters up there, I'll bet."

Even as he spoke, the sound of sirens pierced the quiet of the evening. Glancing out of the window, he saw both fire trucks and police vehicles approaching the building.

"We need to scram," he said urgently. Chao was harmless now—or, rather, for the next twenty years—and he needed medical attention. But the police could handle that. The Campbells needed to beat feet out of there.

As they dashed down the back stairs toward the back-alley exit that would, with luck, keep them away from the police, Deanna spoke in a terse whisper.

"When we get back to the hotel, I'll call Marty and arrange for a flight home."

Feeling magnanimous after the successful hunt, Samuel added his own two cents.

"And then you can call Jack, Little Miss. Maybe the two

of you can have dinner together."

Deanna shot him a look that expressed surprise, but Mary shook her head.

"That's okay, Dad. I mean, we could all have dinner with him, as a thank you, I guess."

They ran out of the back door, heading toward the street that ran behind the building.

"I thought you liked the boy."

"He's nice," Mary said, "and it was good to see him. But, like you always say, Dad, romance and hunting don't mix." She grinned. "Except for you two."

Deanna chuckled as they headed toward a bus stop.

"Let's go home."

Albert inhaled sharply, then sat up quickly.

His knee felt fine.

Putting a hand to his head, he found that the gash had closed over, and he wiped the blood away.

Unlike the simple punch from the previous night, this was a pair of wounds, and it took a bit longer for them to heal back up. First the knee injury, which sent paroxysms of pain throughout his entire body. When he hit the wall, he *did* pass out for a few seconds—but he heard bits of conversation among those three *gaijin*, including the girl speaking—with an *awful* accent—the words to the other spell he'd found in the library.

But by the time they'd finished casting the spell and left, he was whole again. Whatever link he had with the Heart of the Dragon, it still existed.

He could not be hurt—at least not permanently.

He yanked up his bloodstained pant leg, exposing the bare flesh. There was blood on his knee, but the skin itself was unbroken and unscarred.

He grinned. It was like magic.

In fact it *was* magic—very *good* magic.

While Albert had no idea who those three *gaijin* had been, he knew that they thought the battle was over—at least for the next two decades.

But by the time twenty years rolled around again, Albert intended to be ready.

Three police officers appeared at his broken door.

"Don't move!"

"What's going on, officers?" he asked innocently.

"We got a report of gunshots being fired," one of them said.

"No, sir, officer," Albert responded in as deferential a voice as he could manage. The last thing he wanted right now was trouble with the police.

Another officer inspected the shattered lock.

"Your door looks like it's been kicked in."

"Yeah, I've been trying to get the landlord to fix that for weeks," he replied.

The officer snorted. "I'll bet." Then he looked down. "What happened to your leg?"

"Got the pants from Goodwill. Can't afford to be picky these days, you know?"

The police had a few more questions, but other than the door, there was no evidence of a crime, and they didn't seem eager to pursue it.

As soon as they left, Albert smiled.

That taken care of, he now had two decades to figure out the best way to put the power of his ancestor to his use.

2009

TEN

"Y'know," Sam Winchester said, "it still freaks me out a little."

Dean was still staring at the printout of the forty year-old *San Francisco Chronicle* article.

"What, that Mom and our grandparents were hunters?" Dean remembered how stunned he'd been when a nineteen year-old girl had started beating the crap out of him—and then he'd seen the protective charm bracelet she was wearing and put two and two together.

Mom really knew how to kick ass.

Family history had never been a huge priority for the Winchesters while they were growing up, though. Dean's grandparents were barely remembered faces on faded pictures that had hung on the staircase wall. The only family that had mattered after Mom died were Sam and Dad, and later folks like Bobby—who had become a surrogate uncle to the boys, and more as they grew older. And Caleb and Pastor Jim.

Sam smiled when he answered Dean's question.

"No, somehow it makes sense that they would be hunters," he said. "But it's weird that we were named after them, and Dad never told us."

Dean snorted derisively.

"Add it to the list of things Dad never told us. We could fill a damn—" Suddenly, he got a faraway look in his eyes. "—book. *Sonofabitch*."

Bolting from the kitchen into the living room, Dean made a beeline for the worn duffel bag he always traveled with and pulled out the leather-bound notebook that had been an integral part of their lives as hunters these past four years— ever since Dad had disappeared, and Dean had gone to Stanford to drag Sam back to the life that he'd left behind.

Dad's journal.

Furiously, he started flipping pages until he found the section that covered the late 1980s and found what he was looking for.

"Here we go," he shouted over his shoulder. "Heart of the Dragon—San Francisco, 1989. Twenty years later—and Dad faced it!"

Sam got up from the kitchen table and followed his brother.

"Okay, yeah, that's starting to ring a bell. There was a sword involved, wasn't there?"

"Yup," came a voice from the back room. Bobby wheeled himself into the living room, a long, thin package wrapped in brown parcel paper and twine sitting on his lap as he navigated his wheelchair until he was sitting next to the brothers.

Staring up at them from under the bill of his omnipresent baseball cap, he held up the parcel.

"If you two're goin' after *Doragon Kokoro*, you're gonna be needin' this."

Sam took the package.

Expecting a katana, Dean was surprised when Sam undid the twine, ripped off the plain brown paper, and unwrapped a hook sword. It had a hilt with a wrist guard and an additional piece beyond that, with the long blade that curved around at the very end to form the hook.

That wasn't the interesting part, though: that was the runes in Asian characters—Dean could never tell the difference between Chinese and Japanese—etched into the sword's blade.

"When your father faced off against *Doragon Kokoro* twenty years ago," Bobby began, "this is what he used to send the spirit away. We were hopin' it was permanent, but we knew we'd probably just accomplished what your grandparents apparently did, and got rid of it for two decades.

"S'why I kept the damn thing."

Dean snorted again. Bobby didn't need a reason to keep anything—he was the classic pack rat. And as they'd discovered time and again, in this line of work, it didn't pay to get rid of anything that might be useful in the future.

Sam looked at Dean.

"It's been years since I read that part of Dad's journal. What's it say?"

Dean looked back down at the leather-bound notebook.

"A whole bunch, actually."

1989

Eleven

John Winchester pulled into the yard, the smell of incense still stinging his nostrils. It had been a difficult fight, but the spell he'd cast had gotten rid of the poltergeist once and for all.

Part of him had been tempted to stay behind in Henderson and get a good night's sleep, but he'd been away from the boys for far too long. He had enrolled them in a school in South Dakota, giving the Singer Salvage Yard as their address, and the fall semester was almost over. Once it ended, he'd stop abusing Bobby Singer's hospitality.

John wasn't comfortable making use of it this much, but he also understood the need to give the boys as much continuity in their schooling as possible—especially six year-old Sammy.

He'd see where the work took them from here on in.

There was another reason he felt the need to see them. That poltergeist had targeted two young girls, and the danger they'd been in hit too close to home. John knew his boys would need to be able to defend themselves against whatever was out there—he'd already started that process with Dean, Sammy's ten year-old brother. Dean was a crack shot with John's M1911, and could load the shotgun with iron rounds and fire them off in one smooth motion.

Eventually he'd need to train Sammy, too.

But not yet.

He'd been driving all night, and the Impala's engine was starting to make an odd clunking noise. He'd need to borrow Bobby's tools and check it out, once he got a good night's—or day's—sleep.

The sun was rising in the east when he pulled in, shining haphazardly through the assorted cars, trucks, and wrecks that surrounded Bobby's house. Squinting as he clambered out of the Impala, he walked stiffly toward the porch.

Sam ran out before he could even reach the front door.

"Dad!" the boy cried as he wrapped his arms around John's legs.

Unable to help himself, John grinned.

"Hey there, Sammy."

"I'm so glad you're home!" the boy said, peering up at his father with an angry expression. "Dean's being a creep."

Looking up, John saw Bobby and Dean standing in the doorway. The former had on his usual: flannel shirt, ball cap, and jeans, and a look of irritation. The latter was sulking.

"I'm *not* a creep," Dean protested. "I just ate the last donut. It's no big deal!"

"But Bobby said I could have it!" Sam wailed from his position still wrapped around John's legs.

"I *said* you could both have two each," Bobby said in a long-suffering tone. He'd told John several times that he didn't mind watching Dean and Sam, because he'd never had kids of his own. Right now, though, it looked as if he was coming to understand that there were benefits to being childless.

John started to walk toward the house, but as Sam still clung to one of his legs, it was more of an awkward shuffle. Before he got five feet they were both giggling at the ridiculousness of it. After a second, Bobby and Dean started laughing, too, and minutes later they were all sitting around Bobby's kitchen table, back in a good mood.

Dean and Sam told him all about their adventures while he was gone. On the weekends they played games of hide-and-seek amidst the cars in the yard—a paradise for two young boys. During the week they went to school, though only Sam seemed interested in talking about that. Then again, he was in the first grade, so the course load was easier than Dean's.

"Miss Roach said I could do third-grade work!" he said proudly.

John was surprised.

"That's 'cause you're a dexter," Dean said.

"No, it means he's smart, Dean," John said. "And that's good. I'm proud of you, Sammy."

Sam stuck out his tongue at his brother.

"Dean's doing third-grade work, too!"

"Screw you, Sammy!" Dean said, who was now in the fifth grade.

John put on the voice that his drill sergeant had always used in the Corps.

"Hey! Enough of that!" he said sternly. "I hear any more, and you won't like what happens."

Both boys clammed right up, looking down at their laps abashedly.

"Sorry, sir," Dean said.

"Sorry, Dad," Sammy echoed.

"That's better."

After a while, the boys went off to play, and John followed Bobby into the living room. They sat on the couch, each holding a bottle of Budweiser, and John filled him in on the poltergeist.

"Sounds like you handled it okay," Bobby drawled.

John chuckled at Bobby's talent for understatement.

"Yeah. The Impala's engine's acting up again, by the way. I need to sleep off the drive, but I wanna put it up on the blocks later on."

"No problem." Bobby had been part of the community of hunters for a few years longer than John, and he'd already gained a reputation as the go-to guy for car repair. But John was a fine mechanic in his own right, and he knew the Impala's engine better than anyone.

John rubbed his eyes, an action that cleared his vision but only served to increase his fatigue. The post-hunt adrenaline had kept him going on the road, but now that he was back with the boys, exhaustion was starting to cover him like a flannel blanket.

"Anything cooking?" he asked.

Bobby had his finger on the pulse of the hunting community better than anyone outside of Harvelle's Roadhouse. What John really wanted to know was if he'd received any information that would lead them to Mary's killer.

"Actually, yeah." Bobby got to his feet and started rummaging through some of the many papers that were strewn about the desk in front of the fireplace. "*Doragon Kokoro*'s back."

The name didn't ring any bells.

"What's that?"

"Nasty-ass spirit. Twenty years ago, it showed up in San Francisco killin' folks. Now it's back, and I got the only thing that'll stop it."

Suddenly alert, John immediately started calculating the mileage in his head.

"San Francisco's a long way off—especially with the Impala's engine acting up. But I can probably get out there—"

Bobby held up a hand.

"Whoa, there, John. You just said yourself that you're wiped out. And you ain't spent time with the kids in a dog's age."

John agreed with him, but at the mere mention of another hunt, another killer to destroy, another chance at maybe—maybe—finding out who killed Mary, his exhaustion fell away like autumn leaves.

"You got someone else who can do it?"

Bobby hesitated, and that was all John needed.

"You said people are dyin', Bobby. That's all that matters." And revenge, but he didn't need to mention that. "What do I need to do?"

Reaching behind his desk, Bobby pulled up a sword from the floor. John was confused as to why it wasn't in a scabbard, then he saw that it was a hook sword, of the sort that came from Asia. Those things didn't really holster well....

He also saw the *kanji* characters etched onto the blade.

"Magic sword?"

Bobby shook his head.

"Nah, just a fancy label. The characters just mean 'Pierce the heart of the dragon.'"

"How do you know?" John asked.

In response, Bobby reeled off several phrases in what sounded like Japanese.

"Oh," John said lamely. He should have known better than to assume that there was something Bobby *didn't* know. "I'm guessin' you just told me to screw off and die," he added.

"Somethin' like that," Bobby replied, grinning. "And that's all you got to do—run this through the heart of the dragon. End of story—at least for now." Then the grin fell. "Look, I'll take a gander at the Impala's engine, get her good as new while you're gone."

"How'm I supposed to get there? Especially with that." He gestured at the sword.

"Take a plane," Bobby said. "I'll ship the sword, and it'll be there waiting when you arrive in San Francisco."

"Okay, that could work." John hadn't thought of that. But then again, Bobby had a legitimate and regular source of income. Just buying a plane ticket and shipping stuff you couldn't get through airline security tended to be outside of John's budget. He was struggling enough just to keep the Impala going, especially with gas over a dollar a gallon.

Bobby explained that *Doragon Kokoro* was the spirit of a *ronin* that had been brought back by a half-Chinese, half-Japanese man named Albert Chao. A spell had been cast by a hunter—from what Bobby heard, it was a man named Jack Bartow—that banished the spirit for twenty years. And that was exactly two decades back.

"What happened to the hunter who cast the spell?"

"Bartow? He died later on, savin' a couple from a vengeance spirit that was hauntin' 'em. I met him right after I started in the business, and he left me a bunch of his stuff—including this."

With that he hefted the sword.

"Where'd he find it?" John asked.

"Got it from a fella at Berkeley, in the Oriental Studies Department. Guy helped Bartow out twenty years ago, along with a couple of other hunters, then came across this and figured Bartow would know what to do with it when *Doragon Kokoro* came back. Now we got us some dead folks in

Chinatown, burned to a crisp and cut to ribbons."

"Chinatown?" John rubbed his stubble-covered chin. "I thought this was a *Japanese* spirit."

"It is—like I said, Chao's a half-breed. Don't know much beyond that." Then he peered intently at his friend. "You sure you wanna do this? I can probably head on down to Harvelle's, find someone who could handle it. Couple days won't make that much difference."

John didn't answer at first. Instead, he looked over at Dean and Sam in the dining room, playing that oh-so-common game of "I touched you last."

Christmas was coming up, and he did want to spend it with the boys….

But if all that was needed was for this sword to penetrate the Heart of the Dragon—like it said on the blade—then the job would only take a couple of days. He'd be back in plenty of time.

"Burned to a crisp, you said."

Then the image came back into his head.

His wife Mary, pinned to the ceiling, blood pooling outward from her stomach, fire surrounding and consuming her.

He'd dedicated his life to finding out who or what did that. True, he had other reasons for hunting—people were dying at the hands of monsters that most refused to believe really existed.

At the age of eighteen, John Winchester had been drafted by the U.S. Marine Corps, but had gone willingly, because he believed what his superiors in the Corps taught him: that being a Marine would save lives. A year in Vietnam had cured him of that notion, but the urge was still there.

Yet the saving of lives was like a side benefit. Because when he did return from 'Nam, he did so with but a single thought: *I want to spend the rest of my life with Mary Campbell.* And for ten years he did, until that *thing*—demon, monster, whatever it was—took her away from him.

No, his true reason for hunting—the reason that drove him, day in and day out—was to find out what had killed his wife and destroy it once and for all.

Perhaps the Heart of the Dragon would provide another clue to where he could find it, and finally achieve the vengeance for which his heart had cried out for the past six years.

John turned to Bobby with renewed resolve.

"So what time's my flight?"

TWELVE

Tommy Shin really hated having to deal with the Old Man.

Unfortunately, he didn't really have much of a choice. The Old Man still commanded respect among the people with whom he did business. There was simply no way Tommy would be able to keep his crack cocaine supplier without the Old Man's help. And there wasn't a person in Chinatown who didn't owe the Old Man a favor.

So Tommy put up with him—but only because he had no choice.

Some day, he promised himself, he'd finally have the respect he deserved, and be able to put the Old Man out to pasture. For now, though, he needed him.

Especially with everything else that was going on.

Tommy called the Old Man into his office, which was located above the Shin's Delight restaurant on Pacific Avenue in San Francisco's Chinatown neighborhood. As usual, the

Old Man sneered at him as he walked in. When this had been the Old Man's office, it was decorated with paintings and artifacts from China.

But Tommy hadn't liked that. So when the office became his, he put up framed posters instead—of movies like *Batman* and *Lethal Weapon 2* and bands like REM and Public Enemy. He had even repainted the walls.

Tourists expected a Chinese restaurant to have red walls with gold trim, and it didn't do to alienate the tourists—not as long as they had money. But Tommy had insisted that his office be redone in black. He'd read a magazine article about how dark walls made people nervous, and Tommy liked people to be nervous when they were in his presence.

Now the Old Man looked at the movie and music posters with that disdain of his, then he turned it on Tommy.

While the Old Man's paper-white hair was done in an ordinary bowl-cut, Tommy had his moussed and spiked; and where the Old Man wore traditional Chinese garments, Tommy had on a white linen jacket, with the sleeves rolled three-quarters up his arm, over a dark-blue polo shirt with the collar turned up.

"You continue to disrespect our traditions."

That was what the Old Man always said when he saw Tommy, and he said it in Mandarin, of course.

Tommy's response was just as rote, though he spoke in English.

"Those traditions remain in China. We're in America now. We should act like it."

The Old Man sat in the guest chair across from Tommy and continued to speak in Mandarin.

"I assume that you didn't summon me here so I could remind you what an imbecile you are."

Smiling, Tommy decided to indulge the Old Man and continue the conversation in Mandarin.

"Not that I don't enjoy it, but yes, there is a reason." He opened the top drawer of his desk and retrieved a manila folder. Handing it to the Old Man, he said, "We have a problem. I could use your advice on how to fix it."

Taking the folder, the Old Man snorted.

"*Now* you wish for my advice?"

"I always want your advice on things that *matter*," Tommy said, still smiling. Then he let the smile fall, for this was serious business. "Three of my lieutenants are dead. That is a copy of the police file—I got it from my cop on the inside."

"Why do you take such absurd risks?" the Old Man asked. "The police are not to be trusted."

"I pay this one good money to provide me with intelligence," Tommy said with a scowl. "It's useful."

"It's a waste of money. The police know nothing of our ways, so they cannot enforce their laws on our people. By adopting their ways, you make it easier for them to complicate our operations. And by putting one on your payroll, you risk discovery."

Tommy leaned forward, his hands flat on the wooden desk.

"Profits are *up* since I took over, and the only arrests have been of low-level workers who know nothing of consequence. I know what I'm doing."

Now the Old Man smiled.

"Then why do you need my help?"

Tommy leaned back into his chair.

"Read the file."

The Old Man finally opened the manila folder, looked through it, and grimaced.

Tommy had had much the same reaction when he first heard about the deaths of Teng, Li, and Lao. Whoever killed them had overdone it: broiling them and cutting them up. Lao's body had been found by Tommy himself in an alley behind the restaurant. The sight had made him ill, and the subsequent vomiting had ruined a very nice pair of moccasins.

"Someone," Tommy said as the Old Man closed the folder, "is going to a great deal of trouble."

The Old Man nodded.

"This is more than simply killing several of your lieutenants. If it was just a bullet to the back of the head, I would expect that they had done something idiotic. But this…." The Old Man sighed. "This is a power play by someone who has access to considerable resources."

Frustrated, Tommy threw up his hands.

"What kind of 'resources' could accomplish *this*?"

"Ones not of this world," the Old Man said, "but the next."

Tommy rolled his eyes.

"That's absurd."

"Really? Did you actually *read* the report your policeman friend supplied?"

"What do you mean?"

The Old Man opened the folder to a particular page and shoved it forward on the desk.

"See this medical examiner's report? The bodies had third-degree burns evenly distributed, yet there was no sign of fire anywhere near the corpses. The bodies were too fragile to be moved."

"So?" Tommy asked, wondering what difference any of that made.

"So, you young idiot, these deaths were not natural."

Tommy laughed.

"Then what, they're *super*-natural?"

"Do not mock me," the Old Man said gravely. "You are too young to remember, but this has happened before. Several citizens of Chinatown were killed in just such a manner, twenty years ago. Rumor had it that the Heart of the Dragon was responsible. It is possible that he has returned."

Tommy rolled his eyes once again.

"That's just a fairy tale! I heard about that evil spirit when I was a teenager. It was stupid then, and it's stupid now."

The Old Man shrugged.

"Mock it if you wish," he said. "They are *your* lieutenants being killed, so what does it matter? But it is obvious that someone has summoned the Heart of the Dragon once again. And it is just as obvious that you must find that person, and kill him before he kills *you*."

With that, the Old Man got up from his chair. Pausing once to sneer at the image of Mel Gibson and Danny Glover on the poster near the door, he turned and gave Tommy one last parting shot.

"You think you're better than me," he said, "but you're just a fool who got lucky."

Tommy shook his head in disgust, but didn't bother to reply. He stabbed a finger at the intercom that would put him in touch with the foyer outside the office, where his one surviving lieutenant—Benny Hao—was waiting.

"Get in here," he said in English.

Hao, broad-shouldered, well-muscled and imposing, strode into the room.

"Yeah, boss?"

"Tell Mai-Lin to find out whatever she can about 'the Heart of the Dragon.'"

For a brief instant, Benny laughed, then he saw that Tommy wasn't sharing in the humor, and stopped.

"You sure, boss?" he asked tentatively. "I thought that was just a story."

"Maybe—but I want to be certain."

"Uh, okay." He started for the door, then turned. "Oh, and Al's outside."

"What does *he* want?" Tommy snarled.

"Said he had an appointment."

Just as he was about to tell Benny to shoot Al in the head, Tommy recalled that he had, in fact, made the appointment—he'd just forgotten about it in the chaos surrounding the deaths.

"Shit," he spat. "Fine, send the little twerp in."

Nodding, Benny left the room.

Al came in a moment later, wearing a polo shirt, jeans, and moccasins of the same type as Tommy. His shoulder-length dark hair was tied back into a tiny ponytail.

"What do you want?" Tommy asked impatiently. He could hear Benny on the phone in the foyer, talking to Mai-Lin.

"I wanted to talk to you about my ideas for improving the collection taking."

Tommy blinked in confusion.

"What?"

"We've been having problems with the collections of the protection money, and I think I know why. We always collect on the first day of the month."

Tommy couldn't believe he was having this conversation.

"Al, I don't know if you've been paying attention, but a bunch of our people are *dead*."

"Uh, okay. I just—" Al cleared his throat, and pressed on. "When we collect on the first day of the month, usually the owners have already deposited all their cash into their bank accounts, so claim they don't have any in the till. If we do all the collections on the first Saturday of every month, it'll work better. The banks are closed on Saturday, so the owners can't say they don't have the cash."

As pissed as he was at being interrupted, Tommy had to concede that it wasn't a bad idea. Taking protection money on the first of the month was one of the Old Man's policies, and Tommy had continued it out of habit.

But he was more than happy to get rid of another outmoded notion.

Now, however, was not the time.

"Al, it's a good idea, but not now, okay? We'll do this next week."

Al looked deflated, but nodded.

"All right, boss."

The man turned to leave, but Tommy stopped him.

"Hey, you ever hear anything about something called 'the Heart of the Dragon?'"

Albert Chao just shrugged.

"Nope—never heard of it."

THIRTEEN

John looked around at the room he'd been given at the Emperor Norton Lodge on Ellis Street. It had probably been a nice hotel once, but the décor looked like it was straight out of the 1960s. Were John still a teenager, that would have been fine, but times had changed, and the flower-power wallpaper and garish carpet just didn't feel right.

The place even had a rotary phone; John hadn't realized there were any of those left.

Still, it was cheap, and that was what really mattered.

It had been all right at first. He and Mary had saved plenty of money—okay, so it was originally earmarked for Dean and Sammy's college funds, but that was less of a priority now—so after she died, he'd been able to finance his hunt for vengeance.

But he'd had no idea it would take this long. A year or two, maybe, but not the six years he'd already spent.

And there was no end in sight.

Which meant he'd been progressively downgrading the type of hotel he was willing to stay in. Besides, cheap places like this were less intrusive, and the staff asked fewer questions.

The money he saved on lodging went to weapons and ammo and other equipment. Not to mention food, gas for the Impala, and paying for that storage unit in upstate New York.

Sooner or later, the bank account was going to run dry. But John was already practicing a few tricks that would enable him to keep going....

One advantage to this particular dump was its proximity to Chinatown, where the three murders he knew of had taken place.

As promised, Bobby's package was waiting for him upon arrival, and he set it down on the rickety desk that stood against one wall of the room.

Just a day earlier, Dean had helped him put the package together. Dean tended to wield Bobby's tape gun like it was a weapon, which John had found at once charming and unfortunate. He knew that the boys needed to know how to defend themselves. Even if they found the thing that killed Mary, he doubted it would end there.

John knew too much about how the world really worked, Dean was starting to learn, as well—and it wouldn't be long before Sammy would find out, though John still held out some hope that his six year-old might have something resembling a normal life.

If he could find Mary's killer soon.

Yet as he brought the heavy package into the hotel room, he wondered if the quest would *ever* end.

He thought about the Heart of the Dragon as he ripped the box open, and the fact that the hunter who had stopped it before—this Bartow guy—had died. John would never be able to find out what he knew. And that raised a disturbing possibility that he tried not to think about too much.

What if some other hunter had come along and killed the thing that took Mary away? John would never even know. It wasn't as if there was a hunter's newsletter or anything, and the folks at places like the Roadhouse weren't exactly forthcoming with details of their hunts. Boasts, yes, tall tales, certainly, but actual solid information was hard to come by.

So someone might have killed the thing that took Mary, and no one would ever know. Monsters didn't generally provide resumés of their previous kills.

There was a very real chance that John's hunt was entirely pointless.

But it didn't matter. Because he couldn't stop on the basis of a random possibility. He needed to find what had killed Mary, and destroy it. Until that day, there would be no respite.

One of the most important lessons Daniel Elkins had taught him was that the first step of any hunt was to gather information. It was something of a miracle that John hadn't gotten himself killed in his first few months of hunting, because what he hadn't known back then could fill volumes.

So his next step was to visit the San Francisco Public Library's main branch at the Civic Center. He took the bus there, since his car was back in South Dakota, and that gave him the opportunity to see the City by the Bay.

Unfortunately, most of what he saw was construction—right up to and including the Main Library itself. The Bay Area had been hit by a brutal earthquake in October—ironically right in the midst of the first World Series between the Oakland A's and the San Francisco Giants. While nowhere near as devastating as the famous 1906 quake, there had been a lot of damage, and the city was still in the process of rebuilding.

When the quake hit, John had actually been at the Roadhouse watching what was supposed to be the third game of the Series with some fellow hunters. The Roadhouse owners, Ellen and Bill Harvelle, had planned it all out: for the duration of the '89 Series, the place would—for once—be run like a normal sports bar, with guys drinking beer and talking about Mark McGwire and Jose Canseco, and about Will Clark and Rick Reuschel, and about the death of the commissioner, and all sorts of other things that hunters normally didn't have the time or energy to think about.

But then while the players warmed up for the third game, the earth shook. Al Michaels, Jim Palmer, and Tim McCarver turned from sports announcers to newscasters.

Immediately the patrons of the Roadhouse tried to figure out what kind of omen this might be, what the signs were, and what they might have missed. But it soon became apparent that no mystic forces were involved—it was just the San Andreas Fault with a case of the hiccups.

Now, as he got off the bus, John realized that he had no idea who actually won that Series.

To his relief, the section of the Main Library that included recent newspapers was still open to the public, and wasn't among the areas closed off for post-quake repairs. He immediately started digging through all the local papers, trying to find out everything he could about the three murders.

But the stories themselves didn't offer much, although the *Chronicle* had managed to locate pictures of the victims from before their deaths. They were all Chinese-Americans, they were all employed by the Shin's Delight restaurant— and they all had tattoos on their forearms.

While the quality of the black-and-white photos was sufficiently poor that John couldn't make out what the tattoos depicted, he *could* tell that they were of the same design—whatever it might be—and in the same place. These days, ornate tattoos were mostly the purview of bikers, Marines, and gangsters—John had the same tattoo on his forearm that all the members of Echo 2/1 boasted.

Chinese-American biker gangs weren't really the norm.

He also checked the sports sections from late October. The A's had swept the Series in four games.

Go team.

When he got back to the hotel, John made a phone call to Lucas Jackson, a fellow Marine who'd gone to work for the VA after serving his tour. He left a message asking if there were any Marine veterans named Jack Teng, Michael Li, or Johnny Lao.

While waiting for that phone call to come back, John

went to the hotel gym. It was a pitiful affair, with only a few weights and one of those stairmaster things, but it would do.

One of the great vampire hunters Daniel Elkins had been an invaluable storehouse of information about the supernatural. He had urged John to follow his example and keep a journal, so that if he died, it would provide Sam and Dean with a roadmap on how to continue his work.

It was astonishing how little John knew of those who had come before him. Bobby had reinforced that need with his own account of how he got into hunting. Like John, Bobby had lost his wife. And like John, Bobby had no idea who or *what* it was that had taken her from him.

But where John's first instinct was to fight—no doubt born of his Marine training—Bobby's was to learn. He had sworn that he would never fail someone due to ignorance.

John had taken both men's lessons to heart.

He had also embraced the lessons the Marines had taught him, which included the idea that it was never good to be idle. As Sergeant Lorenzo had always said, "You're only as strong as the last guy who kicked your ass."

So he worked out with the weights while he waited for Lucas to call back.

By the time he returned to the room, sweaty and sore—but the good kind of sweaty and sore—the message light was blinking on the room's rotary phone. Picking it up, he dialed zero.

"Front desk."

"This is Room 220. There's a message for me?"

"Uh, yes, sir." John heard the man shuffle through some papers. "It's from Lucas Jackson. The message is, 'no soap.'"

John smiled.

Back in country, Lucas had never gotten tired of telling the awful, 'No soap, radio' joke, mostly to new recruits who didn't get it—because, of course, there was nothing to get. That proved to John that it was really Lucas returning the call, and also that he hadn't found any records for the three dead men.

Which wasn't a surprise. Still, he'd needed to be sure.

So they were gangsters.

Stripping off the t-shirt and shorts he'd worn to the gym, he took a quick shower, then changed into the warmer clothes he'd need to go outside in San Francisco in December.

Time, he thought, *for a nice dinner at Shin's Delight.*

FOURTEEN

The second-best day of Albert Chao's life had been when Tommy Shin took over as the official of this branch of the Triads.

The best, of course, had been the day Moondoggy Verlander had completed the spell that would allow Albert to summon the Heart of the Dragon. Nothing before that—and nothing since—had matched the sheer magnificence of having such power.

He needed to get that power back.

While it had healed his wounds, and continued to do so, without the presence of the spirit itself his greatest weapon remained maddeningly out of reach. Until the spell that banished the spirit wore off, *true* power would be denied him.

He couldn't be hurt or killed—though, for some reason, he continued to age. The spell kept him from permanent harm by healing any injury to his person—though the graver the injury, the longer it took for him to recover.

And invulnerability wasn't the same as having the ability to hurt people. Once he realized that, Albert took advantage of the kung-fu craze of the early 1970s, when martial arts dojos were opening up all over the place, filled with students all eager to be the next Bruce Lee. There his rapid healing gave him a distinct advantage, and he quickly developed the fighting skills he needed.

As soon as Albert felt they were sufficiently honed, he offered himself up to the local Triad group. At first he was refused, but he persisted, and found a branch that would have him.

Growing up in Chinatown, he had always known how much of the power in his community was wielded by the Triads. So he committed himself to working his way up the Triad ladder, and did so for the next two decades.

Unfortunately, he spent most of that time on the bottom rung. His status as a half-breed—as usual—was a frustrating impediment.

Eventually, however, he was permitted to work as a low-level enforcer. He acted as a bodyguard for the prostitutes, minded the door at the clubs, and occasionally took care of people who didn't pay their protection money or repay their loans.

Never, however, was he permitted to express an opinion. Half the time, they wouldn't even let him speak.

That all changed, though, when Tommy Shin took over from the Old Man.

* * *

No one had any idea why the Old Man chose to retire. The announcement came out of the blue, and he seemed deeply unhappy about it. Rumor had it that the higher-ups back in China were displeased with something the Old Man had done, and had made it clear that new blood was required.

Tommy considered himself an American who happened to live in Chinatown, rather than a Chinese who happened live in America. And he did something nobody else in the Triad hierarchy would do: he spoke directly to Albert.

"This is the land of opportunity," Tommy had said then. Albert was pretty sure Tommy hadn't cared who he was talking to—he just liked to hear the sound of his own voice. But that didn't matter—what mattered was that it was Albert who was standing there.

The television was on, and it was tuned to a newscast. There were people in East Germany climbing over the Berlin Wall, unopposed by the security forces that months earlier would have shot them for even attempting such a thing.

"We can't let ourselves be tied down to old ways of doing things," Tommy continued. "Look at that—the Iron Curtain doesn't even exist anymore. Who'd have believed that any of us would live to see that? So yeah, Albert, I want to hear what you have to say, because the fact that your mother was Japanese isn't a good enough reason *not* to listen to you."

That was all he needed to hear.

Now, a month later, Albert had moved up in the ranks.

Tommy talked to him, and, reluctantly, so did the others—because Tommy did.

Which was good, because that was only step one of the plan.

Step two came on the penultimate new moon of the year, November 28. That was when the spell cast by that stupid blonde *gaijin* girl finally expired, and Albert once again commanded the Heart of the Dragon.

Once again he spoke the words, and once again the flames erupted—flames that didn't burn the surroundings, yet emitted waves of intense energy. Albert basked in the glow of that power, and planned his next move.

His original plan had been to simply kill everyone who stood in his way, then take control of the Triads, but he hadn't counted on it taking quite so long to advance in the organization.

Plus his years working for the Old Man—and then for Tommy—had illustrated the fact that it took more than sheer power. Yes, it helped to wield such a magnificent weapon, but a genuine leader also needed to command respect, and no spell could grant that.

Albert did not have the respect of his peers, nor of the Triad masters back in China. He would not yet be accepted as the new commander, regardless of the magical resource he now controlled.

But he could systematically eliminate Tommy's support system, leaving the Triad boss with only one man he could rely on: Albert Chao. When that day arrived, only Tommy would stand between Albert and the seat of power. It would only be a matter of time before he controlled this branch, and eventually *all* of the Triads.

He had to be patient, and methodical. His training at the dojo had instilled that in him.

Tommy had called him in for a meeting, so he entered through the restaurant. Albert was hoping it was about his collection proposal. The shop owners were always looking for ways to wriggle out of paying protection money, and Albert's solution, while simple, would solve those problems.

He'd just timed it poorly.

As he entered the restaurant, he scanned the tables out of habit from his days as a bodyguard. The vast majority of the patrons were locals, with only one or two round-eyed tourists who had made the effort to dig deeper and find a more authentic eatery.

Then there was the man with the stubble. He was wearing a Sony walkman, eating his dumplings with a pair of chopsticks that he wielded with surprising ease for an American. Looking more closely, Albert saw dogtags around the man's neck. Given his age, he'd probably served in Vietnam and learned how to use chopsticks there.

As Albert walked past, the man looked up sharply. Then he stopped the tape in his walkman and rewound it.

Albert made a quick detour to Lin, the *maître d'*.

"Keep an eye on the man at table seven," he whispered. "I don't like the look of him."

Lin just stared at him.

"He's a paying customer."

"Yeah, but he looks like a cop," Albert said. The SFPD, he knew, was full of guys who had served in the military.

"Lotta cops in here since Jack, Mike, and Johnny died," Lin persisted. "Maybe he just likes the dumplings."

Albert scowled at him and headed toward the back, to talk to Tommy.

He'd been trying to figure out who the Heart of the Dragon's next victim should be, and now he was pretty sure it was going to have to be Lin.

While climbing the wooden staircase that led to Tommy's office, he started whispering the spell.

John cursed himself for his obviousness, but he couldn't help looking up sharply when his electromagnetic field detector—which looked like a normal Sony walkman—started spiking.

The person the EMF was responding to, a man with a pointed nose and dark hair tied into a little ponytail, had already been giving John the hairy eyeball, and it only grew more intense when John looked over at him so suddenly.

John hoped it was just the standard reaction to an American in a place dominated by Chinese—he'd had similar experiences in Vietnam, and had learned the hard way to stick to places that catered to American soldiers. But given the spike, he couldn't take the chance.

Out of the corner of his eye he saw the guy talking to the

maître d' and gesturing in John's direction. That pretty much clinched it—he had to assume that he'd been made.

Which meant that guy might well have been Albert Chao, the one responsible for bringing back the Heart of the Dragon. Bobby hadn't had a picture, or even a physical description, so he couldn't be completely sure.

But he could find out.

Quickly gulping down the remainder of his dumplings, John shrugged on his bomber jacket, left a ten-dollar bill on the table without bothering to wait for the check—he didn't want to lose time—grabbed the large mailing tube from under the table, and headed for the exit.

The *maître d'* didn't even acknowledge John's departure. He wasn't sure if that was a good sign or not. Bobby had mentioned that Chao was a half-breed, and that was a type that full-blooded Chinese often ignored, so John might have caught a break.

Once out on Pacific Avenue, John turned and went into the alley that ran between Shin's Delight and a souvenir shop. To his relief, the alleyway was open—many large cities these days had taken to gating them to keep out homeless people.

He reached the back of the building, where three dumpsters contained all the restaurant's garbage. The stench of rotting food assaulted his nose, but he didn't let it slow him down—he'd smelled far worse over the past six years. Along the way, he stepped in brackish water that simply joined the dozens of other unidentifiable stains already present on his hiking boots.

Once he got past the third dumpster, he found a large metal door that was covered in chipped brown paint the same color as the bricks. Using the trash receptacles to hide himself from street view—not that many people were staring down the alley, in any case—he removed the hook sword from the mailing tube.

The door had two locks, one on the knob, and a deadbolt above it. Trying the knob, he found that it turned all the way, so it wasn't locked—but the door didn't budge, which meant the deadbolt was in place.

Reaching into the inner pocket of his jacket, John pulled out the lockpicks that had been a gift from Caleb two years earlier. Well, half a gift—the other half had been showing him how to use them. After eighteen months, he finally started getting the hang of it.

After a few moments of fiddling, the tumblers dropped into place.

Turning the knob, John had to yank to get it open, and cursed silently at the sound it made. As he did so, he held up the sword in a ready position.

But there was nobody there. Just a dark hallway that led along the back of the building.

Slowly stepping inside, John closed and locked the door behind him—it wouldn't do for someone to notice anything amiss—then waited for his eyes to adjust to the dark. There was a light somewhere down the hall, providing him with some illumination. He almost tripped over a couple of giant Hefty bags filled with refuse that hadn't made their way out to the dumpsters yet. The walls were covered in cracked wooden paneling.

He could hear chatter in Chinese, coming from the direction of the light, and the crackling sound of oil frying. He moved slowly and silently toward the sounds, and found an entryway to the kitchen, as well as a spiral staircase that went up to the second floor.

Dozens of people dressed in dirty white uniforms moved about the kitchen, the chatter and the cooking creating a constant stream of sound, enough that the kitchen staff didn't notice John moving quickly up the staircase.

The stairs emptied out onto another hallway with similar wood paneling, but in better shape. One wall boasted pictures in both black-and-white and color, showing various people on streets that could've been here in Chinatown, or in China itself. Closer inspection, however, revealed the flower-lined twists and turns of Lombard Street visible in the background.

The other wall had three closed doors and one open one. As he slowly moved down the corridor, staying close to the wall to avoid creaking floorboards, John heard two voices. Both, to his surprise, were speaking English.

Moving closer, John could start to make out the conversation.

"I understand," one of them said, "but we still have to consider—"

"Right now, Al, the only thing I'm 'considering' is how to kill whoever's responsible for this. I've lost three good lieutenants, and someone needs to *pay* for that!"

"Of course, Tommy, I understand, but we also have to make sure that business as usual goes on."

John had a suspicion it had been 'Al' who had set off the EMF spike and given him the evil eye, since that matched the first name Bobby had given him.

Before he could act, though, he heard a piercing scream from the direction of the large wooden staircase at the far end of the hall—followed by dozens more screams, all emanating from the restaurant below.

FIFTEEN

Lin Sun loved his job.

It was a simple job, one that didn't require a great deal of effort, but which allowed him to talk to people. Lin had always been what Americans referred to as a "people person."

As a boy he'd come to San Francisco with his family, and immediately started making friends. Unlike his older brother and younger sister—who were reserved at best, chronically shy at worst, just like Mother, Father, and Grandfather—Lin got along with everyone he met.

As he'd grown, he'd hoped for a career working with people. Perhaps as a librarian, or something else that involved serving the public.

But he quickly realized that what he hoped for made no difference, especially once he became old enough to learn the truth about why his parents had uprooted them from China.

The Triads had done Mother and Father a favor. To repay

the favor, they had been forced to move to San Francisco and promise that all three of their children would serve under a boss known only as "the Old Man."

For his sister, Lien, that meant serving as a hostess at one of the brothels. To Father's relief, she was not asked to be a prostitute. All she had to do was bring drinks, and occasionally let a customer buy her a drink.

For his brother, it meant being a personal errand boy for the Old Man.

Lin was grateful that the Old Man had actually *met* the children before giving them their assignments within the gang, because as soon as he did so, he recognized that Lin had a gift for talking to people. Thus, by the time he was sixteen, he was a waiter in one of the Triads' restaurants, eventually working his way up to *maître d'*.

That meant that he got to spend every day talking to people, greeting them, seating them, making sure they were enjoying their meals, and simply reveling in meeting other members of the human race.

Every day he recognized that his lot could have been much worse. His brother, Quan, had been killed in a drive-by shooting just last year. And while Lien wasn't forced to sleep with her customers, her life was a grim one, and not likely to get any better.

Lin didn't think very highly of Tommy Shin. The Old Man had kept things running smoothly, but Tommy kept trying to change things for their own sake, regardless of whether or not they worked. It was as if his only concern was not doing things the way the Old Man had done them, regardless of whether it was the right way or not.

Even worse, he let half-breeds like Albert Chao work for him, and move up in the ranks. That may have been acceptable to Americans, who had no proper sense of racial identity, but for true Chinese like Lin and his family such practices were not to be encouraged—certainly not by rewarding mongrels with positions of power.

As a result, Lin hadn't bothered to "keep an eye" on the stubble-covered American who'd been dining with his headphones on. He'd assumed that the man was listening to what passed for American music—all of it too loud for Lin's taste—and remained oblivious to all that was happening around him. Or maybe he was just impolite. Lin had come to expect that from Americans, though he hadn't seen as much of it here.

Shin's Delight wasn't included in most of the guidebooks, catering as it did to locals rather than tourists, so rarely did any Americans wander in off the street. The ones who made the effort to find the place usually had better manners.

Regardless, if Chao wanted Lin to keep an eye on the man, then it was clearly a waste of time.

Besides, he had more important things on his mind. With the deaths of Tommy Shin's lieutenants, Lin feared that Chao would rise to an even higher position in the Triads, and no good could come of that. There was nothing to be done about it, of course—Tommy wouldn't listen to a lowly *maître d'*.

The most Lin could do was quietly fume about it, standing at the podium near the restaurant's entrance.

Suddenly he realized he was sweating. Another thing that annoyed Lin about Tommy was his insistence on keeping the heat turned up whenever the temperature outside dipped in the slightest. That was why Lin liked his position at the podium, it allowed him to enjoy the occasional cool breeze when someone opened the outer door.

But this was hotter even than Tommy liked it. Wondering where the unusual waves of heat might be coming from, Lin turned around—

—and found himself facing the most horrific sight he'd ever experienced.

There was a man standing in a column of fire that climbed upward toward the ceiling. Already only a few feet away, the man moved toward him and raised a sword wreathed in flames.

Lin couldn't scream.

Couldn't breathe.

Couldn't move.

He was transfixed by the fire that surrounded the man, and by his horrible eyes....

Hook sword held at the ready, John took the stairs two at a time and ran into the main part of the restaurant. He registered several things in a single glance.

First, the restaurant's patrons were screaming, pointing, shouting, and tripping over tables and chairs trying to get away from something, even though the source of their terror was blocking the only exit.

Second was the *maître d'*, who was standing stunned while everyone around him was panicking.

And third was a *samurai* encircled by fire wielding a flaming katana.

That's new, he mused.

The *samurai*—which John figured just *had* to be the Heart of the Dragon—was making a beeline for the *maître d'*, who remained rooted to the spot.

John found himself having to shove the panicking patrons out of his way in order to get to the front of the restaurant. The tables were crammed far too close together, and people were literally stepping on one another to get away. Shouts mixed with the piercing sound of shattering glass and porcelain as plates and glasses were knocked onto the floor.

By the time he reached the front, *Doragon Kokoro* was practically on top of the *maître d'*.

Standing behind the creature, John swung the sword so the hook caught the *ronin* as if it was a cane yanking a poor performer off a vaudeville stage. But he couldn't manage to get a grip.

The spirit didn't even notice.

Yanking the sword back, John took another swing, this time at the spirit's neck.

The demon whirled around, swinging his flaming sword. John was barely able to duck as the flames singed his hair.

He only burns his intended target, John realized. *He can fry me as easily as he fried his other victims.*

But after that one brief attack, the *ronin* turned to focus again on his prey.

However, John's distraction seemed to have shaken the *maître d'* out of his reverie, and caused him to move his ass. With a sudden cry, he bolted through the front door as fast as his feet could carry him.

John moved swiftly to place himself between *Doragon Kokoro* and the exit.

"You ain't gettin' past me," he said, holding the sword in a ready position.

Through the flickering flames, John could see the patrons continue to scream at one another in Chinese as they tried to escape via the kitchen or the rest rooms. Behind them, at the foot of the same staircase John had run down, he saw Albert Chao standing alongside a young man with spiked hair.

Chao looked pissed.

Raising his katana, the Heart of the Dragon swung downward.

John leaned back, avoiding the flaming blade by a hair's breadth. The spirit came back with a side thrust. John parried with the hook sword, the clash of metal on metal shaking him so hard he almost lost his grip.

Tightening his hands around the hilt, John swung once again, this time aiming right for where the *ronin's* heart had beaten when he was alive. Bobby had said that the inscription translated to, "Pierce the heart of the dragon," and maybe it meant exactly that.

Unfortunately, it did no more good than the other two strikes. The hook sword went straight through, as though what he was fighting was nothing more than flames. Yet the strike of the katana on the hook sword had been *quite* substantial.

Again, *Doragon Kokoro* swung his weapon. Again John raised his own sword to parry.

He had wielded a sword in the past, during his training as a Marine, but that was primarily for ceremonial functions. Then Caleb had introduced him to a middle-aged woman named Lara, an expert swordswoman with amazingly fast hands. He never forgot the best piece of advice she'd given him.

"*Go on instinct. Don't think about what you're doing, just do it!*"

When the Heart of the Dragon attacked, John didn't think. He just acted.

Each sword strike got closer. Each parry from John came later.

The thrusts were impossibly strong and never varied. John, on the other hand, was only human, and would tire as the scrap wore on.

He needed a new plan, since the sword didn't seem to be doing the trick.

Then the fires that surrounded the spirit started to dim. Glancing toward the stairs, John saw that Chao was muttering something.

In a moment, the spirit faded away. The floor beneath it remained untouched.

A few people were still milling about and John saw that both the spike-haired man and Chao were trying to plow through the chaotic restaurant toward him.

Not having any desire to answer their questions, John followed the path of the *maître d'* out of the door. Luckily, Pacific Avenue was even more packed than the restaurant had been. Tourists of all shapes, sizes, and colors joined the locals to jam the sidewalk. He was able to lose himself in the crowd, doing his best to hide the hook sword beneath his bomber jacket.

He worked his way to a bus stop—walking gingerly to avoid stabbing himself—knowing that the first thing he needed to do when he got back to the hotel was call Bobby and tell him that his sword was a dud.

Albert couldn't believe it. He just couldn't.

Everything was going so well, and yet here was some *gaijin* messing things up—just like those people from twenty years ago. This one even had a sword of some kind.

Quickly, Albert banished the spirit. There were too many witnesses, and Lin had already run off.

Unfortunately, the damage had been done. Tommy had run out front, along with two of the waiters, to go after the *gaijin*.

Albert, however, stayed behind, so he was able to survey the damage that had been done. He cursed himself for a fool, letting his dislike of Lin overcome his good sense. The point was to wield the Heart of the Dragon with subtlety, to weed out those who stood in his way.

Lin wasn't in Albert's way, he was just an idiot.

Albert was *never* going to succeed if he kept making stupid mistakes like that.

With a sigh, he started walking back through the restaurant, glass and ceramic crunching under his feet. The patrons were starting to calm down, some checking themselves for injuries, all of them whispering breathlessly to one another.

After a few moments, Albert realized that they were all saying the same thing: that after twenty years, the Heart of the Dragon was back.

At first he was tempted to shout them all down, tell them they were giving in to superstition and foolishness, but he quickly realized that it would be a mistake. To begin with, they could hardly deny the evidence of their own eyes.

Besides, since he'd already opened Pandora's Box, maybe he could use the situation to his benefit.

Tommy stomped back into the restaurant, bellowing furiously.

"What the hell *was* that?"

"From the looks of it," Albert said, "that was the Heart of the Dragon. It was trying to kill Lin."

"That's not what I saw," Tommy said. "It was trying to kill that tourist with the sword." He smiled then. "For some reason, the Heart of the Dragon was trying to protect us."

Then the smile fell.

"Al, I need you to find out everything you can about this thing—where it came from, what it wants, why it's helping us.

And *who* the hell it was trying to kill."

One of the waiters—Albert couldn't remember his name—spoke up.

"Boss, isn't that the thing that killed Johnny and—"

"True." Tommy rubbed his chin. "We need more information. C'mon, Al, you've always got ideas—so what is this thing, and what does it want with me? Can you get me some answers?"

Albert bowed respectfully.

"Absolutely, Tommy."

Sixteen

Bobby Singer was about to make dinner for himself and the boys when the phone rang. He grabbed his new cordless appliance off the wall-mount and held it up to his ear.

"Hello?"

In response, the phone rang again.

With a sigh, he held it in front of his face and pushed the "talk" button.

"*Hello?*"

It was John Winchester.

"What the hell you tryin' to pull, Bobby?"

Now Bobby scowled, wondering why, exactly, he put up with this sort of crap.

Voices from the living room wafted into the kitchen.

"*Deeeeean!* That's my pen!"

"So get another pen, Dexter Sammy."

He ran his other hand through his thick hair.

"I ain't pullin' a damn thing, John," he replied, holding his temper as best he could. "What the hell are you talkin' about?"

"You send me out here, ship me this sword, and I'm stuck flailin' around like an idiot. The damned thing doesn't work."

Bobby started to rub his eyes, but noticed that there were tufts of red hair between his fingers. He was starting to go bald, and in his uncharitable moments he blamed it entirely on John.

"Look, why don't you go talk to that Berkeley professor that gave Bartow the thing?"

There was a long pause before he heard John's reply.

"What's his name?"

"Marcus Wallace."

Bobby went into the living room. Dean was standing on his tiptoes and holding his left hand as high in the air as he could—Sam's pen clutched between his fingers. Sam, for his part, was jumping up into the air trying to grab it from his much taller older brother.

Shaking his head, Bobby rummaged through the papers on his desk.

"Hang on—okay, here it is," he added as he liberated the letter that had been packed away among Bartow's effects. Finding Wallace's direct line at the UC-Berkeley campus, he read it off.

"All right," John said, "I'll give him a call. If he doesn't pan out, though, I'm gonna need to get creative. It's that, or end up shake-and-baked. I'll talk to you later, Bobby."

"The boys are just fine, by the way," Bobby said quickly, before John could hang up.

Lowering his arm, Dean turned toward Bobby.

"Is that Dad?"

Sam took advantage of the distraction to snatch the pen from his brother's hand with a piercing "Ha!" of triumph, but Dean barely noticed.

John sounded impatient on the other end of the line.

"I figured they were, since if they weren't, you'd have said something," he said. "I need to go, the long-distance charges are murder."

With that, he hung up.

"Can I talk to him?" Dean asked pleadingly.

Pushing the "talk" button again to close the connection on his end, Bobby let his hand drop to his side.

"Sorry, Dean, he, uh—was on his way out the door. But he told me to tell you both to behave yourselves and do what I tell you. And that he loves you."

Tilting his head, Dean gave Bobby a sidelong glance.

"Did he *really* say that?"

"'Course he did. So I'm tellin' you right now, boy—stop stealing from your brother. You need a pen, ask me for one, all right?"

Dean nodded.

"Okay. I did all my homework already anyhow."

Now it was Bobby's turn to give Dean a sidelong glance.

"Really?"

Unlike Bobby, the ten year-old boy wilted.

"Well, most of it."

"That's what I thought. You get it done before I'm finished cookin', all right?"

"Okay."

Dean sat down next to Sam on the couch. Sam had gone back to the homework he'd been working on when Dean stole his pen.

Dean looked up at Bobby again.

"Can I have a pen?"

Bobby grinned.

"Sure." He opened the top drawer of his desk and fished out a ballpoint he'd gotten from one of the hotels he'd stayed in during a hunt.

He handed it over, and headed back into the kitchen.

"It won't write!" came the voice of a ten year-old. "This pen *sucks*!"

As he went into the fridge for butter to spread onto the pan, Bobby decided it was the entire Winchester family that was making him bald.

John had imagined that a college professor's office would be a large room with a grand wooden desk, a leather chair, and walls lined floor-to-high-ceiling with bookcases.

So when he arrived at the University of California Berkeley campus and went to the building on Fulton Street that housed the recently renamed Asian Studies Department, he was strangely disappointed.

Marcus Wallace's office was a tiny rectangle of a room

with no windows and less air. A dull gray metal desk sat against one wall, taking up so much space that the professor's simple leather chair butted against the opposite wall, leaving room only for one small particle-board bookcase in the corner.

The desk was covered with papers, some of which were precariously stacked in two wireframe in-boxes. Otherwise the desk boasted a phone—on which Wallace was speaking when John entered—and a personal computer screen, though the keyboard had been buried under more papers. Bright green letters glowed from the monitor, shining on the side of Wallace's face and contrasting oddly with the fluorescent bulb overhead.

The office's walls had probably been painted yellow once, but had faded to a dirty mustard.

Wallace himself was a pleasant-faced man who looked seriously out of place in an Asian Studies Department, with his squared-off Afro that was cut close to the skin at the temples.

While talking on the phone, he gestured for John to sit in the folding chair crammed between the desk and the wall next to the door.

"Yes, I understand that, but—" he said, then fell silent. "Yes, I *know* that, but— The students aren't going to—" More silence, and he was beginning to look pissed off. "Yes, sir. Yes, sir. Okay, sir. Good-bye."

Slamming the phone down with considerable force, Wallace snarled at it for a second, then composed himself.

"Sorry about that," he said sincerely. "We just got a new

department chairman, and his solution to everything seems to be to change how things've been done for the twenty years I've been here, whether it's a good idea or not. Swear to God, man, academic politics makes the folks in Washington look like pikers." He took a breath and held out his hand. "Sorry— I'm Marcus Wallace. You must be John Winchester."

John accepted the firm handshake.

"I guess you talked to Bobby after we spoke?"

Wallace nodded.

"So the hook sword didn't work as advertised?"

"That's an understatement," John said somewhat bitterly.

"Take it easy, man—it isn't Bobby's fault. Ever since *Doragon Kokoro* first showed up, some twenty years back, I've been trying to find out everything I could. I helped Bartow out, and since then, I've been doing research up the yin-yang to try to find out more. But it isn't easy."

He started rummaging through the papers on his desk while he continued.

"Nevertheless, I think I may have found something that might be of some use. Where is it?" After going through a few more sheafs, Wallace finally found what he was looking for. "Here it is!"

It was a booklet, about half the size of John's own journal in breadth and width. At first he thought Wallace was handing it to him upside down and backward, before he remembered that most Asian languages were written right-to-left.

Flipping through it briefly, John saw the *kanji* characters, along with some line art that John might have found pretty under better circumstances.

"What the hell'm I supposed to do with this?" he asked.

Wallace shook his head quickly and grabbed the booklet back.

"Sorry, man—I forget sometimes that not everybody reads the language." He flipped through to a back page. "Here we go." He handed it back to John and pointed at the drawing that appeared there. "I'm guessing a picture will be worth a few thousand words."

Again taking the booklet, John saw line art that took up the entire bottom half of the page: a man holding a very familiar-looking hook sword, crouched in a ready stance facing off against a man who was wreathed in flames while wielding a katana.

Of particular note to John was that the *kanji* characters on the hook sword were glowing.

Looking up, he saw that Wallace was nodding toward the book.

"If this thing's the real deal—and I've been translating this sucker for a while now—then it isn't the sword, it's the engravings." Turning away, he used his forearm to sweep the papers off the keyboard, and began typing. "I went ahead and wrote out the characters on the sword phonetically for you. The next time you face the spirit, you need to focus your concentration on it and then cast the engraved spell.

"My guess is that that'll get rid of *Doragon Kokoro*."

"Your *guess*?" John didn't like the sound of that.

Wallace regarded him levelly.

"Look, man, you and I both know that this sort of thing doesn't always come with an instruction manual."

With a sigh, John relented.

"Yeah, okay."

Rising to his feet, the professor gestured toward the door.

"C'mon, the printer's down the hall."

John followed him out of the cramped office and into the cramped hallway to a table that sat next to a bunch of wooden mail slots with people's names written on small white labels affixed to the front. One of them, John noted, had Wallace's name, there was an envelope propped up in the slot. The professor nabbed it as they walked past.

The printer was a daisy-wheel that worked very slowly, but it was still done by the time they arrived. The sheet it spat out contained only a few words.

Wallace pulled a lever that let loose the paper, and yanked it out.

"Here you go, Mr. Winchester. Hold the sword near *Doragon Kokoro*, chant this, and stand back."

John took the proffered paper.

"And if that doesn't work?"

Wallace's face broke into a wry grin.

"Run like hell?"

John rolled his eyes.

"Thanks a lot."

SEVENTEEN

Tommy Shin hated the fact that the Old Man had been right.

Mai-Lin had followed his instructions and provided him with a dossier of information about the Heart of the Dragon. Tommy didn't know as much as he'd have liked, but he knew enough to take action.

To his irritation, one of those actions had to be to talk to the Old Man again. When the Old Man had proposed that a spirit had been responsible for the deaths of his lieutenants, Tommy was barely able to even consider the idea. Now he would be forced to eat his own words.

But he couldn't deny the evidence of his own eyes. He'd *seen* the Heart of the Dragon in the restaurant, saw it advance upon Lin, and saw it disappear as if by magic. So Tommy had to accept that the creature truly existed. Which meant that once again he had to ask the Old Man for help.

The wild card in all this was the white man with the

sword. Tommy had no idea what to make of him—and that didn't sit well. On the one hand, the *gaijin* had brought that strange sword into the restaurant. On the other, he'd risked his own life to defend Lin—a perfect stranger.

Why would he do something like that? Tommy wondered. *What does he stand to gain?*

He also seemed to have *expected* the Heart of the Dragon to appear. Why else would he bring a sword into Shin's Delight in the first place?

Still, until he learned more about the man, there was nothing Tommy could do about him. Other preparations, however, could be made—and had been.

Tommy summoned Benny and Al to his office, and both men showed up almost immediately.

"Have a seat," he said, indicating the two guest chairs that sat in front of his desk. "I've received a report about the Heart of the Dragon—the flaming warrior—since it appeared in the restaurant downstairs."

Al seemed to become agitated.

"So have I," he said without waiting to be asked, "and I think it was that ga—uh, that foreigner who summoned it in the first place."

Benny turned to peer at him.

"Why would you think that?" he demanded. "Everyone I spoke to said that he seemed to be fighting it."

"It's obvious!" Al stared back at Benny as if to imply that he was an idiot. "The foreigner came in here carrying a sword! People don't do that sort of thing unless they plan to use them. I'll bet he called up the demon so that it would help him with whatever twisted plot he planned to carry out."

"Then why fight it as he did?" Benny asked.

Al shrugged.

"Who knows? Maybe it got out of control. That would explain why it went after Lin. I mean, Lin isn't anybody important, after all." He turned to face Tommy. "No, I think he was after *you*, and the reason he revealed himself when he did was in order to stop it from killing the wrong person." He looked very smug at his own reasoning.

Tommy nodded, considering what had been said.

"It's not a bad theory, Al," he admitted.

A knock came from the doorway. The door was open, and Mike Zhang—one of the bodyguards from downstairs—was standing there.

"Excuse me, boss? We got somebody."

Tommy waved his hand to indicate that Mike should enter.

"Come in, come in," he said eagerly.

Mike stepped into the office, followed by Jack Wu and an unshaven white man wearing a bomber jacket. Jack stood six-foot-eight, with massive shoulders.

Mike held up a hand to reveal a hook sword.

"Well well well," Tommy said, walking around his desk to face the foreigner, "returned to the scene of the crime, have you?"

Jack had huge hands with which he held the foreigner's shoulders in a crushing grip. Despite this, the white man was defiant.

"I'm not the one who's committing a crime here," he said with conviction.

"Who are you?" Tommy demanded.

"Name's John Winchester—and I ain't here to cause you any harm."

At that Al stood up and placed himself next to his boss.

"You're lying!" he said in a voice that was a little too high. "You're trying to destroy the Triads, starting with Tommy, aren't you? You think he's weak, but you're wrong!"

Winchester just smiled at him. It was a disturbing smile, because it was at once both completely wild and frighteningly sane. This, Tommy quickly realized, was someone who'd stared into the abyss.

He had seen that look only once before—on the Old Man.

"There's only one thing I'm tryin' to destroy, son, and it's not in this room."

Al turned to Tommy.

"You should kill him now, before he destroys you!"

Now it was Tommy's turn to smile.

"Oh, I may very well kill him, Al," he said calmly. "But not because he summoned the Heart of the Dragon."

"What are you talking about?" Al asked, and the blood drained from his face.

Tommy started to pace back and forth between the movie posters on the wall.

"Mai-Lin's research revealed a great deal about the Heart of the Dragon, including something you left out of your little report," he said. "You see, the creature is the damned spirit of an ancient warrior, Yoshio Nakadai, and John Winchester here cannot possibly have brought him back to the land of the living. No, that can only be done by a blood relative—a descendent of the *ronin*."

He turned to stare right at Al.

"Her information was very thorough. And since Yoshio Nakadai was Japanese, there's only one person I can think of who could possibly qualify. Someone who himself is half-Japanese, and might start to call a foreigner '*gaijin*' before correcting himself. Someone who has ambitions within the Triads. Someone who never got along with Lin."

At first panic swept across Al's features, and he glanced around the room as if to seek a way out.

Then his shoulders slumped, and he looked back at his boss.

"Very well, Tommy. You got me."

Before anyone could react, however, he muttered something under his breath.

Tommy felt the heat warm his face almost instantly.

There, in the middle of the room, was the Heart of the Dragon, looking just as he had downstairs.

"How the hell—?" Benny said, rising to his feet and backing away instinctively. He pulled out his Beretta.

Tommy and his bodyguards were frozen with fear. Winchester, who was still held in Jack's grip, was the only one who seemed to have kept his wits about him.

"He must've cast most of the spell before he came in here," he shouted. "What he just said had to've ended it."

"Very good," Al smiled, like a teacher praising a clever pupil.

Benny pulled the trigger three times, but the bullets evaporated instantly in the flames.

The Heart of the Dragon raised his katana.

Benny was about to shoot Al instead of the creature, but before he could do anything, Winchester started muttering some words of his own in Japanese.

As he did so, the lettering started to glow on the sword in Mike's hands.

Without warning the fiery spirit leaned his head back and screamed, his katana still raised. It was a hollow, agonizing sound—only vaguely human. The fire started to burn brighter, and Tommy had to shield his eyes from the glare.

Then the flames dwindled to nothing, and the spirit was gone.

Al cried out in anger.

Tommy gestured to Benny, who got the idea immediately and pointed his Beretta at Al.

Winchester moved quickly, however, elbowing Jack hard in the gut, then punching him in the face with the back of his fist. A kick of his booted heel caught Jack in the groin, and as the bodyguard doubled over, Winchester took a swing at Mike. One punch did the trick.

He always did have a glass jaw, Tommy thought absently. As Mike hit the floor, the Caucasian scooped up his sword.

Tommy never carried a gun—that was what he had guys like Mike and Jack for. Since Benny was aiming at Al, that freed Winchester to bolt for the door.

"Boss?" Benny asked, not taking his eyes off Al.

"Let him go," Tommy said, having fully regained his composure. "He's not our enemy. If he comes back, I'll deal with him then." He ran a hand through his spiked hair and turned to Al.

"You, however, I'll deal with right now."

Defiant to the last, though with nowhere near the conviction Winchester had shown, Al responded.

"Go ahead and do your worst, Tommy. Tell Benny to shoot me."

"If you don't shut up, I *will* shoot you, you half-breed piece of crap," Benny said.

"Like I said, go ahead. I have nothing more to say to you."

Tommy considered this.

"You may believe that, Al, but I don't. You see, you could be very valuable to me. After all, you know how to summon the Heart of the Dragon."

"Not anymore," Al said bitterly. "That—that *gaijin* banished the spirit. He's gone."

Shrugging, Tommy gestured to Benny.

"All right, then, shoot him."

With a grin, Benny squeezed the trigger three times, emptying his clip into Al's chest. He fell to the floor of the office, blood pluming from the wounds.

Tommy turned his attention to Jack and Mike.

"You two all right?"

Jack nodded, looking flushed with embarrassment, but

Mike was still insensate on the floor. Benny shook his head as he ejected the clip from his Beretta and replaced it with a new one. It slid into the grip with a solid click.

Tommy was thinking that he needed to put Mai-Lin on this John Winchester person—find out who he was, and where he came from. Clearly he had considerable knowledge and resources, of the sort Tommy thought he would, perhaps, be able to use.

He looked at Jack, who was kneeling down next to Mike.

Mike, in turn, was beginning to regain consciousness. He moaned loudly.

"Jack, get up and call Doctor Jiang. We'll need to have him dispose of Al's body."

"*Owww!*"

Whirling around, Tommy froze. They all did.

Al was getting up from the floor.

Blood still stained the front of his shirt, encircling the holes made by the bullets, but through those holes, Tommy only saw smooth, unbroken skin.

"What the hell?"

Smoothing his clothing as best he could, Al just stared at him, a huge grin appearing on his face.

"You're not gonna need Jiang for me, Tommy. And you're gonna want to keep me around, too. Remember how I said the Heart of the Dragon was banished? Well, one thing I *didn't* say was that it would be *forever*."

But before he could continue, Benny shot him again, this time in the shoulder.

Al stumbled back against the wall, then snarled and reached out to grab the gun from Benny's grip.

"Damn it, Benny, that *hurts*!"

Even as he pulled the weapon from Benny's hand, Jack got to his feet and put two bullets in Al's back, spinning him around. They burst out through his belly, spraying blood all over the *Lethal Weapon 2* poster.

But Al didn't fall down this time, though he was doubled over when he whirled around, aimed Benny's Beretta, and shot Jack twice in the chest.

Jack most definitely *did* fall over.

Benny leapt forward, trying to grab the gun back. Four hands wrapped around the Beretta's grip, fumbling desperately in an attempt to move it one way or the other, fingers trying to slide in to get purchase on the trigger.

At first they seemed evenly matched. Tommy didn't dare move closer for fear of getting shot himself. At one point the gun aimed right at him, and he ducked behind his desk.

Eventually Benny managed to get the upper hand, pushing the barrel against Al's chest.

With a deafening report, the weapon fired, and Al screamed.

Benny smiled. Thinking himself victorious, he relaxed his grip on the Beretta.

As soon as he did so, Al shoved the gun under Benny's chin and squeezed the trigger.

Brain matter and skull fragments splattered across the ceiling, and even as the body hit the floor, Al turned to Tommy. His shirt was shredded now, and completely drenched in blood, but where the skin was broken, the wounds were healing even as Tommy stared.

The smile that crossed his face now scared Tommy even more than Winchester's had. There was a madness that hadn't been there before.

"All you had to do was give me more authority," Al said grimly. "That's why I killed those three idiots— Teng, Li, and Lao. And these two." Then he turned to Mike, who was still half out of it on the floor, and shot him twice in the back. "And him.

"None of them were going to help you, Tommy. *I* could've helped you. Now I'm just gonna have to help myself. By the time I'm able to summon the Heart of the Dragon again, I'll be the most powerful man in Chinatown."

Tommy sneered at him the way the Old Man had always sneered at Tommy.

"You think you're better than me, but you're just a fool who got lucky."

"And I'm about to get luckier."

The last thing Tommy Shin ever heard was the report that sent a bullet into his brain.

EIGHTEEN

When Nakadai met his death at the hands of the demon, the experience was indescribable agony. Yet even as the flames roared, burning his flesh away from the bone, as the fires drove the life from his body, he knew that the demon had a plan that stretched far beyond turning a peaceful town into a bloodthirsty mob.

The intensity of the pain eventually caused him to lose consciousness—for the final time, he prayed. And once the agony disappeared, there wasn't anything to replace it, simply a void of nothingness. For the briefest of moments, Nakadai imagined he had found the peace he had sought ever since the dark days of his former master's disgrace.

That moment of hope, however, was fleeting.

The fires that killed him returned. While he did not feel their heat or their destructive power, somehow they transported him back to the land of the living.

When he arrived, a wizened old woman stood before him.

"*I am Miko*," she said. "*You are my great uncle. And you will do as I say.*" In her hands she held a hooked sword engraved with runes that spelled out the words "Pierce the heart of the dragon."

Try as he might, Nakadai could not speak—not even to verify that this withered crone was indeed the offspring of the pudgy two-year-old nephew he'd known when he lived. Nor could he control his own actions.

Visible through a haze of fire, the woman who called herself Miko revealed that she had learned of the spell the demon had used to damn him, but the power of her birthright had enabled her to summon him back to the land of the living.

She spoke of the foreigners who had come to their shores soon after Nakadai's death, and how their foul ways had corrupted Japan. She told him about her own daughter, who had married a Chinese man and moved across the ocean to the United States, and had given birth to a son.

That had been the final indignity, and it had spurred Miko to action. Disowning her daughter and cutting her off from all contact with the family, she had proceeded to search the family history, hoping to find *something* that might grant her the influence needed to turn the tide of corruption. In doing so, she had learned of the spell that had doomed Nakadai.

She then located masters of the arcane, and studied their arts. They had helped her craft a counter-spell that would return him to the land of the living as a weapon for her to wield. But knowing the dangers that lurked wherever evil was involved, she had set out to have the hook sword forged.

It was to be kept in reserve, in case the demon returned and attempted to assert control.

"*And now you will help me rid our land of the accursed Western plague,*" the ancient woman said, and that was when he realized that her mind had long since given way to insanity. "*Together we will destroy them, and restore Japan to its noble glory.*"

But the years had ravaged her body as much as her mind, and before Nakadai could perform any of the tasks Miko intended for him, it surrendered to the years and she died.

Oblivion returned the moment she breathed her last, and blissfully remained until the day that her grandson, Albert Chao, made use of the same spell. This was the half-breed who had so incensed Miko, and at his hands Nakadai was used to fulfill petty revenge fantasies until blessedly, he was banished again at the hands of a Western woman.

When he returned again eighty seasons later, it was again at the hands of Albert Chao. His descendant had become less petty, but his vicious streak remained, and only Miko's sword—somehow wielded by a foreigner—kept Nakadai from doing more harm.

Again he floated in the void, for what he hoped would be an eternity. But even as he did so, he knew the demon would never allow it to be.

NINETEEN

Dean stood between a fidgety Sammy and a patient Uncle Bobby at the Sioux Falls Airport baggage claim.

Each time someone new came through the door, his ten year-old heart beat just a little bit faster. And each time it wasn't Dad, he deflated.

He just wanted Dad to come back home safe. The safe part, at least, he knew was the case.

Dad had called Uncle Bobby last night after Dean was supposed to be in bed. But unlike Sammy, he hadn't been able to sleep. So when the phone rang, he slid out of bed, snuck quietly onto the upstairs landing, and listened to Uncle Bobby's side of the conversation coming from the kitchen.

"Good.... Yeah, okay." He paused while John talked on the other end of the line. "Yeah, I figured Wallace would know his business. What?... Oh yeah, sure. That makes sense. Well, send the sword back, you ain't gonna want to run that sucker through the metal detector, and I sure as hell wouldn't trust it to the idjits who handle checked luggage. Be lucky if the damn thing don't wind up in Outer Mongolia by mistake....

"Just charge it to the FedEx account, for cryin' out loud.... All right. I'll put it on ice when it gets here, in case we need it again in twenty years. Yeah, we'll meetcha when the flight lands—I'll even bring the Impala. It's runnin' all nice and smooth now, just needed an oil change and some tunin'.

"What?... Yeah, I said 'we.' I'll bring the boys along. They wanna see you.... Why shouldn't I bring 'em.... Good....

"Okay, seeya John."

After he'd heard the beep of Uncle Bobby ending the call, Dean had been happy. Dad was alive—and based on the way he and Uncle Bobby had been arguing, he was as ornery as ever.

That, Dean knew, meant Dad was okay.

Waiting there in the airport, he understood how important it was for Dad to be away so much—more than Sammy ever could. Sammy hadn't really known Mom, since he was just a baby when she died. Dean couldn't imagine that his baby brother would ever truly understand what had happened to her.

If he was honest with himself, he didn't really understand it, either. There were some days—though he'd never admit this to *anyone*—when he couldn't even remember what she looked like.

Some kind of monster had killed Mom, and Dad

wouldn't rest until he found that monster and killed it. Along the way, he'd kill any other monsters who tried to kill other people's moms.

Because Dad was a hero, and that was what heroes did.

Finally, a familiar dark-haired head appeared behind a bickering couple. Dad moved past them, walking quickly, a broad smile widening inside his stubble.

Sammy hadn't been paying attention to much of anything, but as soon as Dad walked through the door, he jumped up and ran.

"Daaaaad!"

"What a baby," Dean said, and he pretended it was no big deal that Dad was back.

"You boys doin' all right?"

"We're doin' great, Dad!" Sammy was practically bouncing up and down. "I beat Dean at checkers and then he won hide-and-seek, but it's okay 'cause I beat him at Yahtzee!"

Dean was about to point out that Sammy only won *one* game of Yahtzee, but Uncle Bobby put a hand on his shoulder and shook his head.

Reluctantly, Dean kept quiet. Sammy was happy to see Dad, and Uncle Bobby didn't want Dean to rain on his parade.

So all he said was, "Good to see you, Dad."

"Glad to see both you boys. Oh, and I've got something for ya!" He reached into the pocket of his jacket and pulled out two tiny plastic rectangles, handing one to Sammy with one hand, and reaching toward Dean with the other.

It was a miniature California license plate, with DEAN

where the number would've been.

Sammy's eyes went wide—his said, SAM.

"Wow! This is so great!"

"Can only get 'em in San Francisco," Dad said with a smile. "Had to get you boys somethin' special."

Since Sammy was so happy to have his, Dean said nothing.

But he knew that items like this could be found in lots of places in California. And that airports in particular had souvenir shops that sold them. He'd only gone flying once, and he *really really really really* hated it, but he remembered those shops.

Which meant Dad probably grabbed these quickly, on the way to catch the plane. Based on Uncle Bobby's half of the conversation on the phone last night, he hadn't even expected his sons to be at the airport.

Then Dad ruffled Sammy's hair and walked up to Dean. He put his hands on Dean's shoulders and gave him one of his most serious expressions, the one he used whenever he was saying something really important.

"You took good care of Sammy, didn't ya?"

Dean swallowed, and suddenly felt incredibly guilty. He remembered, too, the words Dad spoke to him the night Mom died. They were always in his mind, but just now they echoed so very loudly.

"Take your brother outside as fast as you can—don't look back.

"Now, Dean, go!"

So he straightened his shoulders, and looked his father right in the eye.

"Yes, sir!"

Dad smiled. "That's my boy."

"C'mon," Uncle Bobby said, "let's get outta here."

They walked to the parking lot. Dean got a little steamed when Sammy started going on and on about the one and only time he beat Dean at Yahtzee, but then he thought about Dad's words and let it go again.

Dad still fought the bad guys and saved people, but he also cared about his sons.

Because Dad was a hero, and that was what heroes did.

2009

TWENTY

Myra Wu ran through Golden Gate Park under the meager light of a crescent moon, desperate for her life.

Never before had she felt such terror. It clawed at her chest, and wouldn't let go. Even in her darkest dreams, she couldn't have imagined such fear could exist.

Not until the day she'd first heard gunshots.

Myra was a San Francisco native, born to a Chinese-American father and a German-American mother. She'd attended a public elementary school, a public high school, and San Francisco State University, where she majored in theater arts and got average grades, not really excelling at anything, but never failing, either.

Some of the professors insisted on spelling it "theatre," which always amused her.

Regardless, acting had always been a passion for Myra, and

while she didn't get the leading roles, she almost always got a part of some sort. When that didn't happen, she helped out with the backstage crew. It made her feel as if she belonged.

Once she graduated she continued to live at home with her mother and father, who were always willing to let her do whatever she wanted as long as she didn't get into trouble with the law.

That caveat was hardly necessary. Myra had never even been sent to detention in school, and her friends were hardly the types to do anything that might get them in trouble with *anyone*, much less the law. The only police she'd ever seen were the officers who happened to pass her by on the street.

At least until she took the job at Shin's Delight.

While Myra enjoyed acting tremendously, and possessed genuine talent, she'd never felt the drive to pursue it as a *career*. She sent out her headshots and went on auditions, which garnered her parts in a bunch of different plays in the Tenderloin, but nothing that attracted any serious attention.

So, in the time-honored tradition of thespians throughout the centuries, she took a job as a waitress. As she accepted the position, she remembered a joke that had been told by one of her professors at SFSU.

A Man meets a woman at a bar.

Man asks, "What do you do?"

Woman says, "I'm an actress."

Man replies, "Oh yeah? What restaurant?"

Myra's features displayed only her father's Chinese heritage, with the exception of the blue eyes she'd inherited from her mother. Her Asian appearance contributed to her difficulty in getting good roles, but they improved her chances of finding employment in the restaurants in Chinatown.

What was more, Myra spoke fluent Chinese and German, in addition to English, so she was eminently qualified to work in a restaurant that still—even in the tourist-heavy times—catered primarily to the locals.

Shin's Delight on Pacific Avenue was just such a place. Even better, they were hiring.

At first, everything went well. Myra liked talking to people, she liked serving people, and she liked her coworkers. Truth be told, Myra got along with everyone.

With one possible exception—the strange, older man who ran the place.

Albert Chao was a secretive, pointy-nosed fellow who rarely came out of his office. When he did, it was usually to shout at someone in anger—whether justified or not. Or to talk to the police, who came by pretty regularly. Occasionally the visitor was a uniformed officer, but it was far more common to see a detective climbing the stairs.

Myra never understood why the police kept coming to the restaurant. She tried to ask Zhong, the manager, but he just brushed it off.

"It's nothing that concerns us," he said, glancing around the main dining room until his eyes lit on one of the tables. "Table four needs water—take care of it." And he'd clapped his hands to send her on her way.

She'd done as he asked, but refused to be distracted.

Careful not to let Zhong know what she was doing, Myra asked around. But all she uncovered were rumors, and she didn't like what they implied.

So she decided to let it drop.

A nearby small business had decided to celebrate the approaching Christmas holidays by bringing all forty of its employees to Shin's Delight for lunch. That, in addition to the usual crowd, kept the entire staff hopping, and meant that their supplies ran out faster than expected. Soon they were running low on cloth napkins, so Zhong sent Myra upstairs to the supply closet to retrieve some that he had stashed there for just such an eventuality.

Her path took her past Albert Chao's office, and she stepped quietly in order to remain unnoticed. As she did so, she heard what sounded like a car backfiring.

Except the sound came from immediately behind the closed door to the office. She wondered if it could have come in through one of the office windows, but then she smelled smoke.

Followed by laughter.

And then another shot.

Myra froze, clutching an armful of napkins to her chest. And somebody screamed.

The scream ended as abruptly as it had begun, only to be replaced by a whimpering sound. Concerned that someone might be hurt, she overcame her natural instinct—which cried out for her to run as fast as she could—and knocked on the door.

"Hello? Is everyone all right? I thought I heard something!"

The only response was the sound of another report— and then the whimpering stopped.

Once again Myra found that she couldn't move, and to her the silence that followed was even more frightening than the noises had been.

Floorboards creaked, and the door opened slowly.

Albert Chao had a thick shock of white hair that stuck straight up on top and hung halfway down his back, making him look like an Asian mad scientist. He squinted at her with cruel eyes that sat menacingly over his pointed nose. That wasn't the scary part, however. Pretty much every time she had seen him, he had looked like that.

No, what frightened her was the red stain on his chest. Myra had seen enough stage accidents to know *exactly* what a bloodstain looked like, and that was it.

"What do you want?" he asked in a frighteningly even tone.

Myra's heart beat so fast she could feel it pounding against her ribs.

"I, uh—I was coming up to get more—more napkins, and uh—uh, I heard—"

"You heard nothing," Mr. Chao said firmly. "You *saw* nothing. Do you understand?"

She nodded so rapidly that she feared her head might fly off her neck.

"Okay! Of course! I mean—" she stammered. "Do you... do you need any help?"

"Go. Now."

The next thing Myra knew, she was back downstairs with the napkins in hand, thrusting them into Zhong's arms. She had no recollection of actually running down the staircase.

Yet there she was.

Zhong peered at her with concern.

"You all right?" he asked. "You look like you saw a ghost!"

"I, uh—" But she couldn't find the words, so she just stood there. Waiting for her to speak, Zhong finally ran out of patience.

"Well, get over it. We've still got to get through lunch."

Sensitivity had never been his strong suit.

Despite Zhong's business-as-usual attitude, a pall of tension hung over the restaurant. Myra hadn't been the only person to hear gunshots, yet no one would speak of it. What's more, people she knew disappeared—not the dining room staff, but people who worked in the offices upstairs, and she assumed they had quit due to the stress.

But Myra had no such option—she really needed this job.

Things grew worse over the subsequent two days, as more cops than usual came by. And they started talking to the staff. Finally she learned that bodies had been found in Ghirardelli Square, and the deceased had been tentatively identified as employees of Shin's Delight. Tentatively, because they'd been very badly burned.

When it was her turn to be interviewed, Myra was tempted to tell the detectives about the incident with Mr. Chao. But if she did that, she might have to tell them about the rumors too. Rumors she hadn't been willing to believe until the day they'd needed more napkins.

That Shin's Delight was a front for the mob.

Myra didn't know what mobsters looked like. Sure, she'd seen some odd-looking people going up and down the stairs, some of them entering by the front door, others through the back. But they were no stranger than the people employed by theatrical tech crews to do the heavy lifting. She never assumed *they* were gangsters, so why would she think that about the people in the restaurant?

So when the detective from the local precinct—a slightly heavyset man in an ill-fitting charcoal suit—asked her if she'd noticed anything unusual, Myra just told him that she didn't know anything.

In many ways, it was the complete truth, she told herself. Nothing she had seen made sense, so how could she claim to "know" *anything*?

After she talked to the detective, the tension only got worse, and it began to involve her directly.

Each day it seemed as if Mr. Chao came downstairs just to glare at her. She overheard him asking Zhong about her work, and if she was talking unnecessarily with the other employees.

Zhong, bless him, sang her praises—or as close as he ever got to it.

"Haven't caught her stealing anything yet," he'd said flatly.

One December night after work she made plans to go to Golden Gate Park.

A burgeoning playwright acquaintance wanted to do a "table read" of the first act of his new piece, to make sure the dialogue sounded natural, and he'd asked a bunch of actors to help out. Like most up-and-coming writers, he couldn't afford to rent a place to do it, and he didn't live in a large enough apartment to hold them all, so he invited his volunteers to Marx Meadow "for a table read without a table," as he put it.

Located on the edge of the park, Marx Meadow had plenty of picnic tables that were perfect for their use, and nearby streetlights kept the area safe and well populated, even after the early darkness of winter. Myra read the part of Gina, the heroine's best friend—which was exactly the kind of role she always got. A lot of the dialogue was really clunky, she thought, but the playwright took a lot of notes.

When it was all done, most of the others announced that they were going out for drinks, and invited her along, but Myra had to be at work early the next morning.

Besides, she hated drinking.

So she said her goodnights and headed north. Since there were plenty of lights, she cut through the trees toward nearby Fulton Street, where she would catch the bus.

Suddenly there was a man on fire, blocking her path.

"Ohmigod," she said. "Don't move… wait, no! You have

to drop and roll—yes, that's it! That'll put it out. Drop and roll!" She grabbed for her purse to pull out her cell phone and call 911.

But then she realized that he wasn't screaming.

Or doing *anything*, really.

He just *stood* there.

"Can you hear me?" she asked, a shiver running up her spine. She glanced around quickly, but there was no one in the vicinity who might help. So she turned her attention back to the burning man.

Still he remained silent. That was when she saw that, even though they were surrounded by trees and bushes, nothing else had caught fire. Not even the grass.

She opened her mouth to speak again, but nothing came out. As she did so, the man raised his arms, which was when she noticed the big, curved sword.

It was also when the man finally spoke. His voice sounded like it was coming through a *really* lousy sound system—kind of murky and staticky. But whatever the guttural words meant, he wasn't speaking English, Chinese, or German. It sounded to Myra like Japanese, and she thought she recognized the word "dragon" somewhere in there.

Doragon Kokoro. That was what he said.

But somehow, even though she didn't understand the words, Myra knew.

Moving suddenly, he loomed over her.

She ran.

She didn't pick a particular direction, she just started *moving*. Two years of waitressing had blessed her with strong legs, so she was able to move quickly through the trees.

But no matter where she turned, no matter how fast she moved, somehow *Doragon Kokoro* kept up with her, flames always burning upward, sword raised as if ready to slice her in two.

She lost track of where she was. Adding to her panic was the fact that the park—which even on a cool December night should have been at least a little crowded—was empty. Even when she found herself running across what she recognized as Kennedy Place, there was nobody.

She tried to scream for help, but all that came out was a rasping croak, and it only served to make her breath more ragged. Strong legs were one thing, but she hadn't gone running for years. Her lungs were beginning to burn, and sharp pains were starting to shoot up through her calves.

Still she pressed on, hoping that she might lose her attacker.

Where is everyone?

Stumbling more than running, she came to the edge of Lloyd Lake, where she had to stop. And as she turned, she knew what she would see.

The burning man was there, sword held high, firelight reflecting in the dark water.

Finally she found her voice, but rather than a scream, it was a whimper.

"Oh God please no I don't want to die. Please don't kill

me, please. *I don't want to die!*"

Her voice rose, *Doragon Kokoro* hesitated, and Myra stopped, hoping beyond hope that she might have convinced him. She thought for just a moment that she saw sadness in his fire-covered eyes.

"I don't want to die," she repeated.

"Neither did I," he replied as the sword slashed downward.

It was different, this time.

Now Nakadai could communicate with the living. His actions were still under the control of another, but he felt stronger, faster, more capable.

With these changes came a vexing question. He could still feel Albert Chao's presence, but this time he could not be sure that it was Albert whose influence he followed.

He appeared in a forest lit by torches that burned without flame. Within an instant a woman stood before him, and one thing was clear—whoever she was, she had to die.

And so he pursued her until she had nowhere else to run.

"Oh God please no I don't want to die. Please don't kill me, please. *I don't want to die!*" she said plaintively.

Nakadai hesitated, her words reminding him of what it was like to be human. Reminding him of what he had felt the day of his own death. How long ago had it been?

The sword slashed downward.

Moments later he stood over her charred, violated corpse by the still water of the lake, wondering how long he would be cursed to endure this.

"Well, well, well," a voice said from behind him. "It's been a while, hasn't it, Nakadai?"

Turning, he saw a blond-haired young man wearing short pants and a sleeveless shirt.

"It sure is good to see you again," the blond man said with a bright smile. "Of course, this isn't *quite* going according to plan, but it's a start."

"I do not know of what you speak," Nakadai said to the stranger. "But it is of no consequence. I will go now."

"Not so fast, chuckles." The man gestured.

Suddenly Nakadai found that he could not move.

Narrowing his eyes, he stared at the stranger. This was a Westerner—he was no descendant of Nakadai's, so how could he control him, unless…?

"You."

"Yup." Blue eyes and white irises were replaced by solid black. "I like this guy a lot more than Cho the messenger. He was one ugly cuss."

"What do you want?" Though he could speak, the *ronin* still could not move.

The demon grinned, revealing perfect white teeth.

"What do you *think* I want?" he said, and this time there was a hint of the gutteral he had heard in Akemi's voice. "You don't think I had you burned alive just for kicks 'n' grins, do you?"

"I would not presume to understand how your mind functions."

The demon laughed raucously.

"Fair enough," he responded. "But no, I had me a long-term plan for you, Nakadai. Or should I say, 'Heart of the Dragon'? I gotta admit, it tickles the hell outta me that you got stuck with that moniker for over 200 years. You did hate it so."

"A plan?" Nakadai spat.

"Of course! And it's finally time for that plan to bear fruit."

"What is so special about now?"

The demon threw its head back and laughed again.

"Haven't you been paying attention? I realize it's not quite your bag, but the end of days has come! Y'know, 'death comes on a pale horse'? Dogs and cats sleeping together…. Mass hysteria? It's the end of the world as we know it, and I feel fine!"

Having no idea what the demon was babbling about, Nakadai simply stared.

Shaking his head, the demon sighed dramatically.

"You spirits of the damned, you have no appreciation of the classics. Look," he held out his arms, as if to indicate the whole world, "what we're talking about here is the Apocalypse. Demons and angels squaring off, and may the best seraph win. And you, Nakadai-san, are my ace in the hole."

Nakadai frowned.

"I do not understand."

"Surely you've noticed that you've got more mojo this

time around. Before, you couldn't do much more than swing your sword like a flaming fool. But things are different now.

"The seals are broken, Lucifer is free, God's *not* in his Heaven, and all's wrong with the world. So it's time for you and me to go kick some angel ass."

Another sigh.

"Unfortunately, it's not that simple. That grand-niece of yours did a nice job of piggybacking onto my spell, and of creating that counter-spell. It's too bad she was totally binky-bonkers—she could've had one *helluva* career as a witch.

"Be that as it may, what's done is done, and her grandson's got you all sucked into his groove."

Nakadai shook his head in disgust.

"I knew I detected his hand in this," he said. "So he has once again brought me back to commit evil in his name."

"Nope—not this time. Thanks to that bastard John Winchester you were well and truly ensconced in the penalty box."

Nakadai almost flinched at the venom with which the demon spoke. He wondered what the man—this *John Winchester*—had done to earn the demon's hatred.

"But when the new moon came around," the creature continued, "your little schmuck of a descendent didn't even bother to call you back. Truth is, *this* is what you were built for—the Apocalypse. You're our secret weapon.

"Yet Albert's bound to call you sooner or later, and thanks to his loony tunes grandmother, as long as he's got his hooks into you, the best I can do is make you do things on *his* behalf. But in order to keep you around, we need to keep him alive, too. If he bites the big one, then *poof*, you're gone in a flash.

"This chick saw something she shouldn't have." He gestured at the corpse lying at Nakadai's feet. "Can you *believe* that idiot was going to let her live? Moron. And he's got bigger problems, too."

The demon stared at Nakadai thoughtfully for a moment.

"Time's running out. The angels are kicking our asses, and we need you. So just a warning, big guy—you're gonna be playing for the home team soon enough."

With that, the blond-haired head tilted backward, and black smoke came pouring out of his mouth. Once the smoke disappeared into the night sky, the man fell to the grass-and-dirt ground.

Dead.

Then Nakadai began to fade away, to remain in limbo until he was summoned again.

But by whom?

TWENTY-ONE

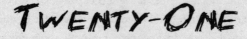

At age ten, Sam Winchester had become obsessed with maps.

It all started when he kept asking his father where they were going next. It was a reasonable question, since the answer was always different, and Sam was still young enough at the time to think it was exciting to know.

However, neither John nor the fourteen year-old Dean had much time for Sam's curiosity. So to shut him up, his dad bought him an atlas.

This proved beneficial all around. John and Dean were no longer being pestered all the time, and Sam had found a hobby.

For weeks after he received the atlas, he would spend every minute of his spare time studying the maps it contained, learning how the highways and byways intertwined and intersected, the arrangements of smaller roads, the way some cities sought to lay out their streets in organized patterns. He studied the effects of topography, and the placements of borders and boundaries.

But the thing that most captured the fancy of his ten year-old brain was the U.S. Interstate Highway System—or, as he breathlessly told his father and brother after a trip to a public library in Indiana, "the Dwight D. Eisenhower National System of Interstate and Defense Highways." He lectured his indulgent dad and an impatient Dean all about the thirty-fourth President's championing of the Federal-Aid Highway Act of 1956, to create a system that would support commerce and serve as arteries should there be a nuclear war.

Sam especially loved the way the interstates were numbered. For the two-digit highways, odd numbers ran north to south, while the even numbers ran east to west. The higher the number, the farther north or east the road was located.

Dean refused to believe him. He claimed it was ridiculous, and that Sam had just made it up, but their father leapt to his younger son's defense.

"A lot of those highways were being built when I was young," John Winchester said, much to Sam's delight. "Where there was a hill, they just cut right through it, and built the bridges over the rivers. Other times they followed the paths for existing roads." He grinned at his sons. "'Course, there wasn't much need for that in Kansas—don't have much in the way of hills there."

Dean just hunched back in his seat and scowled, calling them a couple of dexters.

Like most childhood obsessions, this one burned itself out fairly quickly. But Sam still retained the facility for maps that it had engendered, and it wasn't long before he was doing all the navigating for the Winchester family hunts.

To a great degree Mapquest and Google Maps had subverted the need for the atlas. Even so, Sam didn't entirely trust them. Too often they sent the brothers the wrong way down a one-way street or across a bridge that no longer existed—if it ever had. So for every trip Sam pulled out a traditional map and used it as a backup.

Invariably he was able to find a more efficient route than the one suggested by the computer.

Dean and Sam both knew all the best ways to get from the Singer Salvage Yard in South Dakota to pretty much every major highway. Interstate 80, the one on which they were currently motoring, stretched across the country from New York to San Francisco, and was probably the highway on which the Impala spent the most time. It was a straight shot west from Omaha, Nebraska to the Bay Bridge.

As soon as they finished scouring Bobby's library, looking for everything he had about *Doragon Kokoro*, Sam and Dean had hit the road. It was midday, and Sam took the first leg while Dean—who'd been up all night playing poker—slept in the passenger seat. Then, by the time evening rolled around, Dean took over.

That meant two things.

First, the music from the tape deck got louder, beginning with Metallica's *…And Justice for All*.

Second, it meant Sam had the opportunity to reread the journal. Bobby's books and papers hadn't turned up a lot, nor had the internet, but it was a start, and now he wanted to review what John had written.

Their father's perspective, viewed in light of Bobby's material, added some interesting wrinkles.

"Huh," he muttered.

Dean reached to turn down the music just as 'The Shortest Straw' was starting.

"What?"

Sam blinked. He hadn't meant to speak out loud.

"I was just rereading Dad's notes," he explained. "He had an interesting take on Albert Chao, the guy who summoned the spirit the last two times. Dad saw him as the typical summoner type. Y'know, a weasely little guy who isn't able to make it in the world—or at least not in the world the way he *thinks* it ought to be. So he goes all occult, to make up for his own shortcomings."

"He should try a blue pill, instead," Dean said sarcastically. "Anyhow, it shouldn't matter. From what little I read, Dad didn't think Chao had a snowball's chance in hell of staying alive after the spirit got banished."

Sam shook his head.

"I don't know, Dean. Everything I read at Bobby's says that this Chao guy *has* to be the one to summon it. He's the one with the *ronin* as his ancestor, and according to the texts, the spirit remains tethered to whoever summons it, and renders that person impervious to harm."

"So, what, we can't shoot this guy?"

Sam shrugged.

"Well, we can, but it won't do any good. Best bet is to do what Dad did—cast the spell on the sword. Unfortunately, that'll just banish the warrior for another twenty years."

Dean's expression turned grim.

"You're assuming the world's still gonna be *around* in twenty years. Hell, I ain't puttin' any money on makin' it another twenty *days*."

That elicited a sigh from Sam.

"Yeah, you've got a point. But Cass seems to think this Heart of the Dragon is important, so we've got to do what we can."

Neither brother had much to say after that, so Dean turned Metallica back up. The tape had moved on to 'Harvester of Sorrow,' and Sam went back to trying to decipher his father's chicken-scratch handwriting.

Eventually, he drifted off to sleep himself. By the time he woke up, the sun was coming up in the east and the Impala was zipping out of Sacramento.

"So, we got a plan?" Dean asked without a preamble.

Sam rubbed the sleep out of his eyes.

"Coffee?"

Dean chuckled.

"Next rest stop we see."

Flipping their dad's leather-bound notebook open to the right page, Sam looked for a name.

"We might as well head for the motel Dad stayed in—the Emperor Norton Lodge. It's on Ellis Street, not all that far from Chinatown. Then, I guess we try the restaurant where

Dad banished the spirit last time."

Dean shot him a look.

"Emperor Norton?"

Sam paused before he replied.

"You don't know about Emperor Norton?"

"Not unless you're talking about Art Carney's character on *The Honeymooners*," Dean replied. "And I don't think he even made it to Grand High Exalted Mystic Ruler of the Raccoons."

Sam laughed.

"I can't believe you never heard the story. Joshua Norton was a failed businessman who completely lost it. In 1859, he declared himself 'Norton I, Emperor of these United States and Protector of Mexico.' He dissolved Congress, created his own currency—Oh, and he also levied a fine of twenty-five dollars on anyone who called the city "Frisco."'

Dean snorted.

"Yeah, well, if we run across him, I'll give him a twenty and a five."

"Nobody took him seriously, but everybody loved him. And he had some good ideas. One of his decrees was that they should build the Bay Bridge and construct the BART. In fact, I think I remember reading a few years back that they tried to get the bridge renamed after him."

"Fine, so we'll stay in the royal suite and get some Chinese food. Meanwhile, there's a diner at the next exit."

Sam looked up and saw a blue sign that indicated what eateries were available at the upcoming exit. Besides the diner, there were three fast-food joints and a Starbucks. He was tempted to suggest the Starbucks—thanks to Dean's poker winnings, they could actually afford it—but decided not to open that particular can of worms. They'd been back hunting together for a while now, and things were going well.

But the wounds were still relatively fresh. It wasn't so much that Sam had started the Apocalypse.

No, Sam thought to himself, *that sucks, but what* really *hurt Dean was that I trusted Ruby more than I did him. I lied to him, and I betrayed him.*

He should have known better.

If there's one thing we've got to remember, it's that we're better together than we are apart.

So he decided he didn't need to go to Starbucks.

He just nodded as Dean moved into the right lane.

Albert was in a good mood when he woke up that morning.

Preferring a commute that only required him to go down a flight of stairs, he maintained an apartment over Shin's Delight. As he came out of the bathroom, his cell phone rang.

At first Albert had loved the invention of the cell phone. With cell phones, he could talk to any of his people without delay, and that had been very convenient as he had solidified his power over Tommy Shin's branch of the Triads. Just as Tommy had been far ahead of the Old Man in the exploitation of technology, Albert had become even cannier in its use.

Unfortunately, so had law enforcement. Just as he had used the phones to maintain a constant awareness of their activities, it had become ridiculously easy for the police to track down his people, as well.

The disposable cell phone had alleviated the problem to a great degree—easily purchased at any convenience store, and impossible for the cops to tap into.

So Albert changed his cell phone once a month, like clockwork. The accounts were all in the names of the children who ran errands for the Triads—the most low-level personnel in his organization, who knew absolutely nothing and couldn't be tried as adults, in any case.

The cell phone that was ringing now was registered to the son of the drycleaner two doors down. In return for the use of the boy's name, the father received a slight discount on his monthly payments. Albert reached over, saw that he had a message from Oscar Randolph, and the display indicated that it was Han calling. So he flipped it open.

"It's that waitress Myra Wu," Han said. "They found her body in Golden Gate Park. It was just like Roy and Jack."

Muttering a curse in Japanese, Albert snapped the phone shut.

How can this be possible?

Albert hadn't wanted Myra killed any more than he'd wanted Roy or Jack killed. Sure, she had been a minor annoyance, but he'd checked and confirmed that she hadn't said anything to the police. Indeed, he appreciated employees who kept their mouths shut without needing to be threatened. As for Roy and Jack, they were idiots, and they'd fouled up the gun deal with that motorcycle gang, but Albert hadn't been all that sanguine about dealing with the thugs anyhow.

None of them had done anything that warranted having them killed.

But that wasn't the worst of it.

The Heart of the Dragon is back, he mused, his mind reeling. *But it can't be. There's no one else....*

It had been twenty years since a *gaijin* named John Winchester had cast a spell to banish the spirit for another eighty seasons. That had forced Albert to fend for himself, and he'd found ways to do so. With Tommy Shin's subsequent death, Albert hadn't *needed* occult assistance. He had everything he wanted.

He'd come to realize that *Doragon Kokoro* wasn't a pistol to pull out any time he felt like it. Such a weapon needed to be held in reserve. And no such time had arisen.

Still cursing under his breath, he got dressed and headed downstairs.

Zhong was waiting for him outside his office door.

"Is it true about Myra?" he demanded.

"Yes," Albert replied. He reached into his pants pocket and fished out the key to his office.

"Dammit," Zhong said. "Now I have to hire another waitress."

Under other circumstances, Albert might have smiled. Zhong was never sentimental—it made him a good manager.

He opened the door, and Zhong followed him inside.

"People have been talking," he said hesitantly.

Albert looked up at him, he was surprised as Zhong was never hesitant.

"Talking about what?"

"The Heart of the Dragon," his manager replied. "Look, I wasn't here back then, and I don't give a damn what happened to Lin. If you wanted to spread word around that you controlled some sort of demon, that was your business—Hell, it worked. No one questions your authority. But the chatter is springing up again, and it's getting out of hand. Ever since they found Roy and Jack's bodies in Ghirardelli Square."

Sitting down at his desk, Albert turned his computer on. While it booted up, he turned to face Zhong.

"What if they were true?"

"Beg your pardon?"

"Nothing," Albert said, and he turned back to his computer. On second thought, it didn't make sense to take Zhong into his confidence. Besides, he would probably just think his boss had gone insane. The Heart of the Dragon was just a story, and Albert was perfectly content to keep it that way.

But then, who killed Roy, Jack, and Myra? And why do it in a way that pointed to the spirit?

"You can rest assured, Zhong, that I have not summoned any spirits lately to kill people who annoy me."

"And why not?" came the response.

Albert blinked.

"Excuse me?"

"If the spirit's free," Zhong continued, "why not put it to good use?"

Albert blinked again.

"What're you talking about?"

Zhong grinned. That was even more out of character.

"I'm talking about *Doragon Kokoro*, Albert. I'm talking about the spirit you raised forty years ago, and could've raised again, but haven't. The question is, *why?*"

As he spoke, Zhong's eyes flicked to a deep black that seemed to penetrate deep into his skull.

Albert rose to his feet.

"What do you want, demon?"

Zhong's features expressed surprise.

"You actually know what I am?"

"Ever since I had the Heart of the Dragon ripped from my grasp a second time, I've made a point of learning more about the occult," Albert said, fingering a charm he wore around his neck. He even had a consultant on the payroll—an old *gaijin* named Oscar Randolph—though he hadn't made much use of the man for a while now.

"I know what you are, demon. What I do not know is why you are here."

The creature wearing Zhong's face used it to sneer.

"Because you have something that belongs to me," he said, all trace of amusement gone. "*Doragon Kokoro* is *mine*, Albert Chao. I created him. And I still have control over him but, right now, only if what he does corresponds to your wishes."

"Yet I had no wish to kill those people!" Albert snapped.

"Sure you did," the demon said in Zhong's voice. "Maybe not consciously, but in the back of your mind—in that place where you keep the little boy who was always rejected, who never got what he wanted. *He* wanted those three dead.

"As for what *I* want, it's simple: I want my spirit back. Playing puppet-master is good for a few laughs, but I have some angels that need killing.

"So you're going to hand him over."

Albert smiled. With that declaration, the demon had revealed that Albert had power over him.

He continued to finger the charm, which he'd purchased several years ago from Bela Talbot, a friend of Oscar's. Bela had promised that it was a powerful talisman that protected him from possession, and it obviously worked. If the demon had wanted control of the Heart of the Dragon, all it had to do was possess Albert.

Unless it couldn't.

"Then you have a problem, demon, because I will not relinquish control of my ancestor's spirit. Not to anyone or any*thing*. You'll have to kill me—but, oh yes, you can't, can you?" That last was added with a wide smile. "Not unless you want *Doragon Kokoro* to disappear back into oblivion."

"No—and I can't possess you as long as you have that… *thing* around your neck." Yet strangely, it was the demon's turn to smile. "But don't imagine that I can't hurt you, Albert

Chao. I've already proven that."

"By killing three of my people?" Albert dismissed the idea with a wave of his hand. "*Pfah*. Their lives mattered little to me. Many have tried to hurt me over the years, demon, but I am still here."

"Many *humans* have tried to hurt you, but that's not really a yardstick I'm gonna take too terribly seriously."

The demon sighed. "Look, maybe we can work out a deal."

He leaned over the desk, and his pitch black eyes caused Albert to shudder involuntarily.

"I just need to *borrow* Nakadai for a while. I can make it worth your while."

Albert laughed.

"What will you grant me, demon? A lesson to those who ostracized me? Petty revenge against slights, both real and imagined? Had you made such an offer when first I summoned my ancestor, I gladly would have accepted. In my callow youth, that was precisely what I used the Heart of the Dragon for. I was a pathetic child, treating all injustices as if they were of great consequence."

Albert leaned forward, putting his palms flat on his desk.

"I am no longer that child. It was the *lack* of the spirit that truly granted me my heart's desire. I came to the attention of the Triads through *my own* hard work, using *my* skills to overcome my half-breed status. I have stayed in power for twenty years without the spirit. Having the Heart of the Dragon taken away was the best thing that ever happened to me."

Zhong snorted like an animal.

"Skills. Right. That would be the invulnerability granted to you by *Doragon Kokoro*, yes? Without it, you'd be worm food."

"Perhaps," Albert responded, determined to remain resolute. "But the spirit is mine, to do with it as I wish."

The demon walked up to the desk and leaned into Albert's face. On its breath, Albert could smell the peanut sauce that Zhong slathered on all of his food.

"Then give it to me," it hissed.

Albert stood up straight.

"I will consider your offer, demon. Come back tomorrow for an answer."

The black eyes stared at him for several seconds without blinking.

Then Zhong's head leaned back and a stream of black smoke issued forth from his gaping mouth, funneling upward toward the ceiling like an obsidian tornado.

Then it was gone, and Zhong collapsed to the ground unconscious.

Albert called downstairs for someone to take care of Zhong, then he pulled his cell phone out of his pocket.

He hadn't returned Oscar's message, hadn't even listened to it, because he thought he was done with the occult. Throughout the '90s, he'd been obsessed with learning everything he could, but in recent years he'd had little use for it. He'd even been considering taking Oscar off the payroll. Now, though, it seemed the occult would be useful to him once again.

Opening the phone, he listened to the message.

"Hey yo, Albert, it's Oscar. Listen, I know you ain't been givin' much of a crap about what I gotta tell you, but remember that tracking spell you asked me to cast a while back, looking for that hook sword? Well, you ain't gonna believe this, but the spell just reactivated. Nearly set my damn house on fire, too.

"Look, call me back, okay?"

Albert cursed himself for a fool.

Forty years ago, a bald man and his wife and daughter had thwarted him, and wrenched from him the greatest weapon he had ever possessed. But what he *hadn't* possessed were the resources to find out where they came from.

Twenty years ago, it had happened again—and again, at the hands of a white man. This time he had been able to turn up a name: John Winchester.

But nothing more.

In 1996, Albert found Oscar Randolph, who had a house in Mill Valley that he'd inherited from his father, a doctor who died in the Korean War.

When Albert went to the old house in the San Francisco suburb for the first time, a weathered Caucasian with a thick white beard and very little white hair answered the door. He had on a faded flannel shirt, worn-out jeans, and unpolished cowboy boots.

"What the hell do *you* want?"

"My name is Albert Chao, and I wish to hire you."

The man laughed heartily.

"You wanna hire *me*? That suit your wearin's worth more'n my house, and that tattoo you got means you're Triad. The hell you need me for?"

"The Triads' connections do not extend to the spirit world," Albert pressed. "Yours do. That information is of value to me."

"Yeah?" Oscar scratched the chin under his thick beard. "So you don't want me to kill nothin'?"

"No."

"That's too bad."

Albert frowned.

"Why is that?"

Oscar grinned again.

"'Cause I was hopin' I'd get to kill something. Hell, that's the only thing I *miss* from huntin'." The grin fell. "So whaddaya want?"

"Information."

"Any good reason I should take the offer?"

With a small smile, Albert replied.

"Because you do not wish to starve to death. Your father's inheritance has run out. Your investments have failed. Within six months, you will join the ranks of the homeless and be destitute. I can save you from that."

For several seconds, Oscar stared at Albert. Finally he spoke.

"This information you need—would it involve rattin' out other hunters?"

"Possibly."

Oscar broke into another grin.

"Works for me. Buncha morons, all of 'em. Bustin' their asses to stop evil, and evil keeps getting' stronger. Waste'a time. Sick'a the whole lot of 'em, and I'm more than happy to stick it to 'em."

He thrust out a hand.

"You got yourself an employee, Mr. Chao."

Oscar called himself a "hunter," and from what he said, that's exactly what John Winchester had been, as well.

That Oscar had reached retirement impressed Albert. The information he'd collected in seven years was sketchy, but one thing he'd learned was that most of those who chose to hunt the supernatural didn't live long enough to retire.

Over the years, Oscar had provided more and more information, even as Albert became less and less interested in hearing it. It wasn't all reliable, and much of it was contradictory, but it still provided some insight into the world that had intersected with his every time he summoned the Heart of the Dragon.

Just a year ago Oscar had confirmed as best he could that John Winchester was dead. The stories ranged from word that he had been killed by vampires to possession by a demon, being shot with an antique gun, and eaten by ghouls. One story had him dying the mundane death of being run over by a truck.

However, Winchester apparently had two sons who had

become impressive hunters in their own right. Albert didn't believe all the stories Oscar shared—they were ridiculous even by the standards of the supernatural.

Profits were up. If the Apocalypse was coming, then clearly it was good for business.

At that point, however, Oscar had mentioned that he could cast a spell that would alert him if the hook sword ever came back within the San Francisco city limits. Since the date was approaching when Albert would once again be able to summon Nakadai, he had told the old hunter to cast it.

Then he forgot all about it—until today.

He returned Oscar's call.

"Yo?"

"Where's the sword, Oscar?"

"Good to hear from you, Oscar. How you been, Oscar? Sure has been a long time since we talked, Oscar," the old man said sarcastically.

Albert had no patience for it.

"I was just visited by a demon who is exerting control over the Heart of the Dragon. If the hook sword is in San Francisco, I *need* it. Where is it?"

"Somewhere on Ellis Street," the hunter replied, all traces of sarcasm gone from his voice. "Just got in this morning, and I went right down there to locate the exact spot. I couldn't pin it down 'zactly, but I got close—I'm sure of it. Emailed you a map with the address."

Albert quickly checked his email, then forwarded the missive on to Tiny's account.

"Thank you, Oscar," he said. "And keep your phone handy. I may have need of your services again soon."

"No problem. Want me to whip up a Devil's Trap for you? Might come in handy if you need to go toe-to-toe with a demon."

"That would be excellent," Albert replied. "Bring it by the restaurant today."

"You got it."

Then Albert cut off Oscar and called Tiny.

"I just sent you a map which pinpoints a block. On that block is a hotel, I want you to locate two young men who have checked into that hotel—they're brothers, so they may have the same last name. They have in their possession a hook sword that has *kanji* characters on it. I want that sword.

"Take Jake with you. Don't feel bad about killing anyone who tries to stop you."

"Yeah, Boss."

One of the reasons Albert liked Tiny was that his vocabulary consisted almost exclusively of the two words, "Yeah, Boss." At least, that was all he said when he was talking with Albert, which was what mattered.

Even though he had no use of the spirit—at least not now—the Heart of the Dragon belonged to Albert.

He would *not* let some smart-ass demon take it from him.

TWENTY-TWO

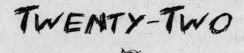

"You said this Emperor Norton dude was crazy, right?"

Sam nodded as he stared at the room they'd been given at the hotel. It was actually better than a lot of the dumps they typically stayed in, but that wasn't saying a great deal. The wallpaper didn't look as if it'd been changed since their father stayed there. The phone was still a rotary. And when he sat on the bed closest to the door, Sam could feel the springs jabbing his butt.

"Yeah," Sam said in answer to Dean's query, "crazy as a loon."

"Well, he had a lousy interior decorator, too," Dean said as he dumped his duffel bag at the foot of the other bed, then lay down on it. "I'm guessin' our Chinese restaurant doesn't open till lunch—that right?" he said to the ceiling.

"I'll find out."

Sam pulled his laptop out of the bag and went to sit at the

tiny desk. He flipped it open and dug around underneath to find an outlet. There were only two, and between the lamp and the television, both were occupied. So he unplugged the lamp.

He knew better than to mess with the television.

Sure enough, Dean grabbed the remote off the nightstand, and clicked impatiently through the hotel's offerings.

It took more than a minute for Sam's laptop to boot up. He sighed, knowing it was only a matter of time before they would need a new one—this one was a few years old and had so much stuff loaded onto it that it was a miracle it still worked at all.

Unfortunately, their only sources of income were poker winnings, pool hustling, and charity from Bobby. But Bobby wasn't being charitable since he'd been crippled. Besides, it was one thing to gas up the Impala or keep them fed. He wasn't likely to pony up a thousand bucks—or more—for a decent laptop.

Once the computer finally finished booting, the wireless card found an unsecure network belonging to the hotel. One advantage to staying in cheap motels was that most of them had their own free wireless networks these days. The fancy hotels charged obscene rates for online access.

First thing, Sam checked the restaurant's hours, and confirmed that it opened at noon. Then he downloaded his email, and also did a web search prompted by something he'd read in his father's journal.

Bingo.

"Hey, Dean," he said, "I've got something that might be useful. Remember Dad mentioning that professor up at Berkeley?"

"Yeah, I think so," Dean replied. "Why?"

"Well, he's still there. He's the Assistant Chair of the Asian Studies Department now. Might be a good idea to go talk with him."

Clambering off his bed, Dean shrugged.

"Might help," he said. "Then again, if we're lucky, we'll just show up at the restaurant, cast the right spell, grab some chicken chow fun, and leave."

Sam just stared at him.

"Dude—have we *ever* been that lucky?"

Dean reached into his duffel and pulled out the hook sword.

"Guess not." He set the sword aside and settled back onto the bed. "Guess you better call the dude."

So while Dean immersed himself in the previous week's episode of *Dr. Sexy M.D.*, Sam called U.C. Berkeley, navigated through an irritating stream of automated messages—made even more so by the rotary phone—and finally got Marcus Wallace's voicemail.

"Hi Professor, this is Sam Winchester—I'm calling on behalf of myself and my brother Dean. Twenty years ago you met our father, John Winchester, and I think you know Bobby Singer, too.

"We're in San Francisco because the Heart of the Dragon's back, and we need your help. If you could call me back, please, that would be great."

Sam provided his cell phone number, then ended the call.

After that, he called Bobby to check in.

"The angel stopped by, and said he'd be comin' at some point," Bobby said, bitterness in his voice. Given his condition, he seriously resented the fact that Castiel no longer had the ability to heal. For his part, Cass didn't seem to care all that much—which pissed off Bobby even more. "I'll let the bastard know you got there, and where y'are, in case you need some heavenly hosting."

"Okay, Bobby, thanks." He wasn't sure Castiel needed to be told, but saying so would just be like rubbing salt into the crippled man's wounds. So he just hung up.

Then he did some more web digging, trying to see if there had been anything reported in the past couple of days. Sure enough, that morning's *San Francisco Chronicle* had a story about two as-yet-unidentified bodies—a man and a woman—found near Lloyd Lake in Golden Gate Park. The woman had been burned to a crisp, with lengthy cuts over a large portion of her body. Strangely, the man was found with no obvious trauma.

"We've got another burned victim," Sam said. "And the wounds are consistent with—"

Sam cut himself off when he heard a familiar snore. Turning around, he saw that Dean had dozed off. Looking over his shoulder at the screen, he saw Dr. Sexy was being slapped by one of the nurses, and winced in sympathy.

He walked over to the bed and gently pulled the remote out of Dean's sleep-loosened grip, hitting the power button so he could use the computer in peace.

That caused Dean to jump.

"Hey, I was watchin' that!" he bellowed.

"Sorry," Sam said quietly, turning the set back on, then handing back the remote. Dean had to surf through to find the show again.

Before he could get there, however, someone kicked in the door.

"So then the one girl just grabs the other girl and starts yankin' on her hair. Now my first thought is, 'Hey, it's a party,' but of course I know they ain't gonna keep it under control, so I figure I gotta intervene."

James "Tiny" Deng grunted as he turned one of Albert Chao's SUVs onto Ellis Street and looked for a place to park. He really hated being paired up with Jake Leung, because Jake just never shut up.

"So I go to try to pull 'em apart, and one of them—the one with the long hair—she goes and claws at my arm! Look at what she did to me!" Jake held up an arm to show the scratches, but Tiny didn't really pay any attention.

There was no parking to be found on Ellis, but Tiny finally found a spot in front of a hydrant, shrugged, and parked there. He pulled a piece of paper out of the glove compartment and put it on the dashboard. It said SFPD – OFFICIAL in big block letters. Tiny had no idea where the boss got them, but they proved handy when you couldn't find parking.

Only once in Tiny's recollection did someone get towed, and the boss got the car back without paying a single penny. Now *that* was how to run a business.

"Anyhow, I had to teach the bitch a lesson, so's I—"

By this time, Tiny had already liberated his six-foot-eight-inch frame from the SUV, and was just staring at his partner, still belted into the passenger seat.

"Uh, Jake? We're here."

"Huh?" Jake looked around, suddenly aware of the fact that the car had stopped. "Right." He opened the door and jumped out onto the sidewalk, just missing the hydrant. "So what're we looking for again?"

Again, Tiny grunted. He had already gone over it, but Jake was so fond of the sound of his own voice that he hadn't paid any attention.

"We need to find a couple'a guys in a hotel," he said. "They've got a sword of some kind, and we're s'posed to get it for the boss. He said to kill anyone who gets in the way."

"Okay. Let's do it. Hope they don't got no bitches with 'em, though. I don't want anymore scratches." He glanced ruefully at his arm, which as far as Tiny could see didn't have a mark on it.

Tiny looked around. He spotted a three-story façade with a framing shop on the ground floor, and a sign next to the door that led upstairs.

"That looks like the place—let's check it out."

Tiny headed for the door, Jake following. Climbing the narrow stairs, they wound up in a lobby with cracked-leather sofas and peeling wallpaper. Beyond were two hallways with frayed carpeting. Sitting behind the battered old wooden desk was an acne-covered young man reading a copy of *Entertainment Weekly*. The nametag on his chest read ELMER.

Without even looking up from the magazine, Elmer spoke in a bored voice.

"Can I help you?"

Exchanging a quick glance with Jake, Tiny pulled out his .45. Jake did likewise. Tiny had a Kimber Ultra Refined Carry Pistol II, while Jake had, as usual, overdone it with a Para-Ordnance Nite-Tac ACP. Most of the time, the guns were just for show, anyhow. When staring down the barrel of a hand-cannon like these, people generally did exactly what they were told.

When he didn't get an answer, Elmer dropped his magazine and jumped out of his seat, knocking it over backward.

"Oh God, don't kill me please don't—"

"Shut up!" Jake yelled. "You sound like a bitch. I hate bitches."

"Just one question," Tiny said, ignoring his partner. "Did anyone check in this morning? Maybe a couple'a guys, mid-twenties?"

Elmer was unable to take his eyes off the barrel of Tiny's Kimber.

"There was—was—was—these, uh, these two guys. In,

uh, in Room 102."

"Thanks," Tiny said. He nodded toward the stairs. "Now get out of here and don't come back for an hour. If you say a word to anyone, we'll find you, and shoot you in the face."

Elmer took the stairs two at a time and burst out of the front door.

Tiny turned and led Jake down one of the hallways, following the sign that indicated rooms 100-150. With his height and broad shoulders, he filled the narrow passageway.

Once they were standing in front of Room 102, Tiny held up three large fingers.

Then two.

Then one.

And he kicked in the door.

Sure enough, there were two little white men in the room. Of course, from his perspective, everyone was little....

One had shaggy brown hair, and he sat at the desk. The other was perched on the edge of one of the beds, the one closer to the window. He was holding a sword—almost certainly the one the boss had sent them to fetch.

He held up his .45.

"Don't move."

"We're not moving," the one at the desk said quickly, standing and putting his hands up.

"Nobody's gotta get hurt, all right?" Jake said. "We're just here to take that little pig-sticker away from you. Might put an eye out, y'know?"

The guy sitting on the bed had short hair. He regarded Jake warily.

"You want this sword?"

"That's right. So shut your ugly face and hand it over!"

Jake crossed the distance between them.

Tiny kept his own weapon aimed at the one who was standing.

Stepping up next to the guy with the sword, Jake pressed his .45 right against the side of his head, then held out his free hand.

"Give it here." He tried to sound menacing. "Don't try nothin' stupid, or I'll shoot you, swear to God."

Tiny knew better, and wished his partner would just *stop talking*. At that range, if Jake actually fired the weapon the recoil would knock him to the floor, plus the shot would go wild. The only time Jake had ever fired his weapon was at a gun range in the Presidio, where the target was standing still.

Suddenly the guy smacked Jake's hand aside, grabbing the barrel and clubbing Jake in the face with the hilt of the sword.

For a second, Tiny didn't react. He'd been an enforcer for years now, and he'd never seen *anyone* do anything other than wet themselves at the sight of a .45.

He was pretty sure that if Jake had stopped talking for half a second, this would never have happened.

The one by the desk leapt at him, and Tiny tried to squeeze a shot off, but it fired harmlessly into the ceiling. Cheap plaster came raining down on them both as the guy tackled him.

Or, at least, tried to. Tiny weighed almost 300 pounds, and most of it was muscle.

The guy punched Tiny several times in the chest.

Tiny just smiled.

Then he punched the guy full-force in the face, sending him flying across the hotel room, where he collided with the desk chair and collapsed in a heap. He lay there, out cold.

Turning, Tiny saw that the other brother had gotten hold of the .45 and was now pointing it at Jake—though from a safe enough distance that Jake couldn't do anything but sweat profusely. Jake sat down on the bed closest to the door.

Crap.

Short-hair set the sword on the bed and held the .45 with both hands.

Pointing his own .45 at the guy, Tiny adopted his most menacing voice.

"Drop it."

"You first, Charlie Chan. Make one move, and I ventilate your boy here."

Tiny shrugged.

"Go ahead. It'll finally shut him up."

"Hey!" Jake said. "What the hell, Tiny, why can't you—?"

Aiming downward, Tiny shot Jake four times in the chest. It'd be easy to convince the boss that these guys had done it. *What's he gonna do? Check for ballistics?*

But he heard five reports, and stumbled backward. A sharp pain lanced down through his arm, from his shoulder.

Even as Tiny killed Jake, the guy had shot *him*.

That *really* pissed Tiny off.

Getting his feet under him, he swung the Kimber upward. But before he could fire, something hit him in the head.

Putting a hand to his forehead, he felt blood trickling down into his eyes. His vision blurred, but he saw the long-haired brother scrambling to his feet. Tiny wasn't sure what he'd thrown, but it *hurt*.

The guy crossed the room in a leap, grabbed Tiny's arm, and chopped down hard. It didn't hurt all that much, but Tiny reflexively dropped his .45.

Using his free arm, Tiny punched him in the face again. It was the arm that had taken the bullet, and it hurt like a bitch.

As the guy fell backward again, Tiny fell forward next to the bed closest to the door. Though he was still conscious, he didn't move.

"Stand up and do *not* go for the gun," said the one with Jake's .45.

But Tiny wasn't even sure where his gun had fallen to. In any case, he had a better idea.

Inserting his fingers into the gap between the mattress and the box spring, he hoisted the mattress up, tossing it right toward the guy with the gun. As he did so, he lumbered to his feet.

The report of Jake's .45 echoed throughout the room, the bullet punching a hole in the mattress.

"Dean!" the other guy cried.

Tiny stepped over Jake's corpse and grabbed the hook

sword off the other bed. The taller one also lunged for it, but Tiny hit him with the hilt the same way Dean had hit Jake.

At first, Tiny was going to finish these two off—then he decided against it. There hadn't been a direct order, just an instruction not to hesitate to kill if he had to. At this point, though, he had blood trickling into his eyes, he couldn't really move his left arm—it hurt like a *sonofabitch*—and he had what he came for.

Best to cut his losses.

He didn't feel great about leaving behind the .45s—it was standard operating procedure to get rid of any guns that had been used in a felony. Somehow, though, he didn't think these two were likely to go to the cops.

So while they struggled with the mattress, he ducked out of the hotel room.

At first Dean had no idea who the two guys were who burst into the room, but once they demanded the hook sword, he figured they had to be working for Albert Chao. Especially the one without a neck who was roughly the size of Cleveland. He had "enforcer" written all over him.

How the hell *did they know where we were?*

For now, there was the simple matter of staying alive.

Luckily for him, the smaller guy was so busy talking he wasn't bothering to watch what he was *doing*. One of the first things John had taught him and Sam—as soon as they were old enough—was how to defend themselves against someone with a gun.

"The best thing," John had said, "is if they get real close. If they keep their distance, you're in trouble, 'cause there ain't nothin' you can do. But if they get close, the trick is to grab the barrel. Even if they get a shot off, your hand'll block the slide. Now it'll hurt like hell, but then he can't shoot again."

Both Dean and Sam had done that drill a thousand times, with and without their father, so when the little guy put the gun right in Dean's face, he almost thanked him.

Three seconds later, he had the gun on the guy.

What Dean *hadn't* expected was for the guy with the thyroid problem to shoot his buddy. While he did, though, Dean threw a shot into the bruiser.

But it barely slowed the big guy down, and before Dean knew it, he was eating mattress.

Then the bruiser was gone, taking the hook sword with him.

Sonofabitch.

Dean ran out after him, shoving the .45 into the waistband of his pants, covering it with his untucked flannel shirt. He wasn't going to have much time if someone called the cops, and he had to get that sword back.

By the time he hit the street, the big guy was getting into a car that was parked in front of a fire hydrant. The Impala was a block away, and there was no way he'd catch up on foot.

No way was he going to fire a gun in the middle of Ellis Street, either.

When he walked back inside, Sam was in the hallway,

but he wasn't coming after Dean. Instead, he was walking back to the room from the other direction, carrying a bucket of ice.

Looking closely, Dean saw that Sam's entire face was red.

"Damn—the Asian Hulk got you pretty good, huh?"

Sam nodded without speaking, entering the room and immediately wrapping ice cubes in one of the bathroom towels. Applying it gingerly to his face, he winced.

"Ow."

"Dunno about you, but those guys screamed 'mobster' to me."

Again, Sam nodded, and when he spoke there was pain in his voice.

"Yeah, it looks like Chao was ready for us—or, at least, ready for the sword. He may not be the pushover Dad thought he was."

"Or maybe he got smart in twenty years. Either way, we gotta be more careful. And we've gotta try to get the sword back."

"What do you think we should do next?"

"First we get rid of Jackie Chan here. Then I wanna take a look at that dead body from last night before we go to Shin's Delight. Dad's notes were good and all, but he didn't actually see any of the bodies."

"Think you better handle that one solo," Sam said. "Federal agents don't usually go into the field with their faces looking like hamburger."

Dean grinned.

"Yeah. At least we got in some shots of our own." Dean looked down at the dead body. "So while I'm gone, can you take care of this guy?"

Sam nodded, then winced.

"I'm on it. I'll need you to help me get him into the car, though."

"Yeah, I can do that." Dean tossed the keys to Sam, who pocketed them, then put the ice-laden towel down so he could start wrapping the body up in the bedspread.

Dean, meanwhile, started to change into his suit.

TWENTY-THREE

Albert was checking over the accounts on his computer, making sure all his enterprises—legitimate or not—were running smoothly. He knew that if he didn't check regularly, one of his accountants would start skimming off the top.

It had happened once before, and Tiny had taken care of it.

Since then, he hadn't had any problems. Indeed, that had probably been the tipping point for him. That was when he'd finally realized he didn't *need* the Heart of the Dragon to do his dirty work for him.

He sat back and thought about it.

Why not turn Doragon Kokoro *over to the demon, then?*

Yet this was *family*. Nakadai was of his own flesh and blood. Didn't that count for *something*?

Gary interrupted his train of thought by sprinting into the office.

"Boss!"

"What is it?"

"Tiny's back. He got hurt!"

Albert got up.

"Where is he?" he demanded.

Gary led Albert downstairs into the back of the kitchen area. The cooks were all preparing for the lunch-hour rush, but there was a small area where Zhong kept an office.

Tiny sat in there. Ronnie was putting a bandage on his forehead, and Tiny himself was using his right hand to clutch a large bloody towel to his left shoulder.

"What happened?"

Quickly, Tiny filled Albert in.

"Those two guys got ahold of Jake's gun. They killed him and shot me," Tiny said. "I was lucky to get outta there alive."

Albert felt anger rising up in him—after all, Jake had been a decent leg-breaker—but he was more concerned about the two men.

"Did you get either of their names?"

"The shorter one was called Dean." Tiny nodded toward a corner of the office, and Albert turned. "I got the sword, though."

"Excellent!" Albert had always hoped to meet up with John Winchester again, and prayed fervently that these two—one of whom he now knew was named Dean—might be the accursed *gaijin*'s offspring. It was the one loose end he most wanted to tie up.

Winchester himself might be gone by now, but Albert

could destroy the man's sons. Family counted for *everything*.

But that was for later. No doubt the boys would come looking for the sword, but right now he was more concerned with his new bargaining chip. This changed everything when it came to dealing with the demon.

"Here are the bodies, Agent Seeger."

Dean watched as the wizened old medical examiner strained to pull a drawer out from the wall. He came close to taking pity on the guy after the third time he yanked on the handle, but then he got it.

Of course, there were two bodies, so he had to go through it all over again. This time Dean did intervene.

"Lemme give you a hand."

The M.E., whose name was Friedrich, let out a long breath.

"Yeah, thanks. Sorry, guess I ain't as young as I used to be."

"Yeah, well, none of us are," Dean said gravely, remembering intimately what it had felt like to be that old. His knees still occasionally cracked, scaring the living crap out of him….

Dean pulled open the drawer and was immediately hit by the smell of burnt flesh.

"*Whoa*."

"Yeah. And this is *after* it's been in the frigidaire all this time." Friedrich shook his head. "Can't believe this is happening again."

Dean shot the M.E. a look.

"Again?"

Friedrich tossed a look right back at Dean.

"Yeah, again, isn't that why you're here?"

With the ease of long practice, Dean tap-danced.

"Well, yeah, but we've been, uh, keepin' it quiet, y'know?"

"Oh, so *you* guys knew the score. Figures." The M.E. turned to peer at the charred corpse. "See, when the first burned body hit a couple of weeks ago, I told the cops it had happened before. Jerks didn't listen to a word I said, like usual. Forty-five years I've been doing this job, and I still can't get anybody to take me seriously."

Stifling a yawn he knew wouldn't buy him any favors, Dean reached for the sheet that covered the female victim.

"Yeah, well, let's see what we—"

He pulled it back and saw the blackened, charred flesh.

"—got."

"See, it's the same thing from forty years back. It was 1969—I remember, 'cause it got lost in all that Zodiac killer crap. You remember, right? No, you're too young—you woulda been a baby."

Dean was tempted to point out that a blind man could see that he was too young by a full decade. But he refrained.

"I assume the COD is burning?" he asked.

"Yeah, but that's not what makes it interesting. Look at this." The examiner pointed at the torso. While the skin was uneven, pocked and charred, there were also several straight slashes.

"This is *just* what happened forty years ago. There was a

Fed back then, too. Bald guy—don't remember his name. He said he'd be looking into it, but I didn't hear *bupkiss*."

This time it was a smile Dean had to conceal. A bald man claiming to be a Fed? That *had* to be his grandfather. Obviously these things ran in the family….

"Didn't solve it in '89, either," Friedrich continued, "'Course we got better toys nowadays. This time I can tell you for sure that there's metal trace in these wounds. And it had to be antemortem."

That surprised Dean, especially since the Heart of the Dragon's MO was to burn and slash at the same time.

"Why do you say that?" he asked.

"Body's too fragile. If I took a blade to this spot on the body right now, the poor girl'd fall to pieces."

Dean nodded.

"Then there are other problems," Friedrich added, pointing at the sword wounds. "Cuts like that should bleed like crazy, right? But according to the crime-scene geniuses, there was *no* blood at the scene, except for what was comin' outta that guy's nose." He pointed at the other corpse. "And that makes no sense."

"Maybe they both happened at the same time," Dean offered, pointing to the burned body. "If the woman was being burned while she was being cut, it might've boiled the blood away."

Friedrich squinted at Dean.

"Huh. That's not a bad theory, actually. Well, okay, it's not a theory, it's a hypothesis—always bugs me, the way people call theories hypotheses, then they say, 'Oh, it's only a theory,' as if it's meaningless, but theories have data behind 'em, and…" Friedrich drifted off. "Where was I?"

"Boiling the blood away," Dean prompted helpfully.

"Right, yeah, okay, maybe. But that still doesn't answer *how*. I mean, this kind of flash-fire could only happen if she was, I don't know, standing on some magnesium strips or somethin'. But those same geniuses checked for that and all kindsa other incendiaries. Bupkiss. What does that tell you?"

It told Dean a great deal, but it wasn't anything he was willing to share with a cranky old dude.

"Not sure yet," he said. "But it *is* an ongoing investigation."

"Yeah, well—first time, everyone had their heads all messed up with that Zodiac thing. And last time—hell, that was the year of the earthquake. Probably kept everybody distracted or something. I don't know, that wasn't actually my beat back then. But there's *somethin'* screwy here."

"Won't get any argument from me." Dean pulled back the sheet on the other corpse.

"That's another weird one," Friedrich said, pointing at the corners of the man's lips. "Look at that. Know what it is?"

"Sulfur," Dean said with a sigh.

"Yeah, sulfur," the M.E. confirmed, looking impressed. "There was some on the other body, too—almost missed it among all the burns. I mean, crazy, right?"

Dean just nodded. Suddenly, this second corpse made a lot more sense.

"Weirdest damn brain hemorrhage I ever saw, too. Usually it's just a blood vessel. This guy burst half the ones he had in his brain. It's like someone set off a detonator or something, yet there was *no* other damage."

Yeah, it meant this poor bastard had been possessed by a demon—and whatever the demon did to him made his brain explode. Dean thought back to Castiel's words: "*A spirit is returning to this plane—one the demon hordes will be able to use in their war with the angels.*" So maybe a demon was sticking its nose into things.

Dean and Sam needed to stay on their toes.

TWENTY-FOUR

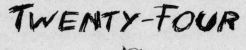

The angel Ramiel knew that Tyler Magowan had spent much of his adult life believing three things.

That God loved him.

That angels watched over him

That some day the Pittsburgh Pirates would stop sucking.

As with most examples of faith, they were things Tyler never expected to see or experience. He would have settled for a winning season from the Bucs, though—something that hadn't happened in his memory.

Therefore, when Ramiel came to Tyler and asked the young man to be the angel's vessel on Earth, it surprised him—to say the least.

But not as much as it might have. Unlike most humans, who lived in blissful and willful ignorance, Tyler had noticed the signs that the Apocalypse was nigh. He'd seen such things before, and thought them to be genuine omens, but they had turned out to be random incidents.

The past six months, though, he'd seen a pattern emerging.

Ramiel came to Tyler in a dream, and spoke to him.

"The Lord needs you to give of yourself in the battle for righteousness."

Tyler was, of course, skeptical. But Ramiel was very convincing.

"This is the wish of the Lord," Ramiel said coaxingly. "The battle is coming, and Raphael has joined us. So, too, will Michael, whose sword will be found."

Until the Michael sword was located, however, the angels had to hold the line against the demons. And that meant sacrifices.

Tyler was perfect. He was young, faithful, and single. He was also unemployed, another casualty of the Earth's inevitable slide into the oblivion of Revelation. Given the opportunity to contribute in the coming battle, he would likely do so with great fire and conviction.

Ramiel had been told that there were demons gathering in San Francisco, at the same time as an interfaith conference was being held at the Moscone Convention Center. This confluence was too good for the demons to pass up—their intent was to possess many of the participants, and slaughter the rest.

The faith of the devout was one of the angels' primary weapons, and the demoralizing effect of such an attack would be devastating on many levels. Thus Ramiel was ordered to join a contingent of angels led by Uzziel to stop the demons.

Ironically, before Ramiel had revealed himself, Tyler had been planning to attend this conference with several other members of his church. Without hesitation, he agreed.

The vast complex of Moscone Center took up an entire city block, with streets on all four sides. When Tyler/Ramiel first arrived, led by Uzziel and accompanied by a dozen other followers, they sensed no demonic presence—disappointing, but not unexpected. Demons were always finding ways to hide themselves. And he had been told from the outset that it was possible that their intelligence was faulty.

Nevertheless, the angels easily infiltrated the conference, pretending to be attendees. For all that it called itself "interfaith," Ramiel realized quickly that it was truly a Judeo-Christian gathering. Still, the two religions—fractured though they were in this modern age—maintained considerable common ground, as well as a desire to exercise greater influence over humanity. They longed to wield the sort of influence their ancestors had enjoyed.

Ramiel thought it was a waste of time. True, everyone in medieval Europe had believed in God, and worshipped and swore fealty to the church, but they had done so because they knew no other way. It was faith by habit. Far fewer people in the modern day's so-called "Western Civilization" considered themselves religious.

Yet in modern America, those who did believe *truly* believed—not because they had to, but because they wanted to. *That* was true faith, Ramiel thought. Tyler Magowan didn't consider himself a Christian out of family tradition or fear that he'd be ostracized from his community if he wasn't. He simply considered himself a Christian, and conducted himself as one.

Better to have one devout follower than a hundred rote ones, Ramiel decided.

Not everyone agreed, however. He had made the mistake of mentioning this preference to Uriel, which had led to a lengthy diatribe on the subject of human ingratitude. Uriel described the rampant lack of faith as "the mud monkeys abusing their own free will."

But Ramiel held his tongue. He had always felt that the whole point of being an angel was to see the best in things. And when Uriel turned out to be a traitor, it had reinforced this conviction.

One thing Ramiel couldn't reconcile was all the death. Too many of his brothers and sisters weren't here now because they'd died—whether in service of the Lord, as victims of the betrayal by Uriel and his allies, or at the hands of demons.

He hoped this day wouldn't add to the ranks of the fallen.

With Uzziel, Jophiel, and Selaphiel alongside him, Ramiel went to a session that was being held in Room 105, which was one of the conference rooms just outside the exhibit hall on the convention center's lower level. The hall itself was currently empty—unlike many who used Moscone's services, the conference boasted no exhibitors peddling their wares or promoting their services. The sole purpose of this conference was for people of faith to talk to one another.

Room 105 revealed a dozen people gathered in a circle. Most of them were well dressed. One was a Lubavitcher, and he had on a black-and-white suit and sported a full beard and a full head of curly hair sticking out from under his hat. Another was dressed in the black shirt and collar of a Catholic priest.

The rest were in suits.

As with every other room they'd entered in the Moscone Center, this one was bereft of any demonic presence.

In the seat that faced the door sat a woman in a lime green pantsuit. She wore a brooch that was oddly familiar.

"Hello," she said, "have you come to join our colloquy?"

Uzziel smiled and spoke in a deep, resonant voice. His host was a pediatrician named Pierce—a large, powerfully built African American who had used that voice to convince his patients that it would only hurt for a minute.

"No, thank you," he replied. "We'd just like to observe, if that's all right."

"By all means," the woman said.

Suddenly, Ramiel recognized the brooch—or, more specifically, recognized the stone in the brooch's center.

There were only four in existence, and three of them were safely hidden in a church in Cordoba. Ramiel had put them there himself in the fourth century, and if the wards he'd placed around them had been penetrated any time in the subsequent 1700 years, he'd have known.

They had been created by Bishop Hyginus of Cordoba in A.D. 381, the year after the bishop had conspired to have an ascetic named Priscillian executed for heresy. Priscillian had learned that Hyginus was consorting with demons, and Hyginus had used his demonic allies to help convince Pope Damascus I to have Priscillian condemned.

Hyginus had created the four stones to hide a demon's essence within a possessed body, even from an angel. Ramiel had been sent to confiscate the stones. He had succeeded in retrieving three of them and casting out the demon who had lured Hyginus away from the Lord. Ironically, history would remember Hyginus as a devout Christian who had rid the church of a heretic, and Priscillian as one of the first such heretics.

And Ramiel had never been able to locate the fourth stone.

Now, standing in Room 105 of the Moscone Center, Ramiel didn't hesitate, didn't give the demons a chance to tip their hands. Nor did he let them know they'd been discovered.

Instead, without a word, he struck.

With but a gesture, he knocked the woman in the pantsuit to the ground.

The angels all turned to stare at him as if he were mad, and only then did he speak.

"She wears the missing Stone of Hyginus!"

The priest jumped up.

"What on Earth are you people *doing*?"

Next to him, a man in a charcoal suit and a Liberty of London tie backhanded the priest.

"Shut *up*, already, will you?" he snarled.

Several chairs started to leap into the air and ricochet off of the walls. Ramiel ducked the one that had been aimed at his head, and it careened away.

"Figures," the demon with the stone said as its vessel got to her feet. "We get stuck with the *one* halo who knows what an ancient stone looks like."

Ramiel leapt across at that demon, catching her squarely in the chest and kicking her across the room. He let his momentum carry him, and then stood over her, shaking his head.

"Only a demon would think of a mere 1700 years as 'ancient.'" His look reflected his contempt. "You're pathetic little creatures."

"Blah blah blah," the demon said, rising slowly as her eyes went pitch black. "Put it in your wings and rub it, halo."

Suddenly she let loose with a kick of her own that sent the angel crashing into the table with what might have been a bone-jarring impact. It was Ramiel's turn to scramble upright, and as he prepared for the demon to follow through, he glanced quickly around the room.

Uzziel had grabbed one of the demons by the head. Smoke poured out of the vessel's mouth, eyes, nose, and ears, dissipating into nothingness even as the man screamed in agony.

The demon with the stone leapt at Ramiel again. Letting his vessel's body go limp, Ramiel let the momentum of her leap carry them through the thin wall that separated Room 105 from a lower-level exhibit hall.

Hitting the hard ground, rolling and getting to his feet, Ramiel faced the demon, standing on the bare concrete.

"Is this really the best you can do?" he asked, his words echoing in the cavernously empty hall.

Grinning, the demon also rose.

"Don't worry, I'm just gettin' started."

She reached into a pocket of the pantsuit and pulled out a knife. Ramiel recognized it as similar to the one Castiel had carried, and he wasn't about to let the demon do anything with it. He reached out and snatched it from her grip.

She offered surprisingly little resistance.

And then Ramiel found he couldn't raise his arms. Or stay on his feet.

His knees felt as if they were crumbling to dust.

His eyesight started to fail, but with a squint he was able to make out the vicious smile on the face of the demon's vessel.

"Not feeling so hot, are you, halo? See, I've been doing some collecting. Hyginus's little trinket was just one of my babies, and me and my buddies are—"

The rest of her sentence was cut off by a hand that appeared on her head.

"No! No! *Yaaaaaaaaarrrrrrrrrrrrrrrrrrrrrrrrrrrhhhhhhhh!*"

Smoke oozed out of every orifice. Moments later the

vessel collapsed to the concrete floor, dead. Her screams continued to echo through the hall.

Only when she had fallen could Ramiel see—barely—that it was Uzziel, recognizable because of his vessel's imposing size.

Still the life was draining from him.

Ramiel dropped the knife to the concrete floor.

"Destroy it, quickly, Uzziel, before...."

Uzziel winced as the *angelus iuguolo* claimed Ramiel. He watched the body of Tyler Magowan die, and with it the angel who possessed him.

Uzziel had always liked Ramiel. He had a good heart—even by the high standards of the angels—and had been a fine warrior in the Lord's cause.

Even if the Lord himself hadn't been much in evidence lately.

Like many of the higher angels, Uzziel was tired of it. Tired of guiding a humanity that neither wanted nor appreciated their help. After centuries of wars, plagues, tyranny, sin—the Apocalypse was something of a relief.

He had thought the twentieth century, with so many genocides, had been the worst ever. Then the twenty-first had begun with lunatics killing each other by the thousands, in every corner of the globe, and Uzziel knew it wasn't going to get any better.

When Zachariah came to him with a plan to bring about the end of days—and sooner rather than wait around for it—Uzziel was on board in an instant.

The only part he hadn't liked was deceiving his fellow angels. Not even when the goal was to draw out *Doragon Kokoro*. The angels had been certain that this assault was going to be the spirit's coming-out party, after which he would serve as a powerful weapon in the hands of demonkind.

Few realized just how powerful a weapon the damned *samurai* would be in the right—or wrong—hands. In so evenly balanced a match, his role could be the tipping point. Zachariah knew that, and he had convinced Uzziel.

When the angelic counter-strike was announced, nobody questioned the orders. Why should they? The host had a very rigid chain of command, and opinions were discouraged. After all, they usually led to betrayal, as had been shown by Castiel.

And Uriel.

And Lucifer.

As it was, the angels had courted disaster. Ramiel's presence had proved a blessing, since Uzziel never would have recognized the Stone of Hyginus. Sadly, Ramiel had paid the ultimate price via the *angelus iuguolo*—but so had six of the seven demons, thanks to Uzziel, Jophiel, and Selaphiel. Only one of the creatures had managed to get away.

Ramiel's sacrifice had served to prove an even greater truth—one Uzziel had suspected all along.

Father had abandoned them. They were on their own.

With a gesture, he atomized the knife. Never again would it claim a sibling.

Then he removed the brooch from the corpse of the woman in the green pantsuit. He planned to place it with the others in Cordoba. Ramiel would, he knew, have wanted it that way.

Leaving the human corpses behind—they were humanity's problem now and not the concern of the host— Uzziel went back to Room 105 to gather up the surviving angels.

And the war raged on.

TWENTY-FIVE

Marcus Wallace lay dying.

The heart attack had come out of nowhere. But then, that was the way of the heart attack—that most unpredictable of killers. Marcus had always laughed at reports of "a sudden heart attack."

As if there were any other kind.

He'd been sitting in his office, grading papers, when his left arm started to hurt. Then he'd had trouble breathing, with fatigue overwhelming him, his body tensing even as he lost control of his limbs.

Somehow, he wound up on the floor.

The new secretary—the one whose name he couldn't quite remember—came running in, cried out in shock, and then grabbed Marcus's desk phone and called 911.

And after that, he must have been hallucinating, because the secretary looked down at him.

And smiled viciously.

He woke up in the emergency room of the Alta Bates Summit Medical Center on Ashby Avenue, surrounded by a doctor and five nurses who told him he was lucky to be alive.

Since then, they'd admitted him, UC-Berkeley's medical coverage being more than sufficient to pay for a stay in a four-person room that currently only had three people occupying it.

For twenty-four hours, nurses came in and checked on him and ran tests and poked and prodded. None of them would answer any of Marcus's questions beyond the platitudes he'd received when he woke up in the ER.

Marcus was pushing seventy. He had gotten used to medical professionals being parsimonious with useful information. Everything was "precautionary," they didn't want to "jump to conclusions," it was always "too early to tell."

Finally, a doctor came in. He was a familiar-looking Asian man with a crew-cut and round cheeks.

"Hi, Mr. Wallace, I'm Doctor—"

"Takashi Iwamura."

The doctor grinned sheepishly as he reached for the clipboard that hung from a hook at the foot of the bed.

"I was rather hoping you wouldn't remember me, Professor."

Marcus laughed, an action that sent shooting pains through his entire ribcage.

"No, I, uh—*woo*."

The grin fell.

"Take it easy, Professor."

Marcus waved him off.

"I'm fine—just shouldn't have laughed," he said, and he caught his breath. "No, it's good to see you. Been a few years since you were three steps from flunking out of my folklore class, Hash. You still go by 'Hash'?"

That prompted another sheepish grin.

"No matter how hard I try not to."

"Well, as long as my heart's in your hands, I'll stick with 'Dr. Iwamura.'"

"Hash is fine, Professor. And speaking of your heart...."

"Yeah." Marcus tugged at the sheets that covered him from the chest down. "What's the verdict? And please—no crap, all right? I prefer Gregory House to Marcus Welby."

Iwamura shrugged as he hung the clipboard back on the hook.

"Fair enough. You had a cardiac infarction and came within a hairsbreadth of dying." He paused briefly before continuing. "Now, this is the part where I'd give you all kinds of reassurances, tell you that there are treatments and medications and diets and all sorts of things. But you want straight, so you'll get straight.

"You've got a heart that doesn't like you very much. It's like a fight with your wife or girlfriend or boyfriend or whoever—you can buy all the flowers you want and apologize all you want, but there's no guarantee you'll be taken back."

Marcus thought about that for a moment.

"So I could take meds that make me sick, eat food I can't stand, and still keel over in six months?"

Iwamura nodded.

"But the chances are reduced *significantly*, if you do all that."

"Great." Marcus let out a long breath. "Okay, thanks for the straight shooting, Hash."

Putting a hand on his shoulder, Iwamura spoke gently.

"Get some rest, Professor. You've got students to terrorize, after all."

That prompted a smile.

"I only terrorize the students who don't appreciate the material. I'm sure your med-school professors were a lot easier on you."

Iwamura coughed a laugh.

"Well, I don't know if I'd go *that* far..." he said.

After Iwamura left, Marcus looked over at the telephone that sat on the table next to his bed. The siren call of voicemail nagged at him.

He looked around, and saw that the other patients in the room were unconscious. Pretty sure he wouldn't disturb them, he reached for the receiver. When he'd started teaching forty-five years ago, he barely even used the phone in his office. He communicated with students in person, during office hours—which were posted on a piece of paper tacked to a bulletin board—and before and after classes.

Now, he rarely had a face-to-face with his students. It was

all email or texting or instant messaging or cell phones. He even had his office phone automatically forward to his Treo. He spent little time in his office these days, anyhow.

At his age, and having had tenure for years, his class load was lighter than it had ever been, and he preferred to spend his leisure time relaxing. Sometimes he'd cross the Bay Bridge into San Francisco and browse through City Lights, or he'd wander the used bookstores here in Berkeley.

If a student needed to talk to him, the call would go right to his pocket.

Unlike many of his contemporaries—who bitched and moaned about it—Marcus actually preferred it this way.

His favorite was Dr. Wang.

"They can call me any time, now. What if I don't want to talk to them?"

Marcus's response was always the same.

"Cell phone's got an 'off' button. Use it—I do. If I don't want to be reached, I can shut the thing down and they can eat voicemail."

He liked not subjecting himself—or his students—to the tyranny of office hours. So many issues that would have been disastrous twenty years ago never even came up, precisely because the students had improved access to their teachers.

His Treo had been in his jacket pocket when he'd suffered the heart attack, which meant it was still draped over the cracked leather chair where he'd left it. His laptop still sat on his desk. Without either of those, checking his email was impossible—despite the nurse's reassurance that the hospital had wi-fi.

However, the landline next to his bed would, at least, allow him to remotely access his voicemail. So he gave in to temptation, and punched in the numbers.

He had six messages, so he grabbed a pen and paper.

The first three were from his students with assorted concerns, none of which he had to sweat until after he was released from the hospital. However, he did copy down their numbers so he could let them know that it would be more than a day or two to get back to them, and for good reason. Knowing the campus grapevine, he expected they already knew what had happened, but Marcus preferred the personal touch.

The next message was from his nephew, and Marcus was tempted to delete it without listening.

"Yo, Unc, some white dude was lookin' for you. Said he met a friend'a yours in Chinatown or somethin' like that. Bought me a beer, so I told him you worked at the hippie school. Just wanted to give you a heads-up, yo. Peace."

Marcus sighed. At least he wasn't asking for money this time. The final message came from an unfamiliar voice.

"Hi, Professor, this is Sam Winchester—I'm calling on behalf of myself and my brother Dean. Twenty years ago you met our father, John Winchester, and I think you know Bobby Singer, too. We're in San Francisco because the Heart of the Dragon's back, and we need your help. If you could call me back, please, that would be great." Then he gave his cell number. The call ended, and Marcus just stared at the phone.

"Son of a bitch."

He found it hard to believe that it had been twenty years since a frighteningly intense John Winchester had come into his office complaining about the hook sword he had given to Jack Bartow. Marcus had thought the man was going to take his head off. From the sound of it, his son was a lot nicer. At the very least, he was more polite.

But that thought was supplanted by another—this one much more ominous.

If *Doragon Kokoro* was back, all hell was gonna break loose. So reading the number off of the note pad, he returned Sam Winchester's phone call.

"Hello?" It was the same voice, slightly out of breath.

"Sam Winchester? This is Marcus Wallace."

"Oh, hi, Professor. Can you hold on one second?"

"Uh, sure," Marcus said, and it sounded as if the young man set his phone down, followed by what sounded like a shovel digging into dirt.

After a few more seconds, Sam Winchester came back on the line.

"Sorry about that—needed to finish something up." As he spoke, Marcus heard the sound of a car engine starting.

"That's all right, son," Marcus replied. "How's your old man doing?"

"Uh, well, I'm afraid he passed a few years ago."

Marcus winced.

"Damn. Sorry about that. He seemed like an okay guy."

"Thanks." Sam sounded awkward. In the background, the traffic noises increased—as if he had just entered a freeway. Whatever the case, he quickly got down to business.

"I'm glad you called, Professor. We've got a bit of a problem."

"Your message said something about *Doragon Kokoro*'s return."

"Uh, yeah, and it gets worse," Sam said. "Some guys came by our hotel and took the hook sword away from us. We figure it was Albert Chao."

"Probably, yeah." Marcus blew out a very long breath. "Well, I'd say you guys are screwed then—and so are the rest of us. You gotta get that thing back."

"That's what I was hoping you could help us with. We need to find the sword again. Chao probably has it at his restaurant, but it'd be good if we could be sure before we try to retrieve it."

"Crap." Marcus closed his eyes and thought for a moment. He'd never *needed* to locate the sword before, because he always knew where it was. Or at least that it was in the right hands.

Even better, he'd put all his notes on *Doragon Kokoro* into a folder on his laptop. Which, of course, was back at his office.

Why is this never easy?

"All right," he said, "I'm gonna need you or your brother to do me a favor."

"Just name it."

"You need to stop by my office. It's at 2223 Fulton Street in Berkeley. There's a laptop on my desk. Grab it and bring it to me here at the hospital."

"Hospital?" Sam sounded confused.

Marcus shook his head. *He couldn't possibly have known.*

"Yeah, had me a heart attack yesterday. I'm in Room 209 of the Medical Center on Ashby Avenue."

"Where on Ashby?"

"Uh, dunno the address—it's right off Telegraph."

"Okay, I'll find it," Sam hesitated and continued. "And Professor, I'm sorry."

Marcus dismissed the sentiment with a wave—not that there was anyone who could see it.

"Forget about it—you didn't know," he said. "And hurry—we can't afford to screw around."

"Okay. I'm on 580 heading toward Berkeley right now. Should be there in ten to fifteen minutes or so."

"Good—and hey, Sam?"

"Yeah?"

"There are no guarantees here. I never needed to look for the sword before, so I don't know if my notes will give us anything that'll find it."

"Yeah, I kinda figured that." Sam paused. "It's still worth a shot, though."

"Oh, definitely. I just don't want you getting your hopes up." Marcus remembered how persnickety Sam's father got, and didn't want to take the chance that the son had inherited that trait.

"I stopped getting my hopes up a long time ago, Professor," Sam said, his voice sounding incredibly tired.

"Yeah, I can appreciate that. Call me when you get to the office." He gave Sam the hospital phone number, then they disconnected.

Lying there in silence, he thought about John Winchester. The man had radiated intensity, a singularity of purpose. Jack Bartow had been a lot more laid back. He knew what he was doing and didn't mess around, but he took things relatively easy.

Winchester, though, was different—he'd carried himself as if his entire existence depended on destroying the spirit.

Of course, neither of them had succeeded in doing so.

If Sam Winchester is anything like his father, then it's no wonder he sounded the way he did.

The next thing Marcus knew, he was woken by the noise of the phone ringing. He hadn't even realized he'd fallen asleep.

"Hello?"

A deep voice spoke.

"Is this Marcus Wallace?"

"Uh, yeah." *Who the hell…?*

"Dean Winchester—Sam's brother. We got the laptop, and we're headin' down to you right now."

"Great—I'll see you shortly." He started to hang up, then pulled the receiver back again. "And hey, like I told your brother, I can't promise nothin'. I may not be able to find the thing for you."

"Yeah, we get that a lot." Dean sounded at least as tired as his brother. "See you in a few."

Marcus hung up the hospital phone, and then rubbed the sleep from his eyes. His connections to the weird world Bartow, Singer, and the Winchester family lived in were tenuous at best. These guys *lived* it.

It had to have taken its toll.

He glanced around to find that both of his roommates were gone. One bed still had a chart on it, so the guy was probably just off getting tests or something.

The other one had no chart—maybe he checked out.

One way or the other, he thought bleakly.

A knock came at the door.

"Hi, Professor!"

Looking up, Marcus saw the secretary whose name he *still* couldn't remember. Despite this, he did recall that she'd been the one who found him and called 911.

"Hey!" he replied with enthusiasm.

She was a mousy little Japanese-American woman with dark hair tied into a ponytail. She had a very bright smile, and was wearing a gray trench coat.

As she walked up to the bed, she seemed to be clutching her purse, as if hanging on for dear life.

"I just wanted to see how you were doing, Professor," she said. "I was so frightened when I saw you collapse like that."

"Yeah, me, too," Marcus admitted ruefully. "But hey, you were the one who called 911, so thanks for that."

"Oh, of course! It would be terrible if you died!" Then

she leaned in close and spoke in a whisper. "Heart attacks are so—so horrible, aren't they?"

Marcus didn't bother whispering back, since they were the only two people in the room.

"Definitely. I'm in no rush to have another one."

Then something about her changed—and abruptly. Her bright smile took on a different aspect, though he couldn't exactly say *how*. With a start, he remembered the strange look she'd given him, right before he blacked out, back at the office.

Her tone changed with her expression.

"Then you'd best tell me what I want to hear."

The smile disappeared, and her eyes went completely black.

Marcus hadn't thought there could be a worse sensation than having a heart attack, but seeing the secretary's eyes suddenly go dark gave him a horrible feeling deep in the pit of his stomach.

"You're gonna help me, Prof," she said, a rumbling undertone to her words. "According to the grapevine, you're the guy to talk to about the spirit of Yoshio Nakadai. I need to take charge of that spirit. Y'see, there's a war on, and my side's been taking a bit of a pounding. I just got my ass kicked and watched six of my buddies die a horrible death because I didn't come through. I'm pretty damn pissed about that, so I'm tired of assing around. I want the Heart of the Dragon back. And that leads me oh-so-nicely to you." As she spat out those last few words, the smile returned.

Marcus said nothing. Whatever this creature was, it wasn't on the side of the angels.

Her face loomed over him, the black eyes deep, hypnotic pools.

"The sword that can be used to bring the spirit to heel," she continued. "I need it. And you're going to tell me where it is."

Marcus stared back at the creature.

"Sorry. Can't tell you," he said, fighting to keep the fear out of his voice.

The creature snarled, a noise that was both frightening and repellant coming from such a delicate-looking form.

"Oh, you think so?"

"Think's got nothing to do with it," Marcus said. "I don't *know* where it is, and I don't know how to find it." He assumed it was with Chao, but even the Winchester boys weren't completely sure of that.

For several long moments those obsidian eyes stared at him. It was as if this monster was looking right into his soul.

"Huh," she said finally. "Looks like you're telling the truth. Well, that sucks." Then the awful smile came back again. "For you, anyhow."

Marcus's left arm started to hurt.

TWENTY-SIX

Sam and Dean were about to enter Professor Wallace's room when several people in scrubs ran in ahead of them, all shouting at each other.

"Helluva time to wind up in an *ER* episode," Dean muttered.

Sam had called Dean following his phone call with the professor and after he had finished burying the gangster's body near the Richmond Inner Harbor.

Rather than deal with going all the way back into San Francisco, then doubling back to Berkeley, Dean had taken the bus from the medical examiner's office to the Civic Center BART station, then the red line to Berkeley. Sam had met him at the station, and they had gone straight to the Asian Studies office to fetch Wallace's laptop and then on to the hospital.

A short Asian woman backed out of the hospital room,

guided by a nurse. She was crying.

"Professor Wallace! Professor Wallace!" she wailed.

"Please, ma'am, you need to stay back," the nurse said in a vaguely reassuring tone. "We'll try to save him."

Dean walked up to the woman.

"Excuse me—what happened to Professor Wallace?"

She looked up at him, tears streaming down her cheeks. He thought she had a nice Lucy Liu vibe going.

"I don't know! We were just talking, and he started acting all weird, and the monitors beeped and it was *awful*!"

Looking up, he saw that Sam was peering into the room.

"They're working on him," he reported, turning around as he spoke.

"Crap," Dean huffed through his teeth. Even if the docs pulled Wallace's ass out of the fire again, it'd be hours before he'd be conscious, much less able to have visitors.

Turning back to the young woman, he tried to figure out a way to gracefully excuse himself from her presence. If she knew Wallace, she probably wouldn't be all that thrilled with them having his personal laptop.

But before he could say anything, she lurched against him, gripping his bicep with one hand. She wasn't heavy, but he didn't dare move for fear of letting her drop to the floor.

"Uh...." He looked helplessly at his brother.

Sam shrugged.

"I'm sorry," the woman said breathlessly. "Need air."

"Let's, uh—let's get you outside, okay? We can check back on the professor in a little while?"

"Yes," she whispered. "Thank you."

Sam stared at Dean, who just glared back.

What else am I supposed to do?

Once they got out into the parking lot, the woman steadied herself and spoke with a stronger voice.

"Thanks very much, Dean."

"Sure, no—"

Then he backed away quickly, his hand moving to the inner pocket of his suit jacket. His fingers closed around the deer-antler handle of Ruby's demon-killing knife.

"Drop the act, sister."

The woman took on a nasty grin, and the black eyes of a demon.

"Ah, well, it was worth a shot. Guy like you, figured you'd want to rescue the hot Asian chick. Got that whole Lucy Liu thing going, right?"

Ahhh, crap. But Dean didn't take the bait.

"You have three seconds to vamoose, chuckles."

"Not that easy, boys," she said, looking at Sam who had followed them outside. "See, you two are even more valuable than that hook sword. Maybe even more valuable than the spirit of Nakadai."

Years of playing poker kept Dean's expression neutral.

The demon continued to address his younger brother.

"You look awful, Sam. Really, you should take better care of yourself," the creature chided. "After all, you *are* Lucifer's vessel. It doesn't do for you to be all bruised up." She shook her head. "Damn me. The Michael sword *and* Lucifer's vessel.

I've really hit the jackpot."

Dean removed the knife from his jacket.

"So've we."

Her face fell.

"Awww, screw it!"

The woman's head tipped back and smoke poured out of her mouth, cascading upward into the sky.

She collapsed to the ground.

"C'mon," Dean said, making a beeline for the Impala. "This is bigger than we thought. We've gotta make tracks."

"Dean—" Sam started, but Dean cut him off.

"We're in a hospital parking lot," he said while fishing the keys from his pants pocket. "Someone'll help her, and we need to get out of here before he tells his demon buddies where we are. We may be hidden from them thanks to Castiel, but Sam, we've been made."

"Yeah," Sam muttered as he ran to catch up his brother. "You're right."

Minutes later the Impala was heading toward I-80 and the Bay Bridge.

"Well, that sucked," Dean said.

"At least we've got the laptop," Sam said. "When we get back to the hotel, I'll see if I can find anything."

"If there's anything there to find." Dean pounded the steering wheel with one hand. "He wasn't even sure. And I'm willing to bet Wallace's heart attack had some encouragement from Smokey the Hot Asian Chick."

"Probably so, yeah."

"You got an hour," Dean said.

"Excuse me?" Sam replied.

"We get back, I change into real clothes, and you take an hour to try to find something. Then we go to Shin's Delight, no matter what you find. That's Chao's HQ, so that's where the dead *samurai* must be. If there's a demon jonesing for this spirit, too...."

Sam nodded.

"Yeah, the stakes are higher than we thought."

"Certainly explains why Cass was the one who gave us the heads-up. Maybe the demons figure a guy like that'd come in handy in a fight."

"Or the angels," Sam suggested.

"Yeah, or the angels." Dean figured most of angel-kind was no better than the demons they fought. In some ways they were worse—having been to Hell, Dean understood how damned souls got that way.

Angels had *no* excuse.

After crossing the bridge, Dean navigated the streets of San Francisco. The first time he'd driven here, it had set his teeth on edge. He spent most of his time on interstates, and even when they went through hilly or mountainous areas, they tended to be mostly flat. But where highways were built by demolishing bits of land to keep the road as flat as possible, the local streets in San Francisco were just draped over the hills.

On that first visit Dean was twenty and Sam was still in high school. John was asleep in the passenger seat, and Dean hadn't wanted to wake him.

By the time they arrived at their destination in the Mission, he thought his knuckles were going to be permanently white. And he let his father drive out, once they took care of business.

But he'd adjusted over the years, to the point where it almost didn't bother him when the Impala felt as if it was at a right angle to the ground.

They entered the lobby of their hotel to find Castiel sitting on one of the badly upholstered sofas, staring straight ahead into space.

"Cass?" Dean said.

Castiel rose from the sofa and stared right at him.

"We need to talk."

"When *don't* we?" Then Dean shook his head, and shrugged in the direction of the stairs. "C'mon."

When they got back to the room, Sam took his position at the desk and opened Wallace's laptop, while Dean sat on his bed. Castiel just stood in the middle of the floor.

"There was a battle at the convention center downtown," Castiel said. "Ramiel was killed, as were half a dozen demons. The Heart of the Dragon isn't in play yet, but it's only a matter of time."

"Yeah," Dean sighed, "we got a taste of that." He told Castiel about their encounter at the hospital. The angel just stared, his face impassive.

"The Heart of the Dragon must be stopped. His power has been gestating for more than a century. Under the influence of demons, he might very well tip the scales."

"Well, I'm open to suggestions," Dean said. "Without the sword—"

Suddenly, the room felt incredibly hot—particularly in the direction of the bathroom.

Whirling around and springing to his feet, Dean saw a man surrounded by fire.

He had to admit, it was an impressive sight. His experience with *samurai*s had been limited to Toshiro Mifune movies and John Belushi skits, so to see one in real life was kind of cool.

The spirit didn't move, nor did the flames spread. Nonetheless, Dean pulled out the demon-killing knife.

Castiel's voice sounded tighter than usual.

"Won't... work...."

Dean looked over to see that Castiel was concentrating furiously—it seemed he was keeping the Heart of the Dragon in check.

Then the spirit spoke.

"You do not have the sword?"

Dean was caught off guard—the figure was speaking Japanese, but somehow he actually understood the words, if not the meaning.

"Say what?" he responded.

"I am under instructions from my descendant to slay you both, but this creature is holding me at bay," the spirit intoned in a deep, hollow voice. "This is good, for you may be able to free me, but only if you wield the sword."

Getting up from his position at the desk, Sam addressed the figure.

"The sword was taken from us, we think by Albert Chao. We're trying to locate it—"

"Ah, Albert Chao," the figure said. "My descendant has planned more skillfully this time, it seems. However, he is not a trusting soul. If he ordered the sword taken from you, then he is keeping it close. You must find it—and when you do, you may finally free me."

"I don't understand," Sam said, "how will it free you? Casting the spell on the sword will just banish you for another twenty years, won't it?"

"You must cast the spell on me as you pierce my heart with the sword's edge. Only *then* may I be free."

Dean shook his head. Sometimes trial and error really sucked. If Dad had known this twenty years ago, a lot of people would still be alive.

Then the spirit raised his sword.

"Cass!" Dean cried.

Sweat was beading on Castiel's forehead.

"I'm trying...."

"I am sorry," the Heart of the Dragon said, even as he advanced on Dean.

A report roared in Dean's ears, and the spirit disappeared in a flash of light, the flames constricting and collapsing into nothingness.

Glancing back he saw Sam holding a smoking shotgun, which was, as always, loaded with rock-salt rounds.

"Nice shot," Dean said.

Sam smiled mirthlessly.

"Nice to know the classics still work."

"Yeah, more people ought to keep those things handy— save a lotta grief," Dean agreed. He started undoing his tie. "We need to get a move on. The rock salt'll only keep Yojimbo there on ice for a little while, and Chao's gonna be pretty pissed when he finds out his pet spirit screwed the pooch." Pulling the tie from around his neck, he looked at Sam. "You got ten minutes to find something we can use. Then we motor to Chinatown."

Sam nodded and sat down, hunching over the laptop.

TWENTY-SEVEN

Albert Chao had been trying to summon the spirit of his ancestor for the best part of an hour, but to no avail.

In his youth, patience had never been one of his virtues. In fact, looking back, he was hard-pressed to find any recognizable virtues at all. He had been a killer, a cheat, and a fool. All those years of inadequacy, and he had blamed it all on people other than himself. Unwilling to accept his own failures, he instead castigated his parents for birthing him, Chinese society for ostracizing half-breeds, racist whites for their treatment of Asians….

Yet he was hardly the only half-breed in San Francisco. He was hardly the only person to suffer misfortunes. But back then he thought his problems were so special that he needed occult intervention. He thought it would solve everything.

It had been a supremely foolish decision, he realized now, to allow himself to make use of a demon's plaything.

But the damage was done. All he could do was move forward.

Finally he was able to bring the spirit to him. As the fiery creature appeared in the center of the office, Albert found himself surprisingly unmoved. Forty years ago, in a tiny apartment in the Mission, he'd never seen anything so glorious. The possibilities seemed endless, then, and he'd felt the spirit's power as if it were a tangible thing.

Now, he just saw a dead *samurai* wreathed in flames.

Albert had power—he didn't *need* the spirit.

"What happened?" he demanded.

"I was unable to carry out your orders, my descendant. The two men had a being of great power by their side, and he was able to keep me at bay until one of them used a firearm. Somehow it banished me."

"How banal." From what Oscar had told him, that was probably a shotgun with rock salt. Standard issue for hunters.

"Then it was fitting for such a banal task," the spirit said.

Albert looked up and stared into the fiery eyes of his ancestor.

"What do you mean?"

"You sent me to kill these two men—these 'Winchesters'—in a childish show of revenge. It is no different from the foul tasks you had me undertake when first you summoned me."

Albert shrugged.

"An indulgence. I cannot avenge myself on their father,

so…." He trailed off.

Why *had* he sent the spirit of his ancestor after the sons of John Winchester? He already had the sword, so he need have nothing else to do with them. True, they would likely come after him, and a preemptive strike was justifiable in that regard.

But that wasn't why he had done it.

"You resist the demon's imploring," the Heart of the Dragon said. "Why?"

"How can you ask that?" Albert said.

"The demon wishes to aid in the destruction of the world. He acts like a child lashing out at parents who have disappointed him. He is no different from you."

Albert dismissed the statement with a wave of his hand.

"That is ridiculous."

But even as he said so, he didn't believe it.

So he banished the spirit.

As the flames faded, he contemplated his ancestor's words.

A knock came at the door.

"Enter."

Ronnie stuck his head into the office.

"Hey, boss. We got the money in from Lady Shiva's. You said you wanted me to tell you."

"Good, Ronnie." He paused and continued. "Please, come in."

"Ah, sure, okay." Ronnie entered the office and stood waiting.

"What's up?"

Albert allowed himself a small smile.

"Nothing, Ronnie. I just wanted to see you for a moment. You may go."

The underling tossed him a strange look.

"You feelin' okay, boss?"

"I'm fine, Ronnie. Go."

"Okay." Ronnie shrugged, turned, and left the office.

Which told Albert all he needed to know.

He stared at the walls, recalling coming in here when it was Tommy Shin's sanctum. Tommy had painted the walls black in order to intimidate people, though he had also decorated it with contemporary movie posters, which somewhat diluted the effect. Albert had taken them down and left the black walls bare.

To his annoyance, he could no longer recall what movie posters had been there.

Leaning back in his chair, he tried to remember, but found that he couldn't.

That irritated him for some reason.

Another knock.

"Uh, boss? I'm back from dinner." It was Zhong, who had sounded subdued ever since the demon possessed him. "I'm sorry, but there's some restaurant business we need to go over."

"Of course, Zhong. Come in."

The man nodded, and he entered the office.

"There is an issue with—"

Albert held up a hand.

"I don't care. I honestly don't have time for this. I simply wished you to come into the room. You may leave now."

"I'm sorry?" Zhong hesitated, standing close to the desk. "Boss, this is important. We need to—"

"I do not care," Albert said in a low whisper. "None of it matters anymore. You will leave my office *now*."

"I—" Zhong shook his head, then looked up.

His eyes were black.

Albert smiled.

"At last. I was wondering when you would return, demon."

"Nice touch." Zhong's darkened eyes gazed at the ceiling. "Straight out of the Key of Solomon." Albert followed that gaze to the Devil's Trap that Oscar Randolph had etched there in chalk. The circle was large enough that anyone standing next to the desk had to pass beneath it. And as long as the seal remained intact, the demon would be unable to leave its boundaries.

"I have more," Albert said. He pressed the intercom button on his phone. "You may come in now."

Seconds later, Oscar entered, holding a notebook in his hand. He was wearing his customary flannel shirt, and a cowboy hat to cover his bald head.

"Aw, you brought Walter Brennan along," the demon said with Zhong's voice. "How cute. This isn't gonna do you any good, y'know. I want the Heart of the Dragon, I want the sword, and your little chalk drawing isn't going to stop me."

"You think so?" Albert asked lightly.

"I *know* so," the demon replied darkly.

Oscar began to read from his notebook.

"*Regna terrae, cantate Deo, psallite Domino qui fertis super caelum caeli ad Orientem Ecce dabit voci Suae vocem virtutis, tribuite virtutem Deo.*"

"Your pronunciation sucks," the demon said.

Albert frowned. From what Oscar had told him, the demon should've already been writhing around in agony.

"*Exorcizamus te, omnis immundus spiritus omnis satanica potestas, omnis incursio infernalis adversarii, omnis legio, omnis congregatio et secta diabolica. Ergo draco maledicte et omnis—*"

Zhong made as if his hands were talking puppets.

"Blah blah blah blah. You're wasting your time. See, Zhong didn't spend his dinner hour on dinner."

"*—legio diabolica adjuramus te cessa decipere humanas creaturas, eisque aeternae Perditionis venenum propinare.*"

Yanking open his button-down shirt, the demon revealed a recently applied tattoo on Zhong's clavicle.

"What the hell is that?" Albert demanded, glaring at the chanting hunter.

But Oscar did not stop.

"*Vade, Satana, inventor et magister omnis fallaciae, hostis humanae salutis. Humiliare sub potenti manu dei, contremisce et effuge, invocato a nobis sancto et terribili nomine, quem inferi tremunt.*"

"It's a binding," the demon said, ignoring Oscar's increasingly desperate incantation. "Zhong doesn't get rid of me until *I* say so. Redneck McGee here can *cantate* to *Deo* all he wants, but it ain't gonna do any good."

He snarled at Oscar, yet the man stubbornly persisted, moving closer to the figure, practically spitting the Latin words.

"*Ab insidiis diaboli, libera nos, Domine. Ut Ecclesiam tuam secura tibi facias libertate servire, te rogamus, audi nos. Ut inimicos sanctae Ecclesiae humiliare digneris, te rogamus, audi nos.*"

The demon spoke over him.

"Something else about a Devil's Trap? All it does is keep me inside its confines. It doesn't actually stop me from doing much of anything."

"That's not what I was told," Albert said. "I suspect you are lying, demon."

"No, you were just given old information. See, times have changed. The gate is open."

At this point, Oscar was practically on top of Zhong.

"*Ut inimicos sanctae Ecclesiae te rogamus, audi nos. Terribilis Deus de sanctuario suo. Deus Israhel ipse truderit virtutem et fortitudinem plebi Suae. Benedictus Deus. Gloria Patri.*"

He practically shouted the last words of the exorcism, but it had done no good whatsoever.

"Aaaaaaand nothin'," Zhong said with a laugh. "Glory hallelujiah and *aaaaaamen*! And you know what else?"

Zhong snapped his fingers. An awful crack echoed throughout the office even as Oscar's head turned to an impossible angle and the old man fell to the ground.

"You walked inside the circle, dumbass," the demon said, answering its own question.

It turned to regard Albert, its expression full of contempt. Albert looked back at it steadily, while at the same time he began to chant the spell that would summon the Heart of the Dragon. He had spoken the words so many times now, he could do it without thinking.

A moment later, his ancestor's spirit appeared.

"Now you die," Albert said calmly, holding the demon's gaze.

The Heart of the Dragon raised his flaming katana and moved into the Devil's Trap.

Yet the demon still seemed utterly unperturbed.

"You made another mistake, there, Al ol' pal," he said conversationally.

"Did I now?" Albert countered.

Zhong nodded.

"See, your office is a bit too small. The outer border of the trap doesn't extend to your chair, so you're safe—but it *does* cover your desk. Which means I can get at what's *in* it."

With a gesture, the demon consumed the desk in an eldritch fire that burned brighter and hotter even than the flames that wreathed the Heart of the Dragon.

Albert leapt back from the inferno, feeling his heart sink as he realized the demon's plan.

Everything the desk had contained was destroyed, with one exception—the hook sword. It lay revealed, and then at a gesture flew into Zhong's hands.

Turning, the demon stared at the Heart of the Dragon and laughed.

"I've been waiting for this moment for a *very* long time," he said. "Y'see, it's true—all things *do* come to the guy who waits. And with the help of my old buddy *Doragon Kokoro*, I'm gonna be the one who wins the day."

"Boy, are you a dumbass."

Jerking with surprise, Albert looked up. Standing in the doorway were two young men. He didn't recognize them, but they matched Tiny's descriptions of the Winchester brothers.

It was the shorter of the two who had spoken, and he continued.

"You actually let yourself get stuck in a Devil's Trap. That makes you stupider than a box'a hammers."

"You watch your mouth, boy," the demon said. "Or just step forward a bit—either works for me."

"He can't," the taller one said, "but I can." And he stepped into the room. "I'm Lucifer's vessel. You do any harm to me, if you even can, and it just might piss off your demon buddies."

Albert watched as the creature stared at the Winchesters, then at the Heart of the Dragon. The ancient warrior swung his fiery katana, but the demon blocked it with the hook sword. The *samurai* attacked again.

"If you two garbanzos had a play," the demon said, Zhong's voice now straining with the effort of fighting off Albert's ancestor, "you'd have made it by now, instead of babbling like idiots."

"Nah," the shorter one said, "y'see we're just stalling. Fact is, I *do* have a plan, and it includes a buddy of ours doing something at just the right moment. In fact, right about—"

Suddenly, Albert felt as if his stomach was being sucked out through his nose. Pain slammed into his head, and he lost all feeling in his legs.

The feeling passed almost instantaneously, but when it did, he was no longer in his office—he was standing in the alley next to the restaurant, between one of the dumpsters and a black vintage car of a type he hadn't seen in decades.

"What the—?"

"Hello," said a deep, scratchy voice. Whirling around, Albert saw a white man with stubble on his cheeks. He was wearing a trench coat and giving Albert the most intense stare he'd ever seen—and this after taking meetings with the Old Man.

"What have you—?" he began.

"My name is Castiel," the figure responded, interrupting him as if he was utterly insignificant. "You will remain here, and not interfere in what Dean and Sam are doing."

Unwilling to listen to this person, Albert started to walk across Ellis—

—only to find that he couldn't move.

Castiel's tone never changed as he spoke.

"As I said, you will remain here. Trying to do otherwise will only cause you difficulty."

Albert seethed.

And then, all of a sudden, it came to him.

Batman and *Lethal Weapon 2*. Those were the posters

Tommy had in his office.

He wondered why he remembered that *now*....

The first thing Sam Winchester did after Albert Chao disappeared was grab the demon-killing knife.

Leaping into the Devil's Trap, he thrust the knife at the man who was possessed by the demon.

The man parried the strike with the hook sword, and the impact sent painful vibrations up Sam's arm.

He had to be the one to use the knife—his status as Lucifer's intended vessel meant the demons couldn't harm him. This one, however, didn't seem to have gotten the memo. Or didn't care, because he swung the sword right at Sam's head.

Sam ducked and thrust upward with the knife, but the demon jerked back, tucking in his stomach so that Sam only stabbed air.

The Heart of the Dragon then swung his katana, flames trailing behind it, but the demon was able to parry that as well.

It backed to the edge of the Devil's Trap, looking back and forth from Sam to the *samurai*, holding the sword heart ready.

"Neither of you is gonna bring me down," the creature snarled. "It's taken a century and a half for this to come together, and you're *not* taking it away from me."

Simultaneously, both Sam and the spirit of Yoshio Nakadai attacked.

The demon parried both strikes, using the base of the sword to block the katana while catching Ruby's knife in the curved hook at the tip.

Then a shot rang out.

The bullet slammed into the shoulder of the body the demon had possessed. He hardly even jerked, and glanced over at Dean.

"What the hell do you think you're—"

The distraction, however, was all Sam needed to slide the blade between two ribs.

Frozen in place, the demon glowed with a light that seemed to come from inside his body, even as he screamed and fell to the floor, dropping the hook sword.

Sam scooped it up, looked straight at the Heart of the Dragon, *focused* on him, and filled his mind with thoughts only of the fiery spirit. As he did so, he recited the same spell that his father had uttered twenty years earlier.

Doragon Kokoro stared at him in anticipation.

When Sam got to the final part of the spell, he raised the blade over his head and swung downward. The curved hook penetrated the chest of the spirit where his heart once beat.

The flames around the spirit burned so bright that Sam had to shield his eyes. It was a pure white flame—a thing of beauty.

As the spirit faded from view, Sam heard one word echo through the office.

"*Arigato.*"

Then the office was empty, save for the two brothers, and the dead body on the floor.

Sam looked at Dean.

"I think we did it."

"Looks like," Dean said with a nod. Peering around, he

shrugged in the direction of the door. "C'mon, let's blow this pop stand."

They went out the back way—the same way they'd come in, just like John Winchester had done twenty years ago— emerging into the alley where Castiel was waiting for them, standing on the other side of the Impala. Oddly, the angel appeared to be alone.

"Where's Chao?" Sam asked.

"We must go," Castiel said.

Dean approached the driver's door, which was on the street side.

"Yeah, but what happened to—?"

"Uh, Dean?"

Sam had run around to the other side to get into the passenger seat. Seeing his brother's face, Dean walked round the car to join him.

What was left of Albert Chao was pretty messy. There were gaping, bloody wounds all over his body, from his head all the way down to his feet.

Castiel spoke again.

"We must go. The authorities will be here soon."

"Yeah," Dean agreed and both boys got into the car.

A moment later Castiel appeared in the back seat behind them. Sam *still* hadn't got used to that.

Dean started the engine and backed out of the alley and into Ellis Street's traffic.

"What the hell happened to him?" he asked the angel.

"The Heart of the Dragon kept Albert Chao alive, and protected him from all harm. When you cast the spell that sent the spirit away—"

Sam nodded.

"He wasn't protected anymore, and it all caught up. God, that must've been, like, every wound he ever got all hitting him at once."

Castiel responded without emotion.

"He did scream rather loudly, which is why I believed it was important to remove ourselves from the scene. I could have simply telepor—"

"No!" Dean bellowed. "Just—no."

Sam smiled, an action that still hurt his bruised face. He didn't see what the big deal was, but he was pretty sure it was mainly because Dean hated any mode of travel that wasn't the Impala.

"You did well," Castiel said, although his face betrayed almost no hint of emotion. "Had the demon been able to control the Heart of the Dragon, it would have been catastrophic."

Sam turned around to question Castiel further, but the angel was gone. He looked at Dean, but his brother just shrugged.

They had solved a problem that had plagued their parents and their grandparents, and kept a dangerous spirit out of the hands of the bad guys in the angel-demon war. Sam wasn't convinced there were any *good* guys in that conflict, but he also knew that he didn't want the demons to win.

The Heart of the Dragon was an advantage he didn't want them to have.

Dean drove them back to the Emperor Norton Lodge, where they packed their bags and went to the lobby to check out.

Dean put the two key cards on the registration desk.

"Checking out of 102," he said to the clerk.

"Sure." The clerk typed at the computer, then quoted Dean a price.

Dean handed over the amount in cash, taken from his poker winnings, plus a bit extra.

The clerk dutifully counted the money. Sam noticed that it took him a couple of tries.

Guess nobody pays in cash anymore.

"Uh, sir? This is twenty-five dollars over."

"I know," Dean said. "I called the city "Frisco' a couple of times. That's my fine for the emperor."

The clerk frowned.

"Emperor?"

"You don't know about Emperor Norton?" Dean sounded incredulous. "Dude, don't you *work* here?"

"Oh, *that* guy," the clerk said, shaking his head. "Yeah, well, I haven't… he wasn't…."

Dean rolled his eyes, then turned and headed out, Sam right behind him.

"Kids today," Dean grumbled, "no sense of history."

Even though it hurt, Sam chuckled.

EPILOGUE

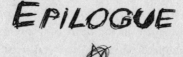

Zachariah loved the view of New York City.

Every once in a while, when he actually had some down time—which didn't happen that often, especially lately—he'd go somewhere that reminded him of the good humans could accomplish if they put their minds to it.

New York wasn't Zachariah's favorite city, but it was probably the one he enjoyed most of those that were left.

Of course, nothing could beat Edo in its heyday.

Or Rome.

Or Constantinople....

Zachariah sighed. He missed the good old days.

Still, New York had its charms. It certainly was the perfect intersection of all the things humanity did right: art, architecture, culture.

It exemplified a lot of what they did wrong, too. Especially now—but just at the moment Zachariah couldn't fault them for it.

After all, if you can't go crazy during the Apocalypse, then when can you go crazy?

He was sitting at the Top of the Rock, sipping an espresso. The restaurant was on the top floor of 30 Rockefeller Plaza in the symbolic—if not geographic—center of Manhattan, in the heart of New York City. It perfectly symbolized what was best and what was worst about those silly little creatures with their free will and their craziness that Zachariah's father adored so very much.

It was as if he was on top of the world.

From up here, on this cool, crisp, cloudless December morning, Zachariah could see the entire lower half of Manhattan, and past it to New York Harbor, Brooklyn, Queens, the Statue of Liberty, Staten Island, New Jersey, and the Atlantic Ocean beyond. The spires of the city reached for the sky at varying heights, creating a lovely pattern.

He couldn't really see the people, and there was no air traffic either, so nothing cluttered the perfection of the buildings.

But that led rather perfectly to the bad. Still there was a gaping hole at the southern end of the island, where two of the city's proudest structures once stood. And the event that destroyed them was why there was less air traffic over Manhattan. For that matter, Top of the Rock had opened up because the destruction of the World Trade Center in 2001 cost the city its Windows on the World.

It was just another example of how mankind had squandered what it possessed. The angels had had enough.

Humanity had pissed away the gifts God gave them, and the host wasn't going to hold their hands anymore.

Zachariah had hoped the war would progress more smoothly. He hadn't counted on so many betrayals by his brothers—Uriel, Castiel—nor that the Michael sword would be such a pain in the ass.

Just as his espresso cup landed in the saucer with a click, Uzziel was there across from him. None of the humans in the restaurant noticed—and even if they had, their recollections would have been that the large black man had always been sitting across from the broad-shouldered, bald white man.

"How'd it go?" Zachariah asked.

"Well enough," Uzziel said. "I destroyed the *angelus iuguolo*, and the final Stone of Hyginus is with the others in Cordoba. We lost Ramiel, though."

"Pity. And the rest of the operation?"

Uzziel smiled.

"The Heart of the Dragon has been banished, as you predicted."

"Of course." Zachariah nodded as he lifted his cup again. "I knew if word leaked to Castiel of the spirit's return—and of the demons' interest—that he'd let the two jackasses know about it." He drank down the last of his espresso. "The Winchesters may refuse to play their parts as they should, but the least they can do is help us out in other ways."

Uzziel's response echoed his frustration.

"Isn't there some other way?" he asked. "Can't we just kill them and move on?"

Closing his eyes and leaning back, Zachariah sighed.

"Oh, how I wish we could. But no, they're the chosen ones. Nobody else can be Michael's vessel—or Lucifer's. Nobody else would be able to handle it."

Zachariah opened his eyes again, and stared right at Uzziel.

"The last thing we need to do is screw up the Apocalypse."

THE END

ACKNOWLEDGMENTS

Thanks first of all to my DC Comics editor, Christopher Cerasi, who liked my other two novels enough to hire me to write a third, and who also provided me with tons of useful reference material (like the fifth-season scripts that told me how to spell Castiel's nickname). Also to my Titan Books editor Cath Trechman, who kept things moving smoothly— or at least smoothly as her deadbeat writer would allow. Cath, Christopher and *Supernatural*'s Rebecca Dessertine had tons of brilliant suggestions that made this book so much better, and I am excessively grateful to them all.

Eric Kripke and his merry band of loonies (in particular Sera Gamble and Ben Edlund) for giving us *Supernatural* in the first place and continuing to write such nifty stories involving Sam, Dean, and the rest.

Jensen Ackles (Dean Winchester), Jim Beaver (Bobby Singer), Ridge Canipe (Young Dean), Misha Collins (Castiel), Alex Ferris and Colin Ford (Young Sam), Kurt Fuller (Zachariah), Amy Gumenick (Mary Campbell), Allison Hossack (Deanna Campbell), Jeffrey Dean Morgan (John Winchester), Jared Padalecki (Sam Winchester), and Mitch Pileggi (Samuel Campbell) for their onscreen portrayals that gave voice, face, and life to several of the characters appearing in this novel.

My ever-excellent gaggle of beta readers: Constance Cochran, Kara Cox, GraceAnne Andreassi DeCandido, Heidi Ellis, Marina Frants, Natalie Jumper, and Nicholas Knight.

Speaking of Mr. Knight, his many volumes of

Supernatural: The Official Companion were immensely helpful reference sources. So were two books by Alex Irvine: *The Supernatural Book of Monsters, Spirits, Demons, and Ghouls* and *John Winchester's Journal.* So were the two comic book miniseries *Supernatural: Origins* by Peter Johnson and Matthew Dow Smith and *Supernatural: Rising Son* by Peter Johnson, Rebecca Dessertine, and Diego Olmos. Props must also be given to Jeff Mariotte, author of the other extant *Supernatural* novel, *Witch's Canyon*, and to Joe Schreiber and to Rebecca Dessertine & David Reed, authors of the two upcoming *Supernatural* novels.

Deborah and Nic Grabien for putting me up (or putting up with me) in San Francisco in March 2009 and answering many questions about the city.

The New York Public Library (Research)—that's the big building with the lions—which was, as always, a magnificent place for research. Also thanks to the SFPL.org web site and to the kind soul who was working the phones in the International Center of the San Francisco Public Library's Main Library the day I called with several more questions.

Shihan Paul and the rest of the folks at the dojo, for constantly enriching my body and spirit.

Finally to friends, family, and felines, for everything.

PLAYLIST

If you purchased either of my previous two *Supernatural* novels—*Nevermore* and *Bone Key*—you know that each of those came with a playlist of suggested songs to listen to while reading the novel. From AC/DC's "Back in Black" playing over the Impala driving down the highway to the brilliant use of such songs as Styx's "Renegade" and Kansas's "Carry on, Wayward Son" to Sam and Dean singing a dreadfully off-key version of Bon Jovi's "Wanted Dead or Alive," music has been an integral part of *Supernatural*'s very soul.

Those two playlists still apply to *Heart of the Dragon*, but as with *Bone Key*, I've made some additions:

America: "A Horse with No Name"

The Band: "Across the Great Divide," "Tears of Rage," "We Can Talk"

The Beatles: "A Hard Day's Night," "Come Together," "I Want You (She's So Heavy)"

David Bromberg: "Suffer to Sing the Blues"

The Contours: "Do You Love Me (Now That I Can Dance)"

Creedence Clearwater Revival: "Fortunate Son."

Crosby, Stills, & Nash: "Suite: Judy Blue Eyes"

The Charlie Daniels Band: "Still in Saigon"

The Doobie Brothers: "Black Water," "China Grove"

Bob Dylan: "Ballad of a Thin Man," "Blowin' in the Wind," "Tangled Up in Blue"

Norman Greenbaum: "Spirit in the Sky"

Arlo Guthrie: "Chilling of the Evening," "Coming Into Los Angeles," "The Motorcycle Song"

Jimi Hendrix: "Purple Haze," "The Star-Spangled Banner"

Iron Butterfly: "In-A-Gada-Da-Vida"

Jethro Tull: "A New Day Yesterday," "Nothing is Easy," "Teacher"

Janis Joplin: "Me and Bobby McGee"

Taj Mahal: "Keep Your Hands Off Her," "Stagger Lee"

Van Morrison: "Caravan," "Moondance"

Kenny Rogers & The First Edition: "Just Dropped In (To See What Condition My Condition Was In)"

The Rolling Stones: "(I Can't Get No) Satisfaction"

Sam & Dave: "Hold On, I'm Coming"

Simon & Garfunkel: "I am a Rock," "Mrs. Robinson," "The Sound of Silence"

Cat Stevens: "Moonshadow," "Peace Train," "Wild World"

The Subdudes: "Papa Dukie and the Mud People"

Paul Thorn: "Angel Too Soon," "Mission Temple Fireworks Stand"

Traffic: "Many a Mile to Freedom"

The Ventures: "Wipe Out"

The Who: "Love Ain't for Keeping," "Won't Get Fooled Again"

The Zombies: "Time of the Season"

—Keith R.A. DeCandido

somewhere in New York City, November 2009

ABOUT THE AUTHOR

This is **Keith R.A. DeCandido**'s third *Supernatural* novel, following 2007's *Nevermore* and 2008's *Bone Key*. Keith has written more than forty novels, as well as a mess of short stories, a smattering of novellas, a bunch of comic books, a dollop of essays, a gaggle of eBooks, and many bits of editing. Most are in various media universes: *Farscape* (most recently the monthly comic from BOOM! Studios as well as several miniseries and one-shots), *Star Trek* (most recently the novella "The Unhappy Ones" in the anthology *Seven Deadly Sins* and a Captain Jellico one-shot comic book), *CSI: NY* (*Four Walls*), *Buffy the Vampire Slayer* (*Blackout, The Deathless*), *World of Warcraft* (*Cycle of Hatred*), *Doctor Who* (the *Short Trips* anthologies *Destination Prague* and *The Quality of Leadership*), *StarCraft* (*Nova, Ghost Academy*), *Resident Evil* (the novelizations of all three films), Spider-Man (*Down These Mean Streets*), and whole bunches more. The bulk of his original work is in the world of his 2004 novel *Dragon Precinct*. Keith is also a musician, currently the percussionist for the parody band the Boogie Knights. A fan of classic rock (Dean Winchester would approve of much of his iTunes "favorites" playlist), Keith is also a black belt in *Kenshikai* karate and a devoted fan of the New York Yankees. Learn less about Keith at his official web site at DeCandido.net, read his tiresome ramblings at kradical.livejournal.com, or email him directly at keith@decandido.net.

SUPERNATURAL
WAR OF THE SONS
BY REBECCA DESSERTINE & DAVID REED

On the hunt for Lucifer, the boys find themselves in a small town in South Dakota where they meet Don – an angel with a proposition.... Don sends them a very long way from home, on a mission to uncover the secret Satan never wanted Sam and Dean to find out.

A brand-new *Supernatural* novel detailing a previously unseen adventure for the Winchester brothers, from the hit CW series!